THE COAL GATHERER

Janet Woods titles available from
Severn House Large Print

Broken Journey
Cinnamon Sky
Amaranth Moon

THE COAL GATHERER

Janet Woods

Severn House Large Print
London & New York

This first large print edition published 2009
in Great Britain and the USA by
SEVERN HOUSE PUBLISHERS LTD of
9-15 High Street, Sutton, Surrey, SM1 1DF.
First world regular print edition published 2007 by
Severn House Publishers Ltd., London and New York.

British Library Cataloguing in Publication Data

Woods, Janet, 1939-
The coal gatherer. - Large print ed.
1. England, North East - Social life and customs - 19th century - Fiction 2. Large type books
I. Title
823.9'2[F]

ISBN-13: 978-0-7278-7740-6

Except where actual histor
for the storyline of this no
fictitious and any resembl

Printed and bound in Grea
MPG Books Ltd, Bodmin,

One

1884

The midwife had left, the infant having finally stopped bawling and fallen asleep.

The Ingram family crowded round the bed to gaze at the latest arrival.

Ranged down one side were the males of the family. Starting with the eldest, and with a year stepping down between each of them, were nine-year-old Chad, Thomas, Joseph and Aaric, the least robust of the boys.

'It's a girl,' Mary Ingram told her children. 'My, but she was born a noisy one.'

Verna, the eldest of the pack at the age of ten, exchanged a glance with the youngest. Jane grinned when she said, 'We'd best get her named before our da gets home. He'll want to call her Agatha after our aunt.'

Jane fetched a piece of paper and a pencil and handed it to Verna. She said, 'We'll start with you, Chad. Nothing daft, mind. Two names apiece.'

Writing the names on small scraps of paper, Verna screwed them up, placed them in a bowl and gave them a stir with her hand.

She held the bowl out to her mother.

Before Mary could choose one the door was pushed open. Ebeneezer Ingram stood there, a whiff of fish about him. There was a grin on his face, now seamed and leathery from exposure to the sea in all its moods, and a lifetime of earning a living on the sea in an open boat.

'Job heard the bairn squallin' on the way past and told me it were likely born.'

Ebeneezer was a short man, not much taller than his wife. He lifted the blanket covering the sleeping babe and inspected her. 'A girl, is it? She's a bonny lass, reet enough.' He gazed around at them all. 'You weren't thinking of naming her wi'out me, were you?'

'No, Da,' Verna said with a sigh. 'Our Chad was about to fetch you from the boat, weren't you, Chad?'

Chad grinned. 'I was that.'

Their da wrote his two names, folded them and placed them on top. They were bigger than the other scraps. Verna stirred them.

'I'll go first,' he said, and picked up one of his own, bringing his second one up to the top. 'Now you, Ma. Best close your eyes so it's all above board. Just pluck one off the top.'

Their mother plucked a paper from the bowl, withdrawing the second of their father's papers.

They all held their breath when their father opened his. 'Calandra,' he said, and grinned round at them in a slightly challenging way. 'Fancy that ... I picked one of my own name choices out.'

Nobody took up the challenge. Their father was a man who was loved and loving, though his word was still law. Only when the drink was upon him, which wasn't often, was he to be feared.

Surprised, his wife stared at him. 'I've never heard of Calandra. It's a fancy name for a fisherman's daughter, Ebeneezer.'

'Don't be daft, woman. You came from trade yourself, so why should it bother you? You hadn't heard of Aaric either, but I got his name from the same place and you said nowt about that.' He ruffled his young son's head. 'You were named after a dead sea captain, tha knows.'

'And which sea captain might that be, Ebeneezer Ingram?' Mary said.

Ebeneezer scratched his head, sucked air through his empty pipe and looked thoughtful. 'It were the Norseman lying in his grave in the cemetery, I reckon. I can't bring to mind his second name.'

She snorted.

'As for Calandra, the fact is, I ducked behind a tombstone last Sunday to have a pipe out of the wind and saw it on the tablet of a passenger that came off that Greek ship two winters ago. Took to it right off, so I thinks to m'self, if we have another lass, Calandra it will be.'

'Lucky you picked it out the bowl then, I suppose,' Mary said, giving a sniff.

Aaric said anxiously, 'What's her second name going to be, Ma?'

Mary opened the paper she'd picked up – the second of her husband's contributions. She gave him a glance, her eyes narrowing at his knowing grin. It was time she taught him a lesson, she thought, unfolding it. 'Why, it's Mary. That was our Aaric's suggestion, wasn't it? Calandra Mary, after his mother. How pretty.' She screwed up the paper and placed it back in the bowl amongst the others, giving it a stir with her fingers.

Her husband's smile faded. He opened his mouth, then shut it again when their mother smiled at him and said, 'It's just as well we don't have to call her after your sister, since the names don't sound quite right together.'

A proud smile flashed across Aaric's face. 'I wanted her to have your name, Ma. She's pretty like you, and her eyes are blue as well, just like yours.'

'Let's hope they stay that way then, Aaric. I feel the odd one out in this family.'

'So you should with your city ways.' Ebeneezer's smile came back. 'Eh, but there's a lad with a silver tongue. Your ma's a bonny one, lad. She kept half the lads in Seafield dangling on a string before she took up wi' me. I've always wondered why she chose me.'

Mary managed to laugh as she said lightly, 'I wonder that m'self sometimes.'

But she knew why, and so did he. She'd been filled with vanity over her looks and her ability to capture the attention of the young men. Ebeneezer had not been an inexperienced lad, though. He'd been a widower looking to wed again, a young man grieving for a wife and children lost to cholera a year earlier.

She'd walked across the sands from Hartlepool when the tide had been out. Dressed in her finery, she'd been parading with two of her friends in front of the local lads. Ebeneezer had been mending his nets and she'd stopped to watch him. His eyes had been bold and dark on her, she remembered, and he'd had a quiet but determined air about him.

'Will you show me how to do that?' she said, wanting his attention.

'Aye, lass.' His eyes had filled with amusement at her first stumbling attempts, but within half an hour she'd mastered it.'

'There's a canny lass, you are ... with nimble fingers. Come and help me another time, all reet?' he'd said.

And the time after that he walked her home, filled her with cider and told her the sad tale of his doomed marriage. Then, when she was feeling sorry for him and crying over it, he'd taken her into the field behind the village when the moon was barely a sliver and the wheat so high that nobody could see what was going on between the pair of them – even if they'd wanted to. With her skirt up over her head and his hands pinning it either side, so her protests were muffled and went unheard, he'd made a proper job of it that night.

Afterwards she railed at him, but he simply lit his smelly pipe and said, 'Stop your nagging, woman. You had the scent on you and you wagged your tail and led me on. Now 'tis over and done with. I can't rightly say I favour another woman more, so I'll wed thee, lass. There's no more to be said.' Which was the nearest he'd got to courtship.

Mary hadn't wanted to marry him but fate had forced her hand.

'I think I'm pregnant,' she told him six weeks later, and he'd smiled.

'Reet, lass. I'll visit your folks on Sunday after the service.'

And so he had. Ebeneezer had been perfectly polite. 'I'm here to ask for your Mary's hand in marriage,' he said to her father.

'That's impossible,' her father had spluttered. 'My daughter can do better than wed a common fisherman.'

'Likely I'm doing the girl a favour, since she's got a bairn inside her. Now, let's talk terms, mister. I'm in need of a new boat so I can earn enough to keep your daughter. I'll settle for that.'

Her two brothers had taken to him with fists flying. Ebeneezer didn't raise a finger to defend himself, emerging from the affray with a broken nose, bloodied but calm. 'The lads had no need to tek to me, tha knows. It won't solve anything.'

Her father had been cold and angry. 'Is what this man says true, Mary?'

Miserably, she'd nodded her head.

'I see. Then you'll leave empty-handed, and

you'll never step over my doorstep again. From this day on you have no kin.'

'William, no!' her mother had cried out in protest. 'It's too harsh. Mary's my daughter and I love her.'

'You no longer have a daughter.' He turned his eyes back to them. 'Now, get out, the pair of you.'

'Not without the boat,' Ebeneezer said. 'It costs a lot to keep a woman and a bairn.'

Money had changed hands and Ebeneezer had smiled. 'Thank you, sir. As for you, lass, go and pack your bag. You're coming with me.'

'She'll go in what she stands up in, nothing more,' her father said, ignoring her mother's protests.

Mary had gone to the altar carrying Verna inside her. And a real quiet wedding it had been, because she'd shamed her folk, who were respectable shopkeepers. There was Ebeneezer's sister Agatha, who ran a boarding house her husband had left her, and who totally disapproved of Mary. Some of the fishing folk had attended too, though Mary had been an outsider in the community because she was a cut above them, and always would be.

Her father hadn't relented to this day, and none of her family had sought contact with her since. Even if she'd had time to visit them between having babies, looking after the family and digging up cockles to sell with the fish door to door, they wouldn't have welcomed her. She'd been dead to them since the day Ebeneezer's hand had slid into the divide of her drawers.

Mary sighed, wondering briefly what her life would have been like if she hadn't met Ebeneezer, though she loved the children they'd produced between them, and mourned the ones she'd lost. Still, there was no point thinking such things now.

She picked the infant up when she began to mew again. 'Put the kettle on, our Verna,' she said now. 'As soon as I've got Callie settled to the breast I'll have a bit of a wash, then get up and start on the dinner. Go into the yard and fill the tin bath with water from the pump, then put the sheets in to soak before the stains set in. You boys can go with your da – except for you, Aaric.'

'Aw, Ma,' the youngest boy said.

'Don't you "aw, Ma" me. I don't want you up coughing for most of the night.'

'For God's sake, Mary, stop babying the lad. It's a fine day and the sea air will strengthen his lungs. I'll carry him down to the boat on my back and he can sit on a rock in the sun and count the fish while the boys and I unload the catch on to Wilkinson's cart. I'm first in so I should get the best price. The cod's got to be on the train to London tonight, and the herring needs salting.'

Their mother nodded. 'Make sure you look after him, then. Jane, you can stay and help me. See the crib? Make sure the sheet is tucked in and the blanket is folded back, ready for our

Callie to be put into. And you can fetch me that little nightgown and the shawl. We'll wrap her up nice and tight, then she'll feel safe.' She gazed round at them all. 'What are you all standing there for? Off you go, there's work to be done.'

Mary lay back on the pillows with a sigh when they were gone. Who'd be a woman, she thought. She'd given birth to ten children in twelve years of marriage, though she'd lost four of them. When would her husband have enough children to help him forget the two he'd lost before her? Perhaps then he'd leave her alone.

Verna would have to take the herring around the houses by herself tonight, otherwise the other fishwives would step in and steal her customers. At least Verna could stand up for herself, Mary thought.

Her eyes went to little Callie. She was a pretty one and, though small, she looked healthy enough. Her hair was as pale and as light as thistledown, her skin so fine it was almost translucent. Calandra's delicate looks must have come from her own family, Mary realized with a pang, for the infant resembled the Brightmans.

'Makes no difference. If you stay round here you'll toughen up and soon lose your looks, girl, same as I did,' she mused. Shaking her head she set the infant to her breast. The girl quickly claimed a nipple and began to suckle. Feeling the strong tug of her, Mary knew that this one was going to be a survivor.

Two

Right from the start Callie ruled the roost. She had the ways of an angel, but feared nothing, not even her father when he was in a temper.

When she was two, and he was in the middle of laying down the law, she climbed up on his lap, her golden ringlets flying all around her, placed a finger against his lips, then scolded, 'Shush, Da.'

Ebeneezer had begun to laugh as he'd gazed at his wife. 'This maiden takes after thee in more ways than one, Mary. She knows her way around a man.'

By the time Callie was three, she'd given up her place in the iron cot to make room for twin brothers. She now slept in the middle of a double bed between her two elder sisters, where she sank into a dent made by her body.

Not much bigger than a pair of dolls, the new twins caught a fever and died two months later. They were buried with their brothers and sisters in the churchyard alongside Ebeneezer's first wife and her children.

'Well, I don't begrudge you my little angels,' Mary told the first Mrs Ingram, which was just as well, since several more would be handed over to her keeping before Mary's childbearing days were finally over.

When Callie was six, Mary gave birth to Giles Ebeneezer, the next survivor.

'Enough,' Mary said tiredly to Ebeneezer eight months later, when the next infant made its presence known. We've only got two bedrooms and the front parlour, and the bairns are already packed like herrings in a salt barrel.'

''Tis in the Lord's good hands,' he said humbly.

'No, it's not. Best you keep your trousers buttoned up from now on. My body's had enough.'

He smacked a hand across her backside and chuckled. 'I married you because you had reet comfortable hips for breeding, and you caught easily. You're my wife and a man needs his comfort, so you'll do as you're told.'

To Mary's mind, her man needed more comfort than most. But she'd married him, and had no say in the matter, although it was something she bitterly regretted.

But Ebeneezer had something else on his mind now. 'I want to talk to you about the lasses. Our Verna has reached the age when she'll soon be looking for a husband. Wilkinson's lad has got his eye on her, and I've had a word with his da. If the lad lays one finger on our Verna before a ring's on her finger, I'll whale the bloody tar out of him and march him up the aisle with the barrel of my shotgun up his arse.'

'Verna could do worse, I suppose.'

'Wilkinson's lad has got a fine horse and cart,

and a good head on him for business.'

'If by business you mean robbing folk of their just due by taking a cut of their produce.'

''Tis no different than a shop buying the merchandise cheap and selling it dear,' he said mildly. 'Robbie can do the figuring out and I can't, since I haven't had no learning.'

'All the more reason why the children should go to the church school,' she pointed out triumphantly.

'They're doing all reet with you teaching them. Besides, I need the lads. I've got two boats to work, and I intend to get a third before they get much older.'

'There's only so many hours in the day, Ebeneezer Ingram. Our Callie isn't doing all right at all. She's clever, like Aaric, and she needs more than I can teach her. And Jane can read a bit, but she needs a teacher with learning in her to help her spell properly. If those three went off to school, Aaric would be able to help keep the accounts later on. Although he's come on a lot, he'll never be strong enough to fish. Surely we can afford tuppence a week each for them.'

'Like as not the lasses won't need no learning since they'll get married soon enough. Jane's nearly of age. Best they marry young so we don't have to keep them.'

'But they might not want to marry. They might want to work. Callie's clever enough to be a teacher, and she has a thirst to learn on her. Just because you've got three brawny lads to help in the boat, it doesn't mean you can ignore the others. They've all got to have a chance.'

Her man said firmly, 'That's another thing. You're putting daft ideas in Callie's head. She's got too much lip, just like you. I never did like an arguing woman, so you'd best shut your gob if you know what's best for you.'

Mary knew when to push him. Hands on hips she shot back at him, 'If I'd known what was best for me I wouldn't have married you. As for mouths, you'd better shut yours else I'll take the skillet to you when you're asleep. Like as not I'll flatten your head, since there's no learning in it. I don't want the rest of my children to follow suit.'

His grin exposed teeth stained brown by his baccy. 'Tell you what. If you can earn the extra sixpence a week, they can go to school,' he said, giving in.

And so come Saturday Mary was down on the sands with the other cockle women. Barefoot, her shirt hitched up and a scarf tied over her head, she dug for cockles, placing them in the basket over her arm. Following the tide out, she used a small spade to dig them up. It was back-breaking work, and the day was hot. The sand stretched to the horizon where a glare of pale blue sea shimmered in the heat. Mary began to fill the sack tied around her waist over the infant she carried.

Another one due in six months' time, she thought wearily. She was fair worn out by it all. She thought of the twin boys she'd lost the year before. Shrivelled in the womb, they were black and small. They'd come early, just slipping from her one after the other.

'Your parts is all worn out,' the midwife had told her. 'Likely there'll be no more.'

But Ebeneezer had planted another one inside her a month later, and this one kicked strongly.

Mary straightened up, holding the small of her aching back. The tide had turned, and a row of sea coal now bobbed along the edge. The lads would be down with their barrows soon, scooping it from the sea, collecting it for sale, or for storing in the bunkers until it was needed.

A shout brought Mary's head up and a smile sped across her face. It was Callie. Her hair had darkened as she'd grown and had settled into a light brown that was streaked through with burnished gold. She'd lost her ribbon and her hair flew free in the wind as she ran like a gazelle towards her mother, her sun bonnet clasped firmly in her hand.

'Give me the basket to carry, Ma. Can I take the cockles round the houses by myself tonight?'

'Eh, I suppose you're old enough. You'll have to mind your manners though, because you're going to the big houses.'

That night Mary lost the infant she was carrying. She felt nothing but relief. The boy was buried with the others, and even though he hadn't breathed or been christened the reverend said a prayer over him as his body was consigned back to the Lord. Afterwards, Mary prayed on her knees that there would be no more.

Verna married a year later in the same church. They stood in the church porch, faces serious, as a photograph was taken. Ebeneezer looked uncomfortable in his Sunday suit. He never went to church, even though he was a firm believer in God.

'I need no preacher to tell me the Lord's ways. He's out there in the fishing grounds with me. Sometimes his face appears in the clouds, and I hear him talk inside my head.'

'That's why he keeps his cap on all the time,' Chad whispered to Tom and Joseph, and the three laughed and punched each other.

Within a year Verna gave birth to her first son. A year later she had another.

Jane, who had taken over Verna's duties, was unhappy when her father began to bring suitors home. They sat at the table, silent young men with nothing to say for themselves, looking awkward.

In 1898, when Callie was fourteen, Jane told her, 'I don't want to stay here for the rest of my life, and I don't want to be wed yet. I've got other plans.'

'But what will you do?' Callie asked her.

'You'll see. Just don't say anything to anyone.'

Jane had surprised them all by getting herself a reference from the reverend and, with their mother's permission, had signed herself on to a domestic agency. There had been an argument, of course, but Jane hadn't let herself be talked out of it. 'I don't want to wed when I'm young and produce babies, and neither do I want to stay here all my life. I want to see a bit of the outside world before I settle down. I've got a job in London through a domestic agency,' she told her da.

'You'll come to no good in London,' Ebeneezer told her. 'You'll be nowt but a servant. You're not going.'

'At least I'll get paid for being a servant there. I'm not spending my life as a slave to one man, like my ma has put up with all these years. And I *am* going.'

'Schooling has put ideas in her head above her station, tha knows,' he said angrily to Mary later.

'That's what it's supposed to do, so things are looking up,' her mother answered. 'If Jane wants to go off to work she can. I put my signature to the contract and it's binding.'

Their da had nothing much to say to that, but he muttered, 'Tha had better still be here when I get home, lass.' And with a face like thunder he got up and strode off without another word. When he came staggering home, rolling drunk and mean with it, Jane had already gone.

Her mother bore the brunt of her father's fists that night. Frightened by his savagery, Callie had run to fetch her brothers. Between them they'd dragged their father into the yard and locked the door on him. After a few threats he'd settled himself in the outhouse and the sound of retching had been heard.

The next morning, looking wretched, Ebeneezer had gazed at his wife's injuries and had begun to cry. Her mother had sent them all out of the house. 'It's the anniversary of her and the bairns that came before us,' she said by way of an excuse for his brutality. 'Leave him be for a while. I have a word or two to say to him.'

Half of Seafield had heard the tongue lashing their da had got. After that, Mary didn't speak to her husband for a week. He slunk about like a whipped cur with his tail between his legs, then he'd gone to Hartlepool and come back with a new hat and a coat with a fur collar, which Mary had worn to church on Sundays ever since.

Two years had passed since then, and Ebeneezer had never allowed a drop of liquor to pass his lips in all that time.

One July morning, on the day Callie turned sixteen, she was first down at the beach. She waved to her da and her big brothers, watching them set off in their cobles for the fishing grounds.

The sea was quiet, like a sheet of pale grey glass. The little fleet looked a fine sight, their single sails set to catch the slightest breeze as they set off into the pearly sea, the tide creeping stealthily after them. It promised to be a warm day, and soon the morning would be golden with sunlight.

The night tide had brought in a good spread of sea coal, but she'd have to be quick to stake her claim, for the Brown brothers were coming with their horse and cart, and would stake out the lot if they could.

The only other person on the beach was a young man sitting on a rock, his bare head bowed to the sketching block in his hand, his eyes absorbing what he saw into their dreamy depths.

One of the summer visitors, she imagined, as she'd never laid eyes on him before and the place was awash with fine folk in the summer. Quakers mostly, for they summered in Seafield and had built a small chapel to meet in at the south end of the village.

Callie wished she had time to draw and paint, too, but there was always too much work to do. 'If something doesn't bring owt for the pocket, or put food in the belly, 'tis not worth the effort of doing,' her da always told her.

'But what about doing something just for the pleasure of it?' she'd argued.

He'd looked at her mother with a grin that had made Mary blush as he'd said softly, 'Aye, I reckon there's that.'

Callie had blushed too, because she was of the age to be aware of what went on between a man and a woman, and in their small terrace house it was sometimes hard not to hear what was going on – and to know what the aftermath was, since hadn't little Kitty been born just two days ago?

Picking up her wooden rake she turned it on end, then dragged a coal line across the sand, heeling in a peg at each end with a strip of rag tied around it.

As was customary, beyond that line, and extending to the water's edge, all the coal the tide left behind on the sand was hers. The sea would retreat for half a mile or so, and be at one with the sky. Already it was sculpting ripples of sand in its wake.

Although Callie could never collect all the sea coal before it was time for school, she had a lot to rake. And there would still be plenty left for others who came after her. She began to gather the black lumps into piles, the hem of her skirt tucked into her waistband and her feet bare.

In a little while her brother Giles – who, at the age of eight, was six years younger then herself – would be down with the barrow. He'd drag the piles of coal on a sack back to the cart, and once that was full they'd haul it home between them.

Callie began to sing to herself as she worked, her arms going back and forth in a steady rhythm. Slender, and with the first signs of womanhood coming upon her, she was nevertheless strong and wiry.

She was looking forward to school. Today they were to write a story for examination, and she'd already decided to write about the fishing fleet putting out to sea in the quiet morning. The words were forming inside her head, like precious gems.

Her hand went to her shoulder as a lump of coal hit her. She turned, her rake held up in front of her.

'Gerroff my patch; I was here first,' she said fiercely.

The elder of Tilly Brown's lads kicked at the pile of coal she'd made, scattering it. 'This is our patch. See, our marker is back there. Now move, Callie Ingram, else I'll give you a good thump.'

She didn't bother arguing, just held the rake in front of her and charged, hoping that Giles would soon arrive. Despite his young age he was a good scrapper when need be. She caught the biggest lad in the stomach and bowled him over. His breath expelled in a painful 'oof'. But the smaller one jumped on her back and began to pummel her. She yelled when he caught hold of her hair and jerked her head back, so she staggered back and tripped over his foot. He sprang to one side and his follow-up kick caught her on the cheekbone.

'That's enough, lads. Only cowards hit girls,' someone said firmly. 'The young lady was here first, so get back to your own patch.'

Callie's fist thumped into the older boy's eye socket when he was distracted by the voice. He grunted, pulling back his own fist. Before it could land the stranger grabbed him by the lapels and hauled him upright. 'Enough, I said.'

Out of breath, Callie struggled to her feet, rearranging her skirt, apron and sun bonnet, while the lads scuttled off to their own patch, hurling insults over their shoulders. She hoped her raggy britches hadn't been on display.

'Are you all right, young lady?'

Breathlessly she told him, 'My face hurts, is all.'

He took her chin between his hands and examined her. He was a young man of about eighteen with a pleasant face, grey-green eyes and long, dark lashes that matched the colour of his hair. 'It looks as though you'll end up with a bruise.' His mouth stretched into a wide smile that lit his face up with mischief. 'That bigger lad will have a black eye, though.'

'Serves him right, mister.' She nodded in satisfaction at the thought, then sent the Browns a scowl. 'They've scattered most of my coal, and I've got to get it gathered before school starts. Here comes my brother with the barrow now. What took you so long, Giles? You knew I wanted to make an early start, and you've missed a scrap with the Browns. Luckily the stranger here hauled them off me.'

'Mr Sutcliffe collared me, reckoned I gave him a bit of lip last week,' Giles muttered. 'I haven't set eyes on him for a fortnight, the old barmpot.'

'That's enough, Giles. You should have some respect for your elders.'

'I will when they show some to me.'

Picking up the rake, the man smiled. 'Let me rake it, while you and your brother put it in the barrow. What's your name?'

'Calandra Ingram. Most people call me Callie, though. This here is my brother Giles.'

He extended a hand to Giles. 'How do you do, young man. I'm James Lazurus.'

'You talk like gentry,' Giles said, ignoring the hand, his dark eyes suspicious. He'd never resembled their father more. Ebeneezer Ingram was beginning to look old now and he walked a bit stiffly, though they'd never heard him complain, or had known him to have a day off work from illness.

'I live in London.'

'What are you doing in Seafield then?'

'I was visiting a relative with my mother's cousin and my sister. My sister was taken ill. My cousin had to go back to London on business while I stayed behind to keep Patricia company. The doctor said the sea air would be good for her.'

'What's the matter with her?'

'It's not our business, Giles.'

James Lazurus smiled at her. 'I don't mind telling you. It started off as a cold, but it got worse and went to her chest, and then it became pneumonia. She's beginning to recover, I'm pleased to say.'

'Between me and Giles we had a sister and two brothers die of pneumonia,' Callie said. 'Now we have a new baby sister, just when my ma thought she was over it. Kitty, her name is. We'd best get on, Giles. Start on that pile where they kicked it over.'

James Lazurus began to rake with a wide sweeping motion. He was fast, and seemed to be tireless as the coal piled up.

Callie grinned to herself. They'd have a cart full in no time if he kept it up – and he did, moving out with the tide. More coal gatherers were coming down to the beach when their cart was full and ready to move. They handed over their patch to one of the cockle women, for there was plenty of coal left to gather.

James stretched, his slim hands holding his aching back. Perspiration moistened his brow.

'Likely you'll feel it tomorrow if you're not used to the work,' Callie said.

'I'm feeling it now, but I enjoyed the exercise. I'm not used to such work. I think my hands are blistered.'

'Aye, they would be.' She smiled at him as she took the rake. 'We must be going. Thanks for your help, Mr Lazurus.'

'Call me James.'

Idly, Giles picked up a round knob of coal.

Shrugging into his jacket, James placed a round straw hat upon his head and picked up his drawing tablet. 'Do you live far away? I can help you push the cart home, if you like.'

'No need. We're used to doing it. Come on, Giles. Let's get this lot home.'

'Just a minute.' Giles grinned at her, took aim and threw his piece of coal. It hit the Browns' horse on the rump. The beast gave a whinny and took off across the sand, scattering its load of sea coal everywhere before coming to a halt. Some way out on the expanse of sand, the brothers continued working, not noticing anything amiss.

James chuckled. 'I hope to see you both again, then. Good day, Miss Ingram. Giles, it was nice to meet you.'

'Tek care, mister.' This time it was Giles who held out his hand. He grinned when James shook it.

* * *

Soon Mary became ill, and Callie had to stay home to look after her.

'Eh, but I don't know what's the matter with me, our Callie,' her mother said tiredly.

Callie did. Her mother was worn out from bearing children. Fifteen of them she'd given birth to, and only nine of them were left alive. And when her mother had thought it was all over, eight years after Giles was born, she'd surprised them all by giving birth to Kitty Agatha at the age of forty-four.

'She's a bonny one,' Callie said, smiling down at the plump, contented-looking infant.

'Aye. All bairns are bonny when they're small. They're an awful lot of work though, and they tire you out.'

'Having fifteen children is enough to wear any woman out,' Callie said gently, kissing her ma's cheek. 'I've got a thruppence I found on the sand yesterday. Likely it dropped from the pocket of the gentry. I'm going to ask the doctor for thruppence worth of blood tonic for you. It'll give you some strength.'

'You're a good girl, Callie. I daresay I'll be all right in a day or two. Tell Giles to drop in on our Verna on his way to school. She might be able to help you with the washing when she's done hers. In the meantime, you make a start on it.'

Callie was loath to miss school, but she had no choice, she realized as she lit a fire under the copper. Grating some Sunlight soap into a bowl, she added some hot water from the kettle on the hob and stirred it until it melted into a thick liquid. Adding it to the boiler, she dropped in the sheets and boiled them until they were spotless. She rinsed them in another tub, carrying pails of water from the pump, then began to feed them through the mangle one by one. After a while her back began to ache and her hands turned red and wrinkled, like those of an old woman.

Verna later came in through the door that led into the lane. She'd been married for three years and already she had a daughter in her arms, two sons hanging off her skirt, and another bairn under her pinny waiting its turn to see daylight.

'Here,' Verna said, 'let me give you a hand with those. When they're pegged out you can boil the whites. We'll let the water cool down then use the same for washing the coloureds. What dost the new bairn look like?'

'She's as plump as a piglet, and has prickly dark hair, like the head of a broom. She takes after the Ingram side, and we're calling her Kitty Agatha.'

Verna chuckled. 'Da got his own way in the end, then.'

'Let's hope it's the end of it. He's had the best years of her and she's worn out with childbirth.'

A sigh issued from Verna. 'It's a woman's lot in life, I'm afraid. I'll go up and see her when the sheets are pegged out. It's a good drying day now the breeze has come up. Johnny, you can be a good boy and hand your aunt Callie the clothes pegs.'

Johnny smiled angelically at her. 'Good un.'

'Hah, the angels must have polished your halo for you when you walked past the church, then.' Callie gave him a hug and a kiss.

'I'll just go in and lay our Daisy down. A letter's come from Jane. We'll read it when we've finished the washing.'

Madam has delivered her second child, a sweet little girl called Emmaline. Mrs Sugden, the housekeeper, recommended me to madam for the nursery maid's position. I'm to be paid an extra shilling a week and it's much easier than being the tweeny maid, where you're at everybody's beck and call from dawn to dusk.

Callie, you should think about leaving Seafield, too. There are so many wonders to see and things to do in London. Theatres, museums, plays and operas. Listening to the band in Hyde Park and watching the horses and riders go by, looking like dogs' dinners in their Sunday best.

Da and my fishermen, Chad, Tom and Joe, keep safe. Aaric, who would have thought you'd become a tally clerk at the wood yard? I hope you're well. It's hard to believe you're twenty now. Verna, I hope you're happy with your Robbie Wilkinson. Callie, give Giles a kiss from his sister Jane. He probably won't remember me after all this time away. Lord, how I miss you all.

Love from your affectionate daughter and sister,

Jane Ingram.

Her mother wiped a tear away with the corner

of the sheet. 'Eh, she writes a lovely letter, does our Jane. And she sent some money through the agency. She's a good girl.'

Callie envied Jane. She wasn't looking forward to leaving school and staying home. For certain she didn't want the hard life her ma had to put up with, though she couldn't say what she wanted her life to be. And she couldn't see how to avoid being a drudge while her mother needed help in the house.

As if her da had read her thoughts, he said, 'Callie is needed here. She's not going off to London town like Jane did. Mark my words.'

But perhaps she would be able to escape, once her mother was back to her normal energetic self, she thought. If Jane could defy him, then so could she.

Then she remembered how her da had lashed out at her mother when Jane had gone. She decided to bide her time.

Three

It was a Saturday, and Patricia Lazurus wore a smile on her face as her brother wheeled her down to the sands in an invalid chair. She'd been confined to the indoors with the servants for weeks, too fatigued to do much but gaze at the sunshine outside the window.

Today, James had surprised her. 'The doctor told me you could take the air for a short time if the weather was fine. But you mustn't tire yourself.'

She'd tired herself already, just by getting dressed, even with the help of the housekeeper. She'd donned a simple promenade dress consisting of a flared skirt in dark blue, worn with a Russian blouse and a jacket over the top. The crown of her straw hat was decorated with a wide blue ribbon gathered into a side bow.

She'd picked up a copy of *Pride and Prejudice*, which she'd already read twice, in case she got bored.

'Dearest James, it must be such a burden having an invalid on your hands,' she said.

He chuckled. 'If you had to be infirm at all, you couldn't have chosen a better time or place. And no, you're never a burden. I don't mind it here at all. There's always something going on at the beach. I thought you'd like to watch the fishing boats set sail this morning. It's a pretty sight. I've been sketching them. I hope to get something on canvas when we get back to London.'

'But you'll be going to Cambridge after Christmas.'

'I'll be home for some of the year. I've got three canvases planned at the moment. The fishing fleet, the cockle women, and the coal gatherer.'

Patricia cast a quizzical eyebrow his way. 'Gathering coal on a beach? How very odd.'

'It's sea coal. It floats in on the tide and is deposited on the sand. The villagers rake it into piles and gather it up. It's hard work.'

'But where does it come from?'

'One of the fishermen told me that nobody knows, not even the experts. Some say that lumps break off from a coal seam under the sea; others that it's from a rotting wooden collier, sunk years before and buried under the sands.'

He pointed to a girl. Rake in hand, she was talking to four of the fishermen. Was one of them her sweetheart? Patricia wondered. But no, the girl was too young, about the same age as herself. The group of men resembled each other. One of them was getting on in age.

She smiled when the girl's voice came to her. 'Bye, Da ... lads ... safe fishing.'

'That's Miss Calandra Ingram,' her brother told her. 'She rakes coal before school.'

'What an odd name.'

'I think it suits her, though everyone refers to her as Callie, I understand.'

She was dressed in a faded and darned checked skirt, plain white blouse, a white apron and a floppy sun bonnet, the strings dangling over her shoulders.

Patricia wondered what it was about the girl that had piqued her brother's interest. 'I think I'd like to meet her, James.'

The girl waved as the Cobles headed out to sea, then she drew a line in the sand and pegged her claim. As she straightened up she saw them, gazed at them for a short moment, then nodded.

A boy came down the beach with a cart, leaving it not too far from where they sat, and carrying on down the beach at a run. He skidded to a stop in front of Callie, scattering sand all over the place. There was a wide grin on his face.

Taking his leave, James strolled over to where they stood. His voice carried clearly to Patricia. 'Good morning. I haven't seen you down here for a few days.'

'Our ma's been off colour,' the boy said.

'Nothing serious, I hope.'

The girl shrugged. 'She just needed to rest for a day or two. The doctor gave her a tonic.'

A frank glance came Patricia's way from the boy. 'Who's that girl with you?'

'Patricia, my sister. She's been cooped up indoors for a while. Come and meet her, Callie. I daresay she'd like having someone of her own age to talk to.'

'I haven't got time to chat. There's the coal to rake.'

'You've marked your patch and the tide is still going out,' James pointed out.

The girl seemed reluctant. 'I s'pose. Giles, you stay here and mind the patch. I won't be long.'

James introduced the two girls. Patricia gazed at the local girl, envying her fine skin, delicate features, and the deep blue of her eyes. 'I'm pleased to meet you, Miss Ingram.'

'Likewise.' Callie nodded and her gaze went to the book in her lap. 'What's the book called?'

'*Pride and Prejudice*. I daresay you've never heard of it.'

'You daresay wrong,' Callie said bluntly. 'It was written by somebody called Jane Austen.'

'You've read it?' Patricia said, startled.

'I can't rightly say I've read it yet, but I've certainly heard of it.'

Patricia felt ashamed of herself. 'If I sounded rude, I'm sorry. I didn't mean to.'

Callie shrugged. 'It's nowt to worry about. It's not the first time I've been given cause to feel offence, nor will it be the last. Because I rake coal, that doesn't mean I lack a brain. Good day, Miss Lazurus. Mr Lazurus. I have work to get on with.'

'Callie?' James said.

The girl turned his way, trying to hide the spark of humiliation in her eyes. 'What is it?'

'That was ungracious of you. I beg you to accept my sister's apology with the grace it deserves. Tish didn't mean to offend you, and she did apologize.'

'I came here to go about my business, not to socialize.' She nodded, then smiled. 'But I reckon I was churlish at that, and since you took the time to point it out, I'm sorry.'

On impulse, Patricia held out the book. 'To make up for my rudeness, I'd like you to have this. I'm sure you'll enjoy it.'

Callie gazed at the book, then at James, who said, 'It's all right, Callie. Take it.'

She took it between her hands, her fingers delicately smoothing over the cover then tracing the gold lettering. There was a wistful smile on her face. 'I've never had a book of my own. This is right nice of you, Miss Lazurus, but somebody might say I stole it. That would shame my folk.' Callie handed it back, turned on her heel and walked off towards her coal patch.

'Well,' Patricia said, giving a quiet laugh. 'She's a prickly one. Did you see the look on her face when she held that book in her hands? I wonder why she didn't keep it.'

'The poor can be proud, since they're used to working hard for everything. A book would be a luxury Callie couldn't afford, and like she said, somebody might accuse her of stealing it.'

'Then I'll write an inscription inside it. Pass me your pencil, James. You can leave the book on the rock next to their barrow, and then she'll have to take it.'

Patricia wrote:

To Miss Calandra Ingram, a gift from Patricia Lazurus, on the occasion of their first meeting in Seafield Village, July 17th 1889. I would be pleased if you will accept this book as a token of my friendship, Callie, and I hope you will enjoy reading it.

Mary Ingram was up bustling around when Callie and Giles got back from the beach. 'How are you feeling now, Ma?'

'Much better. The doctor's blood tonic worked a treat.'

'Well, make sure you keep taking it until the bottle's all finished. Doctor's orders.'

'It sounds more like Callie Ingram's orders to me.'

Callie grinned. 'I don't want you to waste my thruppence.'

'What's that you've got there?'

'A book. It was a gift from Miss Lazurus, who I met on the beach today. She has lovely handwriting – look.' Callie handed the book over to her mother.

'That was kind of her,' Mary said. 'And your writing is just as good as hers. You must write a note thanking her. I'll not have anyone saying my girl doesn't mind her manners. Remember, you're as good as she is any day, and clever with it. How old is this girl?'

'About the same age as me. And how can I be as good as her, when she's gentry?'

'Don't forget, the Brightman family is in trade. They owned a large shop in Hartlepool, and warehouses as well. I heard they moved and opened another one in London.'

'Why don't we ever see them?'

'They cast me out when I married your da. But you and Aaric take after them in your looks, and your ways.'

'Then they're nothing to shout home about.'

'You're right, Callie love. They're not. But I shamed them, though it wasn't my fault. Let it be a lesson to you. Be modest with the lads and don't get yourself trapped into something you don't want. Men will ruin you, given the opportunity – and sometimes they make the opportunity.'

'Is that what happened with da?'

'Never you mind what happened with your da; it makes no difference now. I made the best I could of it, though poverty drags you down, and sometimes you grow weary of the battle to survive. God only knows, although I love my children, if I'd known then what the future held for me, I wouldn't have set foot in Seafield. Improve yourself if you can, Callie. Keep yourself tidy for a man who will treat you with respect.'

'I'll try, Ma.'

'I know you will.' She looked pensive for a moment. 'My folk wouldn't know me if they saw me in the street now, even if they wanted to.' She gazed down at the book and smiled. 'This was a favourite of mine when I was your age. Do you like this Patricia Lazurus?'

'I like her fine, and her brother, too.'

'Then it won't hurt to encourage them. You

never know where such a friendship might lead.'

Kitty stirred at the sound of their voices and began to agitate. 'Likely she's made a clart of herself.' Her mother gave a soft rueful laugh. 'Now there's something I wouldn't have said before I married your da. Fetch me a bowl of water and a flannel, then pass over a clean napkin, would you love. Don't forget to write that note, now. Manners mean a lot to some folks. I haven't got an envelope, but there's some writing paper in the dresser, and a stick of sealing wax. Use the pen, and be careful not to blot. There should be enough ink left.'

'I don't know where they live.'

'With a name like Lazurus it shouldn't be hard to find out. Ask Mrs Staines at the grocery shop, since they handle the letter post, as well. But don't tell her what it's about, lest you want the whole village to know.'

The Lazurus family was at breakfast when the housekeeper brought the letter in on a tray.

'Lord, I haven't seen sealing wax on a letter for years. It's for you, Tish.'

'Me?' Patricia ran her thumb under the blob of sealing wax, opened the fold of paper, and smiled at James. 'It's from Callie Ingram, thanking me for the book. Where is Miss Ingram, Mrs Perkins?'

'I sent her packing, Miss. I thought it was a begging letter.'

'Go and get her, James. Invite her for breakfast. That's all right, isn't it, Uncle Harold?'

'By all means, my dear,' their Uncle Harold said mildly. 'The pair of you have talked about the girl so much that I'm curious to meet her.'

'She's one of the fisher folk by the looks of her,' the housekeeper said, looking down her nose slightly.

'Then she earns an honest living. You may set another place at the table for her, Mrs Perkins.'

Callie was walking rapidly away from the house when her name was called.

'Callie, wait!'

She stopped, then turned to gaze enquiringly at James, a smile on her face.

'You're invited back for breakfast.'

Her heart began to thump. 'I daren't.'

He looked disappointed. 'You don't have time?'

'No ... yes ... I don't know.'

'My great uncle wishes to meet you.'

'Why would Mr Lazurus want to meet me?' She knew why: to look down on her like the housekeeper had.

'Because he's curious.' Mischief filled his eyes. 'Don't you think we're good enough for you, then?'

He'd read her mind, twisting her thought for his own ends. She didn't know whether to be annoyed or to laugh. 'It hadn't entered my mind.'

She giggled when he chuckled, and found herself walking back towards the house. It was large, and set on a corner in the lane that led to the station.

My, but it's grand, she thought. You could have driven a coach and a team of horses through the front door, and with a yard to spare all around them in the hall.

'Uncle Harold, this is Miss Calandra Ingram.'

Harold rose to his feet. 'Please take a seat, Miss Ingram. James, perhaps you'd serve our guest some breakfast.'

Stiffly, she took the seat James pulled out for her. A few minutes later a plate with eggs, bacon and tomatoes, and a rack of toast was set in front of her. Her mouth began to water. It made a change from smoked kippers.

'Tuck in, my dear, before it goes cold.'

Callie's glance took in the table, and she followed James's lead, laying the napkin in her lap, though she only covered up a darn in her skirt with it. She selected the same type of knife and fork as he did from the array of shining silver cutlery on offer.

Feeling self-conscious, Callie took small bites, trying not to laugh as she pretended she was Lady Ingram.

'Would you prefer coffee or tea, Miss Ingram?' Mr Lazurus asked.

'Coffee, please,' she answered, although it was something she'd never tasted.

The coffee was poured from a tall silver pot into a cup so thin that she could see the light from the window through it. The smell rising in the steam coming from the pot was delicious.

'Cream, Miss?' the housekeeper said begrudgingly.

'Yes, please.'

Callie sipped the coffee, and found it disappointingly bitter. When she grimaced, Mr Lazurus the elder raised an eyebrow and gave a bit of a smile. 'Coffee is an acquired taste and you might like to try some sugar in it. Tell me, Miss Ingram, how did you come by the name Calandra?'

'My da saw it on a headstone in the churchyard. It belonged to a passenger on a Greek ship that was wrecked. One of my brothers is called Aaric. He was named after a sea captain from Norway.'

'How quaint,' Patricia said.

The man's eyes came up to hers. 'Aaric Ingram? Ah yes, I believe I've met your brother. He pointed out a flaw in a contract I'd drawn up, which saved his employer a small amount of money, as I recall. A very astute young man. Where was he educated?'

'At the church school.'

'A pity he didn't go on with his education. Mr Ingram struck me as having a good mind.'

'Oh, he has, and he reads books all the time to educate himself. And Aaric can calculate numbers in his head as quickly as a rat can run up a drainpipe.'

Now it was his turn to grimace. 'You have a peculiar turn of phrase, young lady. What about you? You seem to pen a good letter.'

'I go to the church school, too. I'll be leaving

there soon. I like to read, write stories, paint and draw. And I like to learn about history, and the different places in the world, when I've got the time. I'm not as good as Aaric with numbers, but I know my times tables, and fractions.'

'And when you leave school ... what will you do then?'

They were all looking at her now, their eyes alight with interest.

'I'd like to travel, and I'd like to see London town. But wanting to and being able to are two entirely different things. I daresay I'll help my mother look after the family until I'm old enough to wed.'

'How do you fill your time when you're not at school?'

The questions made Callie feel uncomfortable, for she was being made aware of the limitations of her background. Nonetheless her chin tilted up a fraction. 'I have very little time to waste, Mr Lazurus. I think you know that my father is a fisherman. I help my mother in the house, sell fish door to door to grand folk like yourself, and I harvest coal and cockles from the sea. I'm not ashamed of it.' She rose to her feet, and said gently, 'Thank you for the breakfast. It was welcome, but now I really must go. My mother needs me.'

'I'll see you out,' James said.

'Will you be at the beach raking coal tomorrow morning, Callie?' Patricia said. 'I'd like to discuss the book with you.'

Callie gave her a faint smile. 'There's not

much use doing that until I've read it, Miss Lazurus, and I don't get much leisure time. Besides, likely as not I'll be at the church service in the morning.'

'Well, what do you think of her?' Patricia asked as soon as the door closed behind them.

'The girl has a good mind. She's compassionate too, but has an independent nature. I rather like her. A pity she has no prospects.'

'I was thinking that perhaps she could come here of a weekend if her mother can manage without her. I get so bored with my own company, and I'm a nuisance to James. I'm sure he'd like more time to himself to go off sketching.'

Their great uncle shook his head. 'I don't know if Theron would approve of such a scheme. He is, after all, your legal guardian.'

'Our cousin isn't here. Besides, Theron is not as stern as he appears to be. He can be ... *reasonable* at times.'

James, who had just come back into the room, chuckled at the thought. 'Name one instance when Theron Grace has been reasonable once his mind is set on something. Our mother's cousin was born getting his own way. I rather admire his technique, though. When you try to argue with him he just waits until you've finished, then carries on as though you've never spoken in the first place.'

Great-uncle Harold guffawed with laughter, then said, 'Have you taken the girl's feelings into account? She'd be coming into a life she's not used to, then dropped when you leave.'

'I cannot force Callie to visit, nor can I demand her friendship. I can just ask her. I think she'll be quick to realize the benefits that might arise from such an arrangement. Please say yes, Uncle.'

He consulted with his pocket watch, and frowned. 'She appears to be honest, but I'll make enquiries about her character. If that satisfies, I'll approach her father on the matter. Most of the folks round here know the value of a coin.'

'You mean you'll hire her, like a servant?'

'As a companion. At least she'll know where she stands. You can't just befriend these people and show them your hearth. Like stray dogs they'll try and take advantage of you. Besides, her labour adds to her family income, though in an incalculable way. They must be compensated for the withdrawal of that.'

'But Uncle Harold— '

'Theron would approve of the hire,' James said. 'He believes in an honest day's pay for an honest day's work.'

'Which doesn't apply to the charitable work he takes on, of course, nor his reputation of being the advocate for the poor.'

Harold smiled at her. 'Ah, Patricia, nobody would argue with the fact that Theron Grace is an admirable man. He is charming, even when he's being ruthless. I just wish I was cast in the same mould.'

'He's not in the least bit ruthless. As for you,

you're a lovely, sweet-tempered man who can be twisted around my finger when Theron cannot. In fact, you're my favourite great-uncle, and I adore you.'

Harold chuckled. 'Could that be because I'm your only great-uncle? I admit, Theron's mind is an enigma to me, but I like him enormously, too. I must go now. I have a meeting to attend in Hartlepool. Don't worry. I'll see if I can arrange something regarding the girl. Anything that will help you to recover your health.'

There came a knock at the door and the doctor was announced.

'How's my favourite patient this morning?' he said, beaming a smile at everyone.

'Misbehaving,' Harold said. 'She hasn't eaten her breakfast.'

'I drank my milk and it filled me up. Now I'm not hungry.'

'Talk some sense into her, Doctor Forbes. Leave any further instructions with Mrs Perkins, as usual.'

The doctor tut-tutted when the door closed behind their uncle. 'You're looking quite flushed, Miss Lazurus. Have you been overtaxing yourself?'

Patricia, who was feeling decidedly weak after her exertions on Callie's behalf, nodded. 'I rather think I may have...'

Four

Callie had supposed that Mr Lazurus had called after her to complain about her, though she couldn't think what for. It wasn't as though she'd knocked on the front door when she'd delivered her note. She again hoped she hadn't been accused of stealing the book, but Miss Lazurus had written a note in her own hand saying it was a gift, so it couldn't be that. A smile touched her lips. My, but she was enjoying the reading of it, though that proud Mr Darcy needed a good clout around the ear, she reckoned.

She certainly hadn't been expecting to be offered breakfast.

'I didn't think much of the coffee,' she'd told her mother afterwards. 'It left a bitter taste in my mouth. And the table was nearly as big as the back yard. There were knives and forks made of real silver, and a napkin in case I soiled my skirt with food, raggy old thing that it is.' She grinned. 'Mr Lazurus was right inquisitive.'

She gazed through the window out to the street. Her father was sucking through his pipe and looking thoughtful. He still wore his fisherman's cap. Callie couldn't remember ever seeing him without it on his head. She turned to her mother. 'Does Da wear his cap to bed?'

'Only in the winter,' she said with a laugh. 'He's lost most of his hair, and it keeps his head warm.'

She watched the two men shake hands, then Mr Lazurus took something from his pocket and handed it to her da.'

'Mr Lazurus gave him money.' She darted back from the window when her da glanced her way before sliding it into his pocket, even though she was well hidden by the lace curtain. She picked up the sock she'd been darning and applied her needle industriously to the hole, though it was nearly all darns already. 'He's coming back in.'

Her da took his seat by the fireplace and began to pack his pipe with tobacco in his slow, deliberate way. The two females exchanged an exasperated glance. It was no good hurrying him.

'Where are the lads?' Mary asked.

'Chad and Tom are fixing the nets. The William sisters are making a bit of a show of themselves in front of them.'

'It's about time the pair of them took a wife and set up house for themselves. The William girls are hard-working and sensible.'

'Aye, they've got wide hips, so likely as not they'll be good breeders. Joe has gone to the station with our Verna's man to help him load the fish on to the train. Our Joe has a mind to join the navy. I reckon he'll tek off one of these days.'

This wasn't news to Callie, or her mother.

Ebeneezer put a light to his pipe, drawing on it so his head was surrounded by a cloud of smoke, until the baccy began to glow. He leaned back in his chair, and waved the pipe stem towards the window. 'Yon Mr Lazurus came by on a matter of business. He wants our Callie in his home at weekends, to keep company with his great-niece.'

Callie's eyes widened.

'And what did you tell him?' Mary asked calmly.

'We agreed on a wage.'

'Just like that? Have you looked at your daughter lately, Ebeneezer?'

Her da looked at her and smiled. 'She looks like a reet pretty piece to me.'

'Her clothes are in rags. She can't mix with the gentry looking like that.'

'Likely our Verna has got something she can wear.'

'Verna needs her rags for her own back. Better you put your hand in your pocket. You can pass over that money the lawyer feller gave you before you go off to the Seven Moons,' Mary said fiercely. 'Callie has worn hand-me-downs since the day she was born. I'll get her something decent to wear. I can't have her shaming us.'

'Have it your own way, woman,' he said and handed over some coins.

'Is that all, Ebeneezer?'

He shrugged, but found another shilling. 'The

lass is to see the doctor come Saturday, too.'

'For what?'

'To make sure she has no diseases to pass on. Don't worry; yon Mr Lazurus will be paying the bill. His great-niece has been poorly. The only woman in the house is getting on and is nowt but a servant, so not fit company for the girl.'

'Our Callie will be a servant, too.' Mary smiled. 'But never mind. That's better than raking coal up from the beach, and likely she can better herself ... And, Ebeneezer, from now on you'll give Callie a portion of what she earns.'

'I might be able to manage to raise a penny or two for the lass.'

'It's mingy you are, Ebeneezer.'

'Money's not for wasting. My sons earn a man's wage for their labours. That's how it should be. Stop your nagging, Mary. A man wants some peace from his woman when he's in his own home.'

Mary, who'd been about to speak again, pressed her lips together in a tight line. Callie hated it when her da spoke to her mother like that. And she resented him for arranging her life without so much as asking her. It occurred to her that women didn't count for much with her da. She put the thought to the test. 'I don't know if I want to work for the Lazurus family, Da.'

He gave her a measured look that told her he wasn't taking any nonsense from her. 'That's enough from you, maiden. One nagging woman in the house is enough. You'll do as you're told unless you want my strap across your backside.'

And Callie, whose backside had been stung by her da's strap on more occasions than she wished to remember, despite being his favourite daughter, shut her mouth too.

Her mother smiled at her. 'Things are looking up for you, Callie. You're a clever girl, and you never know what will come of this.'

Whether things were looking up or not remained to be seen. Callie wasn't at all sure she wanted to be at the beck and call of Patricia Lazurus. When she was raking coal or digging cockles, at least she had time to think, and to daydream. Best she set the girl straight about that right from the start, so they both knew where they stood.

Callie set out early the following Saturday, for she had to present herself at eight o'clock. She wore a serviceable brown skirt and jacket over a cream blouse that was a bit on the big side. Her mother had bought the dress from the second-hand shop and the material made her skin itch.

'You'll fit into it before you know it,' her mother had said of the blouse. 'You've some growing to do there, yet.'

A sack over her head and shoulders kept the drizzle from soaking through her shoulders, and though her hair was braided, the damp weather caused tendrils to curl away from her hairline.

Shown into the house with a curt warning from the housekeeper to use the servants' entrance next time, Callie found Patricia lying on a couch before the window. She had a discontented look on her face.

It was a big room, the walls covered in paper with bluebirds and yellow butterflies flying amongst a twisting vine. There was plenty of space for a desk and a wardrobe, as well as the sofa Patricia sat on.

'I hate it when it rains,' Patricia said by way of greeting.

'Tell me that the next time the pump runs dry and you're thirsty,' Callie told her.

Patricia's eyes widened. 'Are you going to be disagreeable?'

'Only if you are. There's something I want to get straight between us right from the beginning.'

'Oh ... you *are* going to be disagreeable. Go on then, say it.'

'This arrangement was agreed between your uncle and my da. Nobody asked me what I wanted, or told me what I was supposed to do.'

'I want us to be friends, Callie.'

'You didn't stop to think that it might not be what I wanted. And if you think my friendship can be bought by paying my da, you can think again.'

'That was my great-uncle Harold's idea. Don't you like me then?'

'That's got nowt to do with owt. I don't see how we can be friends if I'm at your beck and call. It makes me feel like a servant.'

'That's your pride speaking.' Patricia grinned as her eyes went to the dress she was wearing.

'You do look rather like a servant.'

Exasperated, Callie glared at her. 'You can take that back, Patricia Lazurus. My ma bought me this dress special to come here in, so I wouldn't shame her. You've no need to mock us. Wasn't it bad enough that the doctor examined my hair for parasites, then asked if I had worms. *Worms!* I blushed to the roots of my hair.'

Patricia giggled. 'And were there any?'

'Certainly not! We might be poor, but we're clean. And what's more, my ma is as good as you are, any day. Her folks were in trade before she married my da.'

Patricia grinned. 'You're as prickly as a hedgehog. I wasn't insulting your mother; I was insulting the garment you're wearing. That's a different thing altogether.'

'That's all right then, because I hate it too.'

Gazing at each other, they giggled at the same time.

Patricia said, 'I'm sorry you weren't consulted, you know. It was none of my doing. I simply suggested that you could come at weekends, and for no other reason than I liked you when I met you. James needs some time to himself and I'm lonely. I'm sorry you weren't asked, Callie. Would you rather not come here?'

Feeling a bit guilty, Callie shrugged. 'I don't mind coming. It makes a change from raking coal, I s'pose.'

'Would you prefer not to be paid, then? My uncle said your labours were valuable to your family, who should be recompensed. So really, *you're* not being paid, your father is.'

'Well, if you put it that way ... .I reckon my family needs the money, at that.'

'And if you feel like a servant in that gown, wouldn't you feel better if you wore a nicer one?'

Now there was a thought. Callie gave a huff of laughter. 'I haven't got a nicer one.'

'I've got a cupboard full. You can wear one of those if you like – that is if you can swallow your pride and allow yourself to.'

Exasperated, Callie knew she wasn't going to get the better of Patricia, so she held out her hands in surrender, palms outwards. 'All right. I give in.'

Patricia beamed at her. 'Have a look in the wardrobe. We have half an hour before breakfast.'

Callie had never seen so many lovely garments. She ran her finger gently over the soft material. 'Eh, it must have taken a long time for you to sew these.'

'Oh, I didn't sew them myself. My guardian, Theron Grace, has a dressmaker who comes in. She's got a sewing machine, and patterns. And she hires people to do the fine work.'

'Don't you have parents then?'

Patricia's smile faded. 'My mother and father died from cholera when they were visiting Egypt eight years ago. Theron Grace is a second cousin of our mother. He was appointed guardian, and took charge of us. He's managing us, and our parents' estate. At least until James has finished his education, since most of it will go to him. I imagine I'll be married off before that.'

'I'm sorry your parents died. What's this guardian of yours like?'

'Clever, bossy, intimidating sometimes. James and I are quite in awe of him.' Patricia lost interest in the subject. 'See that blue house gown – that one would match your eyes. There's a flowered apron that buttons up the back to wear over it, with a lace trim. Come on, you'd better get changed. Great-uncle doesn't like us to be late for meals.'

Half an hour later the two girls entered the dining room, Callie a little self-consciously. The two males rose to their feet.

Patricia kissed her great-uncle when he looked at his watch and frowned. 'I'm sorry we're a bit late. It look us a while to get ready this morning.' Great-uncle Harold merely grunted.

'Good morning, James,' Patricia said.

James Lazurus's smile encompassed them both. 'Good morning, Tish. I heard you coughing during the night.'

'I'm sorry it woke you. It's the damp weather.'

'Tell the housekeeper to light a fire in your room.' He turned his eyes towards Callie. 'How nice to see you again. Are you well?'

Patricia said wickedly, 'Didn't you read the doctor's report then, James?'

'He certainly did not,' Great-uncle Harold interjected. 'It was none of his business. Let me just say that the young lady wouldn't be here if she was not in robust health. Good morning,

Miss Ingram.'

A blush rose to Callie's cheeks as she mumbled, 'Good morning, Mr Lazurus.' She then turned to James to answer his enquiry with, 'I'm well, thank you, Mr Lazurus.'

James laughed. 'You must call me James so you don't confuse us. Otherwise we shall both answer at the same time.' He drew back a chair. 'Will you be seated, Callie.'

'Thank you, James.' Shyly, she took her place at the table next to Patricia.

The men seated themselves and Harold indicated to the housekeeper that she could serve them their breakfast.

Five

Summer began to draw to a close. Spending the weekends with Patricia Lazurus had become a joy to Callie, despite her initial reluctance, for it had taken her a little time to get used to the company in which she found herself.

James used the two of them as models, drawing them from many angles. Callie stood for ages with a sheet draped over her clothes, her arms aching as she posed with one hand on hip, a heavy jug held on her shoulder with the other.

James laughed when Patricia said, 'I hope that one isn't for Theron. He's not keen on classical Greek stuff. It reminds him of the time Lady Bryant brought her troupe of classical poseurs to the charity event he'd arranged. He thought she'd engaged professional dancers, but it was just her exercise group. He was prowling around like an angry leopard afterwards.'

James drawled, 'Theron told me they looked like a herd of elephants tramping about the drawing room. You can relax now, Callie. It was just a practice sketch.'

'You mean I've been holding this pose for nothing,' she said indignantly, inspecting the drawings. One of her arm and one with the jug, her face and a drape of cloth.

'It's not for nothing. You've just furthered my career.'

'Hah,' said his sister. 'You don't think Theron will relent and allow you to become an artist, do you?'

'You know our guardian. Once he decides on something, nothing will change his mind. I daresay I'll study law as he's planned, but I'm sure I'll be rotten at it. Then I'll go to Paris and I'll study art, just as I've planned. I'll have the law to fall back on if I fail.'

'Oh, I'm sure you won't fail, James; your work is too good,' Callie said fervently, for she was totally in awe of his talent.

'Then I shall hire you to write my reviews, as well as be my model. You were good at standing still. I didn't expect you to stay there for such a long time. I'm sorry if I tired you, Callie. You should have said.'

She would have stayed there all day if he'd asked her to. 'Now it's my turn to draw you. Pass me your sketching block.'

'Five minutes is all I have,' he said. 'I want to go out.'

Using all her concentration, she took his sketch pad and pencil and drew him, his mouth curved into that mischievous smile of his as he relaxed in the chair by the window, one leg draped inelegantly over the arm.

'That's good,' Patricia said, looking over her shoulder. 'It certainly looks like James.'

James unfolded himself from the chair. 'Let

me see it.'

She gazed anxiously at him while he assessed it, then his eyes came up to hers, slightly puzzled. 'You have quite a talent, Callie. You should take drawing lessons.' Then, seeming to remember her poverty, he added, 'Or at least you should try and practise.'

She smiled to herself. James had also forgotten she couldn't afford luxuries such as drawing blocks, pencils and charcoal sticks either.

Patricia still tired easily. After lunch she rested, usually sleeping for a couple of hours, which gave her enough energy to get through the rest of the day.

Callie had discovered the library, and asked Harold Lazurus for permission to use it while Patricia took her rest.

'Of course you may, my dear,' he said. 'And there's a piano if you'd like to use that, too.'

'I'm afraid I can't play the piano, Mr Lazurus.'

'I can. You can sing instead, if you like.'

'I don't know any songs.'

'I could teach you one.' He looked sad for a moment. 'My wife used to sing well, you know. She died twenty-five years ago, giving birth to our infant daughter. She didn't live long enough to hold the infant in her arms, or even see her face. Our daughter followed her to the grave shortly afterwards. Such a tragedy. That was before I moved here.'

'I'm so sorry. What was your wife called?'

'Elizabeth, and I named our daughter after her. You remind me of my wife a little. Your hair ... so pretty.'

'You must feel lonely living in this house by yourself.'

'Yes, but I never met anyone else I wanted to spend my life with.' He cleared his throat. 'Are you enjoying your time here, Callie?'

'Yes, sir. I've learned a lot. My ma said I should be grateful for the opportunity to improve myself. And I've tried hard to do so.'

'You have improved, my dear. You were very guarded when you first came here, but you've learned to trust us.'

She grinned and teased him a bit. 'You've learned to trust me, too, Mr Lazurus. I think you expected me to walk off with the family silver at first.'

He gave an easy laugh. 'Good gracious, I certainly did not! You've done Patricia good, you know. She doesn't make friends easily, but she genuinely likes you, and looks forward to seeing you. Her health is improving and she's gaining in strength now she's beginning to eat more. It won't be long before the doctor gives her a clean bill of health.'

'Patricia can walk short distances without becoming so out of breath now. I'll miss her when she returns to London,' Callie said, her face turning pink with the pleasure his words gave her.

She'd miss her surroundings too, she thought. She couldn't help but notice the difference between living in this house and the poverty of her own gloomy terrace, where the sun hardly penetrated and where every penny counted. How hard it must have been for her mother to adjust to her life as a fisherman's wife. Now she'd had a taste of comfort, Callie wanted this life for herself. Surely it couldn't be such a hard thing to achieve.

'Patricia will not be returning to London for some time,' Mr Lazurus was saying now. 'I received a letter from her guardian this morning. He suggested that she might be better off staying here for the winter, away from the London fogs. It will give her lungs time to properly heal. The doctor agrees, and so do I. Theron Grace will be visiting us in a couple of weeks' time, so he can inform Patricia of the arrangement. James will be returning to London with him, of course. He needs to prepare for his entrance to university. Eventually James will join Theron as clerk in his law office.'

'But James wants to be an artist!'

'There's nothing to stop him from painting in his spare time. He has his own attic studio in London, and will be looking forward to using it again, no doubt. But he needs to have a profession, so that when he marries he can support his household.'

Disappointment filled Callie at the thought of James leaving. He was such good company.

'I'd like you to come on Friday evening next week, if you would. James and I are going into Stockton to a dinner to raise money for the lifeboat service, and I don't want to leave Patricia alone. I'll give you a note for your parents. I do hope they won't mind.'

'No, Ma won't mind.' And she knew her da would probably be out on the boats if the tide was right. 'Does Mr Grace know about me?'

'Theron Grace has been informed of the arrangement I've made with your father, and he wishes to meet you. Patricia is very fond of her brother. I think she'll take the parting from him more easily if she knows you're here to fill the void.' He moved towards the bell. 'If I may steal a little of your time before you visit my library, I'd be obliged if you'd take tea with me. Then tonight we shall amuse ourselves singing round the piano ... Oh, and Callie, I'd be grateful if you kept what I've told you confidential, since Mr Grace will wish to inform his wards of what's been arranged himself, as is his right.'

'Yes, sir.' James and Patricia's guardian was beginning to sound more and more like an old ogre, and Callie dreaded meeting him. At the same time, ogre or not, she wasn't going to let Theron Grace get the better of her.

Mr Lazurus smiled at her. 'Good girl.'

It took Callie a moment to realize he wasn't responding to her thoughts.

Theron Grace stepped on to the windswept platform of the railway station with its canopy and small waiting room. He was jaded after a long and tedious journey from London, and the Darlington to Stockton had been running way behind schedule. However, although the train was late, a rather complicated and harrowing court case had been resolved suddenly, so he'd found himself with time on his hands and had decided to come to Seafield a week early.

He was looking forward to relaxing, and also to seeing his wards. He'd been worried sick about Patricia's health, and he needed to talk some sense into James's head.

The lamps at Seafield station stood in a yellow pool of light. He was the only passenger to alight, though the porter and stationmaster had offloaded parcels on to the platform, making room for boxes of fish.

When the train departed in a succession of tortured clanks and hisses of steam, the pair began to amble in the direction of the hotel, passing Theron on they way. The stationmaster stopped and tipped his cap. 'Looks like the omnibus driver has gone home, sir. Likely I can fetch you a ride into Seafield on Wilkinson's fish cart, though 'tis Friday, and you might have to wait until the bar closes.'

'It's only half a mile and I could do with the exercise,' Theron said hastily, for he could smell the fishy aroma of the cart from where he stood.

'Reet you are then, sir. Goodnight then.'

'Goodnight.' He started out towards the lights of Seafield, his long legs carrying him rapidly along the lane, the night dark and solid all around him. There were a couple of gas lamps along the road, which only served to emphasize the stretch of darkness between each one.

How different the air was here. A breeze coming off the sea brought the taste of salt to his tongue. His stomach rumbled and he wished he had a plate full of food to go with it. It had been a long time since his last meal. Maybe he should have gone to the hotel after all.

But the tiredness he'd felt was beginning to evaporate with the exercise and fresh air. He began to whistle a tune, and it wasn't long before he was standing on Harold's doorstep. Lights burned, so he knew they were still up. He knocked on the door. Behind him, the sea shushed against the shore as he waited for someone to answer. He knocked louder.

Upstairs a window opened. He moved out of the porch and gazed up. A curtain was pulled aside, and a pale face stared down at him.

'Who're you?' a girl's voice asked.

It didn't sound like Patricia. 'Theron Grace, from London.'

He grinned when she turned away and said to someone else, 'He says he's Theron Grace, that old lawyer gent who looks after you. Shall I let him in?'

'Be careful, Callie, in case it's a burglar. I'll come down with you.'

'How would a burglar know your guardian's name?' There was a loud sigh, then, 'All right, pass over the poker. I'll fettle him with it if it's not him.'

'Tish, open the door,' Theron called out.

'It *is* Theron. Go and let him in Callie, and shut the window; the cold air is coming in. I'll be down in a minute.'

'Call this weather cold, do you?'

'Yes.'

'Then you'd better make sure you're wrapped up warm, and don't forget to wear your slippers.'

'Oh, stop being a fuss pot, do. You're worse than Great-uncle Harold.'

There was a patter of feet on the stairs and the door was opened. The girl was exquisite, with pale skin and a mass of hair that glinted gold in the candlelight. She was barefoot and wrapped in a robe that was darned and faded. The poker was still clasped in her hand.

'You won't need that,' he said. 'I'm in a harmless mood.'

A faint smile chased across her face and she gave him a frank, assessing look. 'I expected you to be older, Mr Grace.'

'Older than whom? I'm younger than Harold Lazurus and older than you are. Since you seem to need to know, I'm twenty-eight years old.'

She giggled. 'You look younger.'

'Make up your mind! Where's Harold?'

'He's gone to a charity dinner with James.'

'I suppose you're that Callie creature Harold wrote and told me about. Are you going to let me in?'

She stood aside, her nose at an upright tilt. 'I was given to understand that you're always right, so I suppose I *must* be that Callie *creature*.'

'Don't pretend you're offended.' He walked

past her, and grinned as he listened to the definite thud the door gave when she closed it, a substitute for the retort that was obviously trembling on the end of her tongue. She gave a small hiss of annoyance at being thwarted.

Just then Patricia came down the stairs. His grin widened into a smile. 'Hello, my love. How are you feeling? What have you been saying to Miss Callie Ingram about me?'

'I feel all the better for seeing you, Theron. And no doubt you'll believe the doctor rather than me, so I'm not telling you how I feel. As for Callie, I told her how wonderful you are.'

'That's all right then, you contrary miss. You look much better than when I last saw you. Come here and give me a big hug.'

She walked into his arms and held him tight. 'I've missed you, you know. I've had nobody to argue with, except Callie. I would have died of boredom if James hadn't found her on the beach.'

'I'm not a piece of old seaweed that was washed up,' Callie retorted.

She certainly isn't, Theron thought. She was an exquisite sprite. 'Is the housekeeper about? I haven't eaten all day, and I'm starving.'

Patricia shook her head. 'Mrs Perkins has gone home, so you'll have to starve until morning.'

'She left a cold supper for Mr Lazurus and James,' Callie said 'There's some ham left over in the larder, and there's beetroot, cheese and pickles and a crusty loaf of bread. Afterwards, you can have some bottled fruit and cold custard. It will take just a minute to fetch you a plate.'

Theron winked at Patricia. 'Now that's what I call a practical and domestic young lady. A pity you're not more like her. Is my room prepared, Callie, d'you know?'

'Mrs Perkins wasn't expecting you until next week,' she pointed out.

'Then shall I go away and come back next week for the sake of Mrs Perkins?'

Her cheeks began to singe. 'You could. On the other hand, we could abandon this silly conversation and I could make the bed up in the room next to Mr Lazurus's for you.'

'Ouch!' He chuckled warmly. 'I know when I'm on a losing streak, so we'll do just that ... Callie?' he said as the girl made to leave the room.

She turned, head cocked to one side, her eyes alight with curiosity, engaging his directly. They were a beautiful shade of blue, and intelligent with it. She said nothing, just waited calmly.

'Thank you. Go and get your slippers on.'

'I haven't got any,' she said, and walked off.

'Is the girl always so prickly?' he said to Patricia.

'Only if you prod her. Callie is proud, and has a mind of her own.' Patricia smiled. 'James and I adore her.'

Theron hoped James hadn't formed an attachment to the girl. But no, she was too young – and anyway, James would be gone by this time next week. 'I'm glad you like her,' he said, 'because it's been decided that you'll stay here over winter. The doctor thinks that the London fogs on top of your illness will be detrimental to your health. By spring you'll be much stronger if you spend the winter here.'

Shocked, she gazed at him. 'What about James?'

'He'll be going back to London with me next week.'

Tears pricked her eyes.

'Come, Tish. It's only a short while until spring.'

'It might be a short while to you, but to me it's ages. What about Christmas?'

'We'll spend it apart, I'm afraid. You do like your great-uncle, don't you?'

'He's a love.'

'And you'll have Callie for company.'

'But only at weekends. She's at school, or working for her family during the week.'

'I'll arrange it with her family that she comes here every day if you like.'

'You'd better ask her what she wants first. Callie won't want to stop going to school, even though she'll have to when the term finishes. Then she'll have to stay at home and help her mother. She wants to be a teacher, and she makes me write essays. She says she wants to learn everything there is in the world to learn, and tells me I'm missing out on my education by being sick, and there's no reason why I can't exercise my mind.'

The more he heard about Callie Ingram, the more surprise Theron felt. 'That's true,' he admitted.

'But Callie thinks she'll have to get married and have babies. That's what her da wants her to do.'

'Most fathers want a good marriage for their daughters.'

'But it wouldn't be a good marriage.'

'There's nothing wrong with fishermen, if she fell in love and wanted to marry one.'

'You don't understand, Theron. She'd have to marry whether she wanted to or not. Callie is too good to be wasted. Her mother's family were shopkeepers, and Callie says her mother wants her to try and better herself, even if that means running away to London to become a maid, like her sister did.'

'I fail to see how becoming a maid would be a better life for anyone.'

'Since you've never lived my life, I reckon you wouldn't, at that,' Callie said from the doorway, her voice tight with anger at finding herself talked about. 'Your supper's on the table, sir ... your glass of milk too, Miss Lazurus – that is, if you can refrain from discussing my business long enough to drink it. Goodnight.'

'Wait, Callie,' Patricia called out.

But the door shut behind Callie and her feet pattered off up the stairs.

'Oh, dear. Callie only calls me Miss Lazurus when she's really upset with me. I'd better go and apologize.'

But Theron, who'd never apologized to anyone in his life, advised, 'Leave it until morning. She will have cooled down a bit by then.'

'But what if she refuses to come here any more?'

'Then she wouldn't be much of a friend, and you'd be better off without her.' His short acquaintance with Callie had already told Theron that she'd be loyal. Now his mind sifted through the information Patricia had given him. It wasn't long before it provided him with a scheme designed to keep Callie Ingram in his employ until his ward no longer needed her.

Six

'Ma, this is Mr Theron Grace. And this is Miss Lazurus.'

At least Callie had managed to warn her mother they were going to pay her a visit. The small living room had been scrubbed clean and the grate was polished to a high shine with black lead. Her ma, although shabby, was wearing her Sunday blouse and a clean pinny. She'd pulled her hair, now showing threads of grey, into a neat bun at the back of her neck. Love for her mother washed over Callie, leaving tears prickling her eyes. How careworn she looked.

Kitty lay in the cradle, plump and contented, her feet kicking in the air.

Her mother wasn't in the least awed by the company she was in. It was as if her early upbringing had released a different set of manners for the occasion. 'Please be seated, Mr Grace. Miss Lazurus, I'm pleased to have the chance to meet you at last, young lady.'

Theron Grace settled himself into her father's chair. Patricia joined Callie on the couch and smiled at her. 'Oh, I would have come to visit much sooner, since I've been longing to meet you. I haven't been able to go very far because I tire easily. Callie is so much like you.'

'Aye, she is.' Her mother's smile warmed Callie.

The kettle was singing on the hob, and there were scones straight from the oven, with butter melting into the crumbly warm interior. Her ma used the best china teapot, and the cups and saucers that went with it. And even though they were chipped in places, Theron Grace ended up with the only set that was completely intact.

As soon as they were settled with refreshments, Mary said, 'How can I help you, Mr Grace?'

'Because my ward is not yet well enough to return to London with her brother, I'm leaving her in Seafield with her great-uncle until the spring. Since your daughter and my ward have become good friends, I'd like Calandra to be companion to Patricia on a full-time basis while my cousin is here in Seafield.'

Her ma turned to her. 'What do you think about this, Callie?'

'I like the arrangement fine. Mr Grace has pointed out the benefits to me.'

'Perhaps you'd like to relate those to me, Mr Grace.'

'As well as an increase in salary, I'd undertake to continue to educate Callie within Patricia's great-uncle's home. I intend to engage a tutor for a short period – a former headmaster who lives nearby and is totally respectable. His name is Christian Tupper.'

Patricia gave a groan and said, 'Must you,

Theron?' Callie giggled.

Theron bestowed a frown on his ward before turning back to Callie's mother. 'I'll also provide Callie with two sets of clothing for the period of her engagement. I don't approve of her wearing my ward's garments.'

Mary's face flushed and she said sharply, 'You should perhaps be made aware that I bought her something decent to wear.'

'I've seen the garment.'

'It's all I could afford.'

'I can understand that you had to consider something hard-wearing and practical and I'm not criticizing you, or Callie, Mrs Ingram. But the difference between them is too marked and your daughter feels out of place. I imagine you can understand what I'm saying. Girls of their age need something more ... youthful, and *flattering*. You could regard it as a uniform.'

'Well, if you put it that way...' Callie smiled when her ma nodded. 'When would I see my daughter?'

'Saturday evening and all day on Sundays, and you could always visit her from time to time. Perhaps you'd like to talk it over with your husband?'

'My husband is out with the boats, but I see no reason why he should object. It's only for a few months, and it's not as though Callie is leaving the district, is it, Mr Grace?'

Theron's glance reflected for a moment on the two girls. 'I have no plans to extend the arrangement at the moment. I'll leave this contract for you to read then. Perhaps you could ask your husband to sign it when you've read it.'

'I'll ask my son Aaric to go through it. He can deliver it back to you this evening.'

'I'll look forward to seeing him.' Theron leaned back in his chair, seemingly quite relaxed, then took a bite of his scone. 'These are quite delicious. It's a long time since I've had home-baked scones straight from the oven.'

'You're not a married man then, Mr Grace?'

'I haven't yet met a woman who can put up with me. Patricia tells me I'll never wed because I never listen to anyone but myself.'

Mary laughed. 'You're typical of most men, then, but at least you're honest.'

'I confess that I am. Too honest for some. Alas, men are poor creatures when measured against the weaker sex, who are not only more industrious and more delightful to look at, but also more obliging for most of the time. I have yet to meet the one woman perfect for me, though.'

'You're a young man yet, Mr Grace. You still have time. May I pour you some more tea?'

Regret filled his eyes. 'I must get home. Thank you for your hospitality, Mrs Ingram. I enjoyed meeting you, and hope we shall meet again some day.' He stood, a man tall and straight, with eyes like dark liquid velvet. Stooping over the cradle, he tickled Kitty under the chin. When Kitty blew a bubble and cooed at him, a smile touched Theron's lips.

The smile softened him, robbed him of the

tension that seemed to hold him together. His voice was just as soft. 'You have lovely daughters, Mrs Ingram. But then, they have a beautiful mother so I'd expect no less.'

Her ma's hand fluttered to her hair and warmth came to her cheeks, so the flawless ghost of her youth was revealed for a second beneath the careworn countenance. Callie imagined it had been a long time since her ma had received such a compliment. *She'd still look young if she'd married a man like Theron Grace instead of my da*, she thought fiercely. She waited while Patricia was helped into the carriage by Theron.

The women had come from the neighbouring terraces at the sight of the vehicle – some to clean windows, though it was not window day, and some to apply a scrubbing brush to an already spotless doorstep. Three stood gossiping, hands folded on their chests.

Callie hugged her mother tight, whispering against her ear, 'Bye, Ma. I love you.'

'I know, Callie. But these are good folks, and you've got to do what's best for you. I know where you are if I need you.'

'Callie?' Theron said quietly, and held out a hand to slide under her elbow and help her inside.

'Just like a princess,' one of the women remarked.

'She'll be too fancy for the likes of us soon, just like her ma.'

If Theron Grace heard the remark, he made no sign.

Mrs Brown glanced at Callie's mother and her face settled into smug lines. 'That's what she thinks. Agatha tells me her brother's got plans for the girl, reet enough. And they don't include going off to London like that sister of hers.'

With a stab of alarm, Callie wondered what the woman meant as Theron flicked the whip over the head of the horse and they moved off.

A week later Patricia bade her brother a tearful goodbye on the stair landing. 'I'm going to miss you, James.'

'It won't be too long until we see each other again. You take care of yourself, Sis. The next time I see you I expect you to be completely well. I've left a gift for you on my dressing table.'

'What is it?'

'You'll see.'

James smiled when Patricia headed towards his room. He took Callie's hands in his and his eyes met hers. 'Goodbye, Callie. I do hope we meet again, because I've enjoyed your company and I like you a lot.'

Shyness filled her. 'Goodbye, James.'

They looked at each other for a moment, then suddenly James leaned forward and gently kissed her on the mouth.

She blushed at the intimate caress, jerked her hands away and took a step back. Palm against her mouth, she whispered, 'James, you shouldn't have.'

His eyes filled with laughter. 'I know I

shouldn't have. But you look so sweet, and I've grown fond of you, Callie.'

'Please hush,' she pleaded, feeling mortified now. 'Somebody might hear you, then I'd be shamed.'

'It was just a brotherly kiss.'

'Except you're not her brother, James,' Theron said from below them. 'Callie is your sister's companion, a young and impressionable girl. Your conduct towards her on this occasion could be misconstrued.'

'I'm sorry, Callie. I meant nothing by it. I hope you'll forgive me.'

'Of course.'

'The carriage is here. You can go and tell your great-uncle that we're off. He's in the library.'

James clattered off downstairs and headed towards the library.

Callie gazed nervously at Theron Grace. 'I hope you both have a safe journey back to London.'

'I'm sure we shall.' His eyes were fathomless as he gazed up the staircase at her. Suddenly he said, 'I'd rather you didn't encourage James.'

Her blush returned with a vengeance. 'I didn't encourage him. It was unexpected.'

He chuckled. 'I noticed, my dear. I keep forgetting James is no longer a boy. You'd be wise not to form any expectations from the incident. You're a pretty girl and he gave in to impulse – as any young man might.'

What did he expect, that she'd demand James march her to the altar and put a ring on her finger? After seeing what her mother had had to put up with, she didn't want to marry anyone. She grinned at the thought. 'With respect, sir, you seem to be the one that's worried over nowt.'

'Hmmm, I wonder why that is. Perhaps it's because I envy him. I'd be tempted to kiss you myself if you were a little older, Calandra Ingram.'

'Oh!' Callie turned and fled, her heart pounding in her chest and Theron's chuckle echoing in her ear.

Framed by an upstairs window, the two girls later watched the carriage leave. Callie was smiling. As well as the musical box James had left for Patricia, there had been a gift for herself: a sketching block, pencils and a box of charcoal sticks.

'It's going to be deadly dull without James and Theron,' Patricia said morosely.

It wasn't dull for Callie. The morning lessons were a delight. She soaked them up with enthusiasm and couldn't wait for the next day to arrive.

Patricia's sunny nature wouldn't allow her to remain disgruntled forever. After a week she grew used to not having her brother around, and her former enthusiasm came back.

'I hate Sundays without you,' Patricia said one day at the beginning of October. 'Can't I come to your home with you?'

'I go to the church service with my ma, then I

help her with the work. If the tide's right, sometimes I go and rake coal with Giles so he doesn't have to do it by himself on Sundays.'

'I could help your mother, too.'

Callie laughed. 'Doing what? Can you use a flat iron, scrub floors or polish windows? You haven't got the strength.'

'You make me feel useless.'

'You *are* useless. Name one thing you could do to be of help to my ma.'

Patricia thought for a moment. 'I can do embroidery.'

'Nothing in our house needs embroidering. The only sewing skills needed are for darning socks and sewing on patches.'

'You could show me how to do that, then. Or I could watch over Kitty.'

'Sunday is the only time I get to spend with my family,' Callie pointed out.

The sigh Patricia gave was wistful. 'I know; I'm just being selfish. Your mother is so lovely. I wish...'

But Patricia didn't have to finish her sentence, because Callie knew what she wished – that she had a mother of her own. It wouldn't hurt to share with her. 'All right, you can come in the morning and stay for Sunday dinner. But you'll have to ask Mr Lazurus to bring you and pick you up. And I warn you, you won't get any fancy manners from my da or my brothers, and they'll curse without giving it a second thought.'

Patricia's eyes lit up.

* * *

Mary Ingram spent precious money on a piece of beef from the butchers for the occasion, but even so she couldn't afford the best cut.

'Don't go to too much trouble, Ma. Patricia doesn't eat very much,' Callie told her.'

Her mother sighed. 'That's not the point, Callie. If you invite a guest to dinner you have to make an effort.'

That effort saw their best tablecloth darned, boiled and starched, and the bone-handled cutlery that Aunt Agatha had given her ma and da for a wedding present was polished. There was a quick visit to Verna's house to borrow anything that wasn't chipped. Much to her delight, her ma found some table napkins, which, although shabby, would serve to let Patricia know that the Ingram family was not entirely lacking in refinement.

'Look, they've got the initials of Trinity Church sewn into the hem,' Mary said. 'I did some washing for them a while back; must have missed these few. We'll use them, then I'll take them back. I just pray the girl doesn't look too closely at them. She might think we stole them.'

It pained Callie to see her mother worry over such stupid details. She began to wish that she hadn't invited Patricia, and replied flippantly, 'God must have provided them especially for the occasion. A pity he didn't send a side of beef to go with them.'

Her mother flicked the cloth at her, and although she grinned, she said, 'Be content that the Lord has kept you fed with fish all these years. Others are worse off.'

'I know, Ma, and those others include the fish he sends for us to eat.'

'I don't know where you get your answers from, young lady, that I don't.'

'You just have to look in the mirror.' Callie gave her a hug. 'Stop worrying, will you? I'm more worried about how Da and the boys will behave.'

On the day it turned out she had cause to worry. Taking one look at Patricia, Ebeneezer teased, 'That's a skinny one, reet enough. If you were an eel I'd throw you back in the ocean.'

Joseph said, 'Eh, but no eel I've ever saw has a pretty face like that one.' When Patricia blushed, Chad and Tom grinned as they looked at each other.

'Eh, but she's a bonny piece,' said Tom.

'She's summat to admire, reet enough,' Chad answered.

Her father looked sternly at his sons. 'Don't you lads get any ideas. And no cussin'. The lass is a guest in our home, and likely not used to it. Would you like a pot of ale, maiden?'

Rather pink in the face from all the attention, Patricia shook her head. 'No thank you, Mr Ingram.'

'There's nice manners, lass. Best you teach our Callie some. She's like her ma – too pert by far.'

'Perhaps we should say grace,' her mother suggested.

Callie's da picked up the napkin, tucked it into

the neck of his jersey and said, 'Bugger grace. We never had to say it afore, and I've had nowt but a bit of salted herring in my belly all day. Pass the carving knife over, our Mary, then go and fetch the vegetables in.'

Grinning widely at each other, her brothers tucked the napkins carefully under their chins.

'You lot better start to behave yourself else you'll get the dishclowt wrapped round your ears,' Callie told them fiercely.

Chad laughed. 'Like as not she says the very same thing to Mr Lazurus hisself.'

Patricia exchanged a glance with her and the pair began to giggle at the thought.

The men ate heartily, then went off about their business. Sunday or not, there was work to be done.

While she watched over Kitty, Patricia was given a square of linen to hem. It was a part of a worn-out pillowcase, which had been made from an equally worn-out sheet that had been given a new lease of life by being turned sides into middle. Now the remains of the sheet was in the process of becoming a dozen handkerchiefs for her brothers.

Wearing her old skirt, Callie polished the floor upstairs, scrubbed out the wooden-seated privy with lye soap, then washed the windows inside and out with vinegar to make them shine. While her mother started on dinner, Callie boiled Kitty's clowts and hung them in the yard to dry, which would make the load of washing easier for her mother the next day. She dusted the parlour, did the ironing, then picked up the sewing basket and began to sew a button on to her da's shirt.

The tip of Patricia's tongue slid along her lips as she concentrated on the neat row of fancy stitching she was doing. She'd nearly finished one handkerchief when Callie would have finished all six squares by now.

'You don't have to be so careful,' she said. 'Like as not they'll lose them overboard before the week is out.'

Her mother smiled. 'You always do things in too much of a hurry, Callie.'

'That's because there's always something else around the corner waiting to be done.'

'Patricia's shell stitching is beautiful. I'm keeping the handkerchief for myself.' Her mother gazed at the fancy hem. 'You can embroider my name in the corner if you would, Patricia. It's Mary.'

When Patricia's face glowed with pride Callie's heart softened. It must be horrible not to have a mother to turn to in times of trouble, she thought.

As she stitched, Patricia said to Mary, 'Callie tells me your family used to have a shop in Hartlepool, Mrs Ingram.'

She gave a wistful sort of smile. 'They did. It was a general merchandise store. It seems a long time ago now ... another life, in fact. The Brightmans sold up and moved to London, long ago.'

'You must miss seeing your family.'

Relief filled her mother's eyes when a came a

knock at the door. 'That must be Mr Lazurus.'

'Already? I haven't finished my handkerchief yet. Can he come in and wait? It will only take me a few more minutes.'

'I'll make some fresh tea,' Mary said.

A few moments later Harold Lazurus was seated in Ebeneezer's chair and accepted a cup of tea from her mother. 'I see you're making yourself useful, my dear,' he said to Patricia.

Kitty woke from her nap with a start and gazed around her, bestowing a smile on the stranger.

'Now, there's a smile to warm the heart,' Harold said.

Her mother smiled at her latest daughter. 'Kitty's always been the most contented of my babies.'

'Children are a blessing.'

Mary's voice revealed an edge of scepticism reserved for such uninformed observations. 'It seems to me that some are blessed more than others.'

Harold laughed at that. 'And others not at all. My great-nephew and -niece are my only relatives.'

'Patricia is a lovely girl.'

A fond look was bestowed on Patricia. 'Yes, she is a lovely girl. I'm proud of her.' His brow furrowed. 'I rarely forget a face, and I have the feeling we've met before, Mrs Ingram.'

Her mother bent over the cradle to pick Kitty up. 'Like as not we've met, since we both live in Seafield. It's not that big a place, now is it?'

'That's true. And your resemblance to Callie

is great.'

'Aye, we're alike.'

Patricia bit through the cotton and gazed at her handiwork, her mouth twisting slightly before she handed it to Mary. 'It looks a bit lumpy, I'm afraid.'

'The fabric has got no stuffing left in it. It's beautiful stitching and I'll treasure it.'

Harold placed his cup on the table and rose. 'We should be going, Patricia. Callie, will you come with us in the carriage?'

'I'll be along later, Mr Lazurus. There's a chore or two I must help my mother with yet.'

He nodded, fished in his waistcoat pocket and found half a crown. He placed it in Kitty's palm and watched her hand curl around it.

'You needn't have done that,' her mother said. 'We have enough for our needs.'

Harold's eyes met Mary's. 'I know you do. This is a custom. When you meet an infant for the first time you cross its palm with silver. If a strong grip is taken on it, the child will be prosperous later in life.'

'Then I'd better keep this somewhere safe for when Kitty grows up, else it'll end up in the publican's pocket. It will help pay for her education. Thank you for coming in. Not many folks would have.'

'I don't judge people for what they have, only for what they are. I enjoyed your company, even for a short time, Mrs Ingram.'

'So did I.' After a moment's hesitation, Patricia gave Callie's mother a quick kiss on the cheek. 'Thank you so much for your hospitality, Mrs Ingram.'

Mary caressed Patricia's face with her work-worn palm. 'You're welcome, lass. I'm pleased Callie has found a nice girl to befriend.'

'I didn't expect Callie's mother to have such nice manners,' Patricia said to her great-uncle as they made their way along the sea front towards the house. The air had a nip to it and the tide was going out. Small pools were being fed by rivulets of sea water, which eventually leached into the sand, leaving tidemarks of sea coal.

She could see the small figure of Giles Ingram raking his patch. Bare legged, he wore an old pair of trousers cut off at the knee and a cloth cap on his head. He looked up, gazing at her for a moment, and she could almost see the hard life ahead of him etched in the taut lines of his face. He shielded his eyes from the glare of the lowering sun, smiled, then went back to his raking.

Although she couldn't say why, a shiver ran down Patricia's spine. She resolved to add Giles to her bedtime prayers. Callie would join her brother soon, bending her back to lift the coal and take it to the cart. Patricia felt guilty for being so comfortably off. She didn't have to work like Callie and her family. She didn't have to wear garments that were little more than rags.

The Ingram house had been small and dark, like a tunnel through from the street to the yard at the back. The rooms were small, the furniture worn, but it was kept clean. She liked Callie's mother; her hand had been gentle against her face, and she'd wanted to turn her face against it and cry, because it had seemed a familiar gesture, as if her own mother had caressed her in the same way and left a memory of it on her skin.

'Mrs Ingram wasn't born to the life she leads, you know. Her family had a general store in Hartlepool. She told me they'd moved on to London now.'

'Have they, my dear? You can't recall their name, I suppose?'

'Brightman, I think she said her family name was.'

Her uncle's eyes sharpened. 'Are you sure?'

'Yes ... I'm certain she said Brightman. Did you know the family then?'

'I attended school with a Charles Brightman, that's all. It was a long time ago.'

'Her brothers teased me, and so did her father.' Patricia smiled. 'They made me blush, and he pretended to tell them off. Then her father refused to say grace. He's a very short man, isn't he? But he has a look about him that says he'll take no nonsense from anyone.'

'I imagine the life of a fisherman is a hard one.'

'Callie told her brothers she'd wrap a dishcloth around their ears if they didn't behave, only she called it a dishclowt. Then one of her brothers said she probably talked exactly the same way to you.'

Harold laughed. 'Callie's very polite to me,

but she has an inquisitive mind. Mr Tupper is very pleased with her. He said she's easy to teach because she has a good memory. You're very talkative, and don't seem as tired as usual for this time of day. Am I to take it that you enjoyed yourself?'

'Oh yes, I did. Their baby, Kitty, is so sweet. She sat on my lap and fell asleep. Mrs Ingram said I can visit any time. Would you mind if I visited them again?'

'We'll see when the time comes. You must remember that the weekend is Callie's time off to spend with her family. I expect she looks forward to it, so it wouldn't be fair of you to take advantage. And Patricia, my dear, remember that Callie hasn't had the advantages you've had. Your presence in her home might cause both her and her mother embarrassment, especially if they feel they must entertain you. Accept their hospitality by all means, but don't make your visits too frequent.'

They turned into the carriageway of the house. 'I never thought of that,' Patricia said. 'I tried to remain unobtrusive, really I did. Callie did a lot of housework when I was there. And she's probably down at the beach raking coal or gathering cockles now. I feel so sorry for her.'

'Well don't. She's not the type of girl who would welcome your pity. She's a good, hard-working girl who helps her family to make ends meet, and that's how it should be. Please don't get too attached to her, Patricia. You'll have to leave her behind when you go back to London, you know.'

'That's not for ages. I wonder if Mrs Ingram would mind if I gave her some handkerchiefs with her initials on for Christmas.'

'It would be a very nice gift, but there are still several weeks to go before you need to bother about Christmas.'

'Christmas will be lonely without James and Theron this year. I do miss them, so much.'

'I know I'm not much company for a young girl, but I'll do my best to make Christmas enjoyable for you. It's usually a lonely time for me, so I'll be glad of your company.'

Patricia filled the horse trough with feed while her great-uncle unhitched the horse from the trap. Soon the beast was warm in his stable and the pair were inside, helping themselves to the cold cuts Mrs Perkins had left for them in the kitchen.

She couldn't help but compare this kitchen to that of the Ingrams. However small Mrs Ingram's space was, her kitchen was at least filled with movement and mouth-watering cooking aromas. This kitchen on the other hand was scrubbed clean of activity. Black iron pans hung from a rack that could be lowered from pulleys and ropes hooked to the ceiling, all facing the same way and graduating in size. The iron range was cold.

People dodged each other in the kitchen of Mrs Ingram's house, chiding good-naturedly, 'Out of the way, Callie love. Two many cooks spoil the broth,' or, conversely, 'Many hands make light work. Clear a space for me on the table, would you?'

And Callie would anticipate her mother and the pair would exchange smiles, or kiss each other on the cheek as they passed.

Oh, Mrs Perkins was a good enough cook and housekeeper, Patricia thought, but this kitchen had a lonely feel about it. It seemed to be without a heart.

'Uncle Harold,' she said aloud, poking at an unappetizing slice of cold lamb with her fork, because she'd eaten a huge dinner with the Ingrams and wasn't really hungry, 'if you moved to London, you wouldn't ever be lonely, because you'd have us.'

'My business is established here. It takes time to build up a good client list, and I'm too old to start afresh. Perhaps when I retire. By that time you'll be married and be busy with a family of your own, no doubt. That's the way of things.'

And Patricia knew she'd have to be content with his answer for now.

Although Callie's quiet brother Joseph had always dreamed of joining the navy, when he came back from a trip to Hartlepool on the day he turned twenty-one to tell them he'd signed up and sworn the oath to serve queen and country, it surprised everyone because they'd never really thought he'd go through with it. A few days later Joseph came downstairs, a small suitcase gripped in his hand.

'You're finally off to see the world then, lad,'

their father said, shaking his hand.

'Aye.'

The two elder brothers indulged in a bit of jostling. They soon moved apart, in case they embarrassed themselves by giving in to an impulse to hug, which wasn't manly.

'Put our Kitty in the pram and fetch my shawl, Callie. We'll walk to the station with our Joseph.'

'Aw, there's no need, Ma.'

'You're my son. Besides, our Kitty needs to get out in the fresh air for a while, away from the smell of your father's pipe. I'll pack some vitals so you don't go hungry. There's some freshly smoked herring, and you can have a slice of that cake I made. Chad, you can fill a pot with some ale.'

'He can't turn up at the base as soused as a herring, Ma. They'll chuck him out before he begins.'

'More fool them. Do as you're told, and quick about it, else the train will leave before we get there. Da, give our Joseph his wage before he leaves. He can't go off empty-handed.'

'He can't spend money on a ship.'

'I daresay he'll go to some training camp first – isn't that right, son?'

'I reckon. We've got to get kitted out, then learn how to tie knots and fire guns.'

'There you are, Ebeneezer. Now, you fork out his wages, so the lad has some spare money on him if he should need it.'

As Callie left the room their father was

reluctantly moving his hand towards his pocket.

When they were at the station, Callie gave Joseph a hug before he boarded the train. 'I'll miss you, Joe.'

'Aye, I reckon I'll miss you, too. I'll send you a postcard when I can.' He lowered his voice. 'Callie, you watch out for that Sam Brown. He's got an eye for you.'

'Well, he can keep his glances to himself. He's a bully and I don't like him,' she said fiercely. 'I'm not marrying anyone for a long time, and that's for certain.'

'Well, don't say I didn't warn you.' Another hug, this time for his mother. 'Say goodbye to Verna and Giles for me. Thanks for being a good mother to me. I wish I'd been a better son.'

Voice choked up, her mother whispered, 'Ah, Joseph, you've been the best of lads, the quiet one who didn't demand any attention and got lost in the crowd. Damn it, boy, I'm so proud of you this day for following your heart that I could burst. God speed.'

The whistle blew and Joseph got on board. The train gave a jerk, then gathered speed and chuffed noisily out of sight. The two females held each other tight and sobbed together for a few moments.

'You'll be the next to leave,' Callie's mother said suddenly. 'Get out of here when you can, love, but watch out for your father, otherwise he'll have you married off to that Sam Brown.'

'I can't leave you, Ma. And Da can't make me marry Sam Brown.'

'Your father has ways and means of getting what he wants. How do you think he got me? He forced himself on me, that's how; put me in the family way. That's why I was cast out from my family. I wouldn't put it past him to encourage Sam Brown to do the same to you.'

Shocked, Callie stared at her. 'But I'm his daughter!'

Her mother said bitterly, 'Your da hasn't got much time for women. He thinks they're there for one thing: to bear children. He's a hard man when the mood's on him. Mark my words – daughter or not, he'll stop at nothing to have his own way.'

Her mother took a silver locket from around her neck and sprang open the front to reveal a miniature. 'When I was about your age, my father had this little portrait of me done. There's a lock of my hair in the back. See how alike we are? I want you to have it. If anything ever happens to me, I want you to leave as soon as you can. Ask that lawyer, Mr Lazurus, to help you.'

Dumbly, Callie nodded.

Her mother gazed into her eyes and placed the locket around her neck. 'This is for you. Keep it hid, lest your father sees it. He'll only sell it. And Callie, promise me you'll look out for Kitty.'

'Shut up, Ma, you're scaring me. Nothing's going to happen to you.'

'Promise me you'll do your best for Kitty. Giles will be all right. He's older, and he's a lad.'

Callie looked at her sister, who was wide-eyed with wonder as she watched a flock of seagulls fly overhead. ‘All right, I promise. Come on, let’s get home. It looks like it might come on to rain later.’

Seven

Two months after Joseph left, Ebeneezer said, 'I'm tekking our Giles fishin'.'

Mary was horrified. 'No, Ebeneezer; Giles is only eight. He's still at school.'

Ebeneezer ruffled his youngest son's hair. 'Giles is a canny lad; he's had enough schooling. He can tek Joe's place on the Coble and learn how to fish now.'

'Please don't make him go fishing,' Mary begged. 'He's small, and too young to do a man's work. If he stays at school he'll be able to do something better, like Aaric did.'

Ebeneezer cackled with laughter. 'That's a gudden if ever I heard it. You call counting planks of timber better, do you?'

'He does more than that. He figures out the wages, and does the clerking and things. Aaric might make manager one day.'

'Aye, and he might not. Giles is no younger than his brothers were when they started fishing. What he lacks in size he makes up fer in guts. He's coming wi' me, gerrit?'

'Oh yes. I get it.' She gazed at Giles. 'But why not let the boy have a say? What do you want to do, Giles?'

Giles gazed from one to the other, wincing when his da's hand tightened on his shoulder. 'I want to be a fisherman, reet enough, just like my da wants.'

Ebeneezer gave him a push. 'Good lad. It'll be piddling down later, so fetch the oilskins from behind the door for yourself. Like as not we'll have to turn the sleeves up and bunch it up around your middle, but it's better than nowt.'

'I'm telling you he's too young,' Mary said firmly.

Ebeneezer raised his voice a notch. 'And I'm telling you to shut your mouth, and reet now, woman, unless you want me to shut it for you.'

Mary fell silent, though her uneasiness persisted. She supposed she must get used to Giles working on the boats. He was strong and willing, but he was only a little lad, and his older brothers worked long hours.

Chad and Tom would be wed before Christmas to the William sisters, and no doubt they would soon produce kids of their own. In fact, the older of the sisters was already showing a suspicious bulge under her pinny.

As for Ebeneezer, he was still all sinew and muscle. But the long hours spent fishing were taking their toll on him now. He fell asleep in his chair more often, his back pained him at times, and more often than not he was bad-tempered and churlish.

After the men had gone, Mary sat in the chair by the fire with Kitty snuggled against her. There was plenty of work to do, but she just didn't feel like doing it. Gently she rocked back and forth, enjoying the peace and quiet. Sometimes she felt old herself, but she still had her menses. Thank goodness her husband was running out of energy and wasn't as attentive as he'd once been...

It was a Saturday, and Mary was looking forward to seeing Callie, so when the back gate scraped across the flagstones she opened her eyes in anticipation. She was none too pleased when the door was thrust open and her sister-in-law came in.

Agatha Herries was the opposite to her brother. She was tall, almost angular, and had an abundance of grey hair pulled into a bun at the nape of her neck. There was no laughter in Agatha's face; her eyes were mean and dark, her brows straight and thick. Her husband had died from the stomach gripe a year after they'd married, leaving her with a boarding house to run, but it brought her in a good income, with regular boarders all year round.

'Close the door behind you please, Agatha. You're letting the warmth out.'

'You shouldn't be wasting fuel at this time of year.'

'I don't need you telling me what to do in my own house. What are you here for?'

Kicking the door shut, Agatha planted herself on a kitchen chair, sweeping the dirty dishes aside with her forearm. 'Aren't you going to offer me some tea?'

'The kettle's on the hob, and I'm about to give Kitty a feed.' Opening her blouse, Mary allowed Kitty access to her breast, the familiar tugging of her mouth bringing contentment.

'I need someone to work in the boarding house. Ebeneezer said to ask you.'

'And who's going to mind Kitty, and clean my house?'

'Kitty can come with you. And you have Callie to help you. It's not as if you have many kids left at home.'

'Callie helps to rake coal and sell the fish.'

'She's a strong girl.'

'That might be so, but she works for the Lazurus family now. She can't do everything.'

Agatha's voice took on a harping note. 'She doesn't need to sleep there, does she? Besides, mixing with the gentry is giving her ideas above her station.'

'Says who?'

'I do. And my brother agrees with me.'

'You've discussed this with Ebeneezer?'

'Callie is my niece. I have her welfare at heart.'

'Your own welfare, more like. Callie may be your niece, but she's my daughter. I don't like people going to my husband behind my back. No, I won't clean up your boarders' dirt while you pocket the profits from my labour. From now on I'd thank you to keep your nose out of my business. There's the door.'

Agatha swept to her feet, a sneer on her face. 'I've seen the girl in her fancy clothes, strutting along the sea front with her nose in the air, just like you used to do. It didn't take Ebeneezer long to bring an end to your little tricks, did it?'

'Aye, it didn't, and I rue the day I ever set eyes on him. You got what you wanted from your marriage: a piece of property and an income to go with it. I've worked like a slave since I married your brother. Not once have you held out a helping hand to me or my children. I've earned a rest.'

Agatha gazed around her, adding insult to injury by remarking, 'Perhaps it's just as well. Your kitchen looks as though it needs a good scrub.'

Kitty gave a startled cry when Mary leapt to her feet and hissed, 'Aye, and so does your wicked tongue. If you're not out that door by the time I count to three I'll be scrubbing it for you. One ... two...'

The door banged loudly as Agatha went through it.

Callie received a dirty look as her aunt flounced past her in the lane.

'Hurumph!' the woman grunted.

Callie grinned at her mother when she got inside. 'I passed Aunt Agatha in the lane. She looked as though she had a wasp stuck up her snout.'

'Don't mention that sourpuss to me. She wanted me to go and work for her. As if I haven't got enough to do. You're early, love.'

Giving a sleepy-looking Kitty a kiss in return for a smile, Callie said, 'Patricia fell asleep, so Mr Lazurus let me go early. There's plenty of coal on the beach. I thought I could go down and help Giles, though the rake and cart's still in the yard.'

Her mother laid Kitty in the cradle. Thumb in her mouth, Callie's sister fell instantly asleep. Mary poured hot water from the kettle into a bowl and began to wash the dishes. 'Now Joseph has gone away, your father's decided to take Giles fishing with him.'

'What about his schooling?'

'When did Ebeneezer ever worry about book learning? The only reason the boys can read and write is because I taught them how ... Giles is so small.'

'But he's strong and wiry, like Da.'

'He can't swim very far, and the sea is a powerful force.'

'Don't say such things, Ma,' Callie begged, the hairs at the back of her neck prickling. 'It's like tempting fate.'

Angrily, her mother scrubbed at a spot on a plate. 'You mark my words. If anything happens to that lad of mine I'll lock his father out of the house and never speak to him again.'

Callie took the dishcloth from her mother's hands. 'You're going to scrub the pattern off this plate if you're not careful.' She took her mother in her arms when tears began to run down her cheeks, and said gently, 'It isn't like you to let things get you down, Ma.'

'I have a bit of a headache. I'm tired, that's all.'

'Then go and have a lie down while Kitty's asleep. I'll wash up and do the ironing.'

'All right. But don't let me sleep too long, else I won't sleep tonight.'

'I'll make us a cup of tea in an hour or so and give you a shake.'

Her mother did as she was told. Callie got on with the work that needed doing. She'd nearly finished the ironing when a gust of wind blew the door to the lane open, making it bang against the yard wall. Debris whirled upwards with a spattering sound. Callie went outside and pushed the door shut, making sure it was properly latched. With Kitty still asleep, she fetched a pail of water, added vinegar and went upstairs with a cloth.

She stopped short. On the horizon, clouds bruised the sky. They were in for a storm. It was a waste of time washing the outside of the windows; the rain-borne salt would only dirty them again. She started on the inside, her cloth gradually slowing when she made out a line of breakers on the horizon. The tide was coming in strong. It was too late to gather coal.

Giles! she thought, a thrill of fear jolting through her. He was out there with the fishing fleet, and they were such small boats. But her da and brothers were good seamen – the best. They'd braved storms like this one before. All the fishermen had. The weather could change rapidly, especially with winter approaching.

They'd be running before it, making their way to safe harbour.

Usually there were casualties.

Da won't let any harm come to Giles, she managed to convince herself, then whispered aloud, 'Please God, keep my family safe.'

Downstairs, Kitty began to make gurgling noises. The springs of her mother's bed creaked as she restlessly turned over. The sounds seemed so normal and familiar to Callie that she felt nothing could go wrong.

Giles had been as sick as a dog for most of the day. He whimpered as he heaved again on his empty stomach.

Ebeneezer had a frown on his face. 'There's nowt left in your stomach to fetch up, lad, so stop yer complaining. You'll have to toughen up if you want to fish for a living.'

'My stomach hurts, and I'm nithered.'

'We're all nithered. The temperature's dropped.' He held out a bottle. 'Tek a swig of this rum. It'll warm your gizzards.'

He grinned when his son spluttered on the fiery liquid. 'You'll get used to it, lad. Once we get the nets in we'll set sail and head back to harbour after the boys. If the water gets any rougher it'll just tear the nets to shreds. I'll haul them in, you grab any fish that come up wi' it, and throw them in the bottom of the boat. There won't be many, but I can't afford to lose them.'

Ebeneezer started hauling on the nets. He missed Joseph's strength. Giles was next to useless. He couldn't read the sea and was leaning too far over the side of the boat. His hands were cold, the work was unfamiliar, and he fumbled each time he untangled the occasional fish that came in with the net. He'd have to be quicker than that in future.

There was a rumble of thunder and the boat pitched sideways. Rain began to fall. He should have put a line on the lad, Ebeneezer thought as Giles struggled to keep his feet in the unpredictable boat. 'Be careful,' he cautioned, which was all he could do under the circumstances.

As soon as the thought was released a good-sized fish came up with the net. A cod by the looks of it, and it was a lively one.

'Hurry up, lad,' Ebeneezer shouted above the wind.

The fish came free suddenly and leaped from Giles's hands. The boy stood and made a grab for it. He slipped. A wave came up like a swell of liquid glass. The boat rolled one way, then back the other. Giles fell over the side, the heavy fish clutched in his arms.

'No!' Ebeneezer screamed. He rushed forward, grabbing up a hook. He caught a glimpse of Giles, who was in a panic, struggling to untie the belt around his waist. Above it, the oilskin bulged with water, weighing him down.

Then he sank and could be seen no more. Ebeneezer shed his jacket and jumped into the water, using the net to keep contact with the boat. The boy was below him and sinking, then his foot snagged in the net. Regaining the boat,

Ebeneezer pulled on the nets, his lungs nearly bursting as his muscles worked overtime to haul it aboard. Fish and net were tangled together in a heap on deck. It seemed to take for ever but finally the end of the net came up, dragging something heavy. It was his son.

Cutting the net from around the boy, Ebeneezer cradled Giles against his chest. The boy was cold, his eyes wide with panic, his fingers bloody where he'd clawed at the net to free himself. Ebeneezer wrapped his jacket tenderly around his son and set him down, his back against the nets.

'Thank God I found you. I'll get you safely home to your ma now,' he said gently. Hauling up the sail, Ebeneezer turned his little craft towards the harbour.

It was getting dark, and the storm was deepening in intensity. Callie had gone down to the fishing harbour to find that some of the boats had made it to shore and others were behind them. She could see her brothers' boat. Behind it, further out, and flying across the waves, was her father's craft. They'd be safely in port in just over half an hour.

Satisfied that all was well, she turned towards home. The waves crashed against the shore and rolled swiftly up the beach, carrying debris with it.

Out on the sea a freighter was heading towards the safety of the River Tees. Further out, a sailing ship's hull was lost in a welter of high, foamy water, her sails bulging before the wind. The lifeboat men would be watching her, and so would the villagers.

Already the team of sturdy horses that pulled the lifeboat to the shore were dressed in their trappings, ready to attach to the boat's cradle. The available coxswain and crew were beginning to gather. A ship in danger meant that the crew would risk their own lives to save those of others. They'd be joined by the fishermen if need be. If the ship couldn't be saved, the beach would be littered with goods to salvage come morning.

Callie went home and told her mother, 'The boats are coming in. Da and the boys should be home in half an hour.' Her mother sighed with relief.

'I was silly to worry. I'd better put that pot of broth on the stove. The menfolk will be hungry when they get home.'

'Likely the boys will go straight to the lifeboat house, but Da will bring Giles home first.' Callie set bowls and spoons on the table, along with a basket of bread chunks to sop up the gravy with.

Callie grinned as she remembered doing the same at the Lazurus house. There had been silence, and she'd looked up to discover James and Patricia gazing at each other with grins on their faces. Then they'd begun to sop up their own gravy, to put her at her ease. Callie had learned a lesson of manners from the incident, and she'd never made the same mistake again.

Her mother fetched a set of clean clothes for

Giles. She set them to warm on the guard around the stove, hanging them carefully over the brass rail. There was a faded and patched striped shirt, collar already turned, brown corduroy trousers that hung to just under his knees, a flannel vest to wear against his skin, and thick woollen socks. Her mother smoothed her fingers tenderly over the fabric of the vest and said, 'I didn't want Giles to have to grow up this soon. He'll be nithered when he comes in.'

They waited in the twilight the storm had created, one seated either side of the fireplace. Half an hour passed. Then another, and all the while the wind buffeted the house.

Although neither said anything there was an air of unease between them. After a while, her mother said, 'Have a look from the upstairs window, Callie. See if they're coming.' But Callie had no need to, for just then the back door opened and Verna slid through it, her face ashen.

'What is it, girl, what's happened?' her mother cried.

'It's our Giles ... Oh, Ma, come into the parlour. I'll open the front door for them.'

They crowded in, her father first, carrying her younger brother, with Chad and Tom behind him. Verna shooed a couple of nosy neighbours away and shut the door.

'I've brought Giles home to you, Mary,' Ebeneezer said.

'I've got eyes in my head,' Mary said harshly. 'Fetch the doctor, our Verna.'

'Nay, the doctor can't do anything, lass,' he

said, laying the floppy body on the sofa. Giles's head rolled to one side, and he gazed at them through his wide open eyes. Water trickled from the side of his mouth.

Mary gently closed the lids over his eyes. 'Aye, I can see that.' She stood before her husband, her face a picture of despair, and said quietly, 'I told you Giles was too small. I begged you not to take him.' When her hand lashed across his face, he winced. 'You killed him, Ebeneezer. I'll never forgive you for this. Never!' Her hand lashed out again, stinging the other cheek. 'You're no longer my husband. As God is my judge, while I draw breath I'll never willingly speak to you again. Now, get out!'

'Mary, love...'

'Get out, I said!'

'Ma.' Tom took her arm. 'Giles is his son, too.'

She shook the hand off. 'Aye, and Giles would still be alive if your father had listened to me. Get out, Ebeneezer. If you stay I'll stick a knife through your black heart while you sleep. Fetch your father his clothes, Chad. Get him out of my sight. Then go and tell your brother Aaric what's happened.'

Chad gazed at his father, who mumbled, 'Do as your ma says. I'll go to Agatha's until she comes to her senses.'

'I just have. Verna, I told you to fetch the doctor. We'll need to have a death certificate. Tom, you can go for the undertaker. There should be enough money in the funeral club to pay for it. Tell him we'll only need a small coffin. Take your father away with you.'

'Mary,' Ebeneezer said, trying again, and Callie could see the pain and guilt churning in the depths of his eyes.

When her mother ignored him, he turned and stumbled away, Tom and Verna following after him.

'Callie, help me lay our Giles out. I need some warm water, soap and a towel, so I can wash him. And bring his clean clothes. They should be nice and warm now.' Her voice caught in her throat. 'Not that he'll feel it ... Oh, Giles, I'm so sorry I couldn't stop him. I should have been stronger.' She began to sob, and picked up her son's body, rocking him back and forth.

In the kitchen, Kitty picked up on the sadness in the house and began to cry too. Tears in her eyes, Callie went through and picked her sister up to soothe her.

Chad joined her, a bag containing their father's clothes in his hand. 'Do you think Ma will ever forgive him?' he asked.

Slowly, Callie shook her head.

Eight

October had drawn winter into its heart, and the day of Giles's funeral was cold.

The boy's father and brothers bowed their heads in prayer and held their caps against their chests. His sisters cried bitter tears at the tragic loss of such a young life.

Callie gazed across at her da and felt sorry for him. He'd aged over the past few days. He'd turned away when the neighbours had filed through the parlour, their voices muted, their expressions pitying the mother of the pale drowned child in the coffin, as if he knew that his guilt was written all over his face.

Ebeneezer's face was haggard, his eyes bloodshot and running with tears, as though the life was being sucked from him. His breath had smelled of drink when Callie had hugged him. Aunt Agatha was severe in a black coat and hat. Now and again she bore a black-edged handkerchief to her eyes and sniffed loudly, but there was no trace of tears.

Callie's mother was stronger. Back straight, Mary Ingram remained dry-eyed. The rage churning inside her sustained her courage, and as she fed on its heat, it stopped her from thinking of anything else.

Verna stood one side of their mother, Callie on the other. Aaric was by himself, a little apart. He was slender but no longer frail. His face had hollowed into an aesthetic manliness, his hair was a lazy curl of golden brown and his eyes were blue, like Callie's. Aaric's eyes were astute. There was a resilience about him now, and his brothers treated him with respect.

Of all her brothers, Callie loved Aaric the best. He understood her need to learn, and he listened to her when she needed someone to talk to. He must have sensed her eyes upon him, for he looked at her for a moment. And in that moment, something about the way he held himself reminded her of Theron Grace. When she held out her hand to him he took it and moved closer. She laid her face against his arm for a moment or two of comfort. As she did so she noticed Mr Lazurus standing unobtrusively behind the other mourners.

Then it was over. Giles, who'd hardly lived, was lowered into the earth for eternity. She was glad he wasn't still tumbling in the cold sea, his body being torn to feed the fish her father and brothers caught. 'I hope God loves his soul and treats him kindly,' she murmured.

When the burial was over, Ebeneezer gazed at his wife. When Mary turned her back on him, his elder sons led him away.

'I should go, Ma; our Jimmy is due his feed,' Verna said.

'Aye, you go on, lass. I've got Callie and Aaric

with me.'

The three of them linked arms. 'I'll miss young Giles,' Aaric said.

After the others moved off, their mother waved an arm over the nearby graves. 'These are my children. What a waste of life.'

Callie and Aaric exchanged a glance, for both of them suspected that the life their mother referred to was her own.

They found Mr Lazurus waiting at the gate. Patricia was in the rig, a warm blanket spread over her knees.

Harold shook hands with Aaric. 'Mr Ingram, it's nice to see you again, despite the sad circumstances.' He took Mary's hands in his. 'My condolences, Mrs Ingram ... a dreadful thing to have happened to your son. And from Patricia, too.'

'Thank you, Mr Lazurus. It was kind of you to come to the funeral.'

Callie went over to where Patricia sat. 'Thank you for coming, Tish. I suppose you were wondering where I was.'

'No. Someone told my great-uncle what had happened. He was upset for your mother.' Leaning forward, Patricia hugged her. 'Oh, Callie, I'm so sorry. Poor little Giles. Your mother must be beside herself with grief.'

'Aye, she is that.' Callie managed a smile for her friend. 'She'll be over the worse of it in a week or so.' She hesitated before saying, 'She blames my da and has thrown him out. He's living with his sister.'

Patricia's hand went to her mouth and her eyes widened. 'But he'll go back home eventually, won't he?'

'I expect so.'

'You must take as much time off as you need.'

'I can't afford to,' Callie said bluntly. 'Da hasn't gone near his boat since the tragedy. I've already had a week off, and we need my wage.'

'You don't have to worry about that. Great-uncle Harold has given it to your father.'

'I'll be in tomorrow as usual, Patricia, if you can put up with me. It's better to keep active than sit at home. Giles has gone, and there's nowt I can do to bring him back. I'm going down to rake some coal later. The bunker's nearly empty, and we need it now winter's here.'

'If I was strong enough to help you, I'd jump out of this carriage right now and come with you.'

Callie didn't laugh, although she wanted to. Patricia meant well, but Callie couldn't imagine her blistering her hands by raking coal, or digging up cockles, or going from house to house selling fish when the weather was freezing and your hands were numb from the cold and someone demanded that you fillet it for no extra charge. And she couldn't imagine Patricia wearing cheap boots with holes that let in the wet, or repairing clothes until there was more darns than fabric to attach it to.

She buried her resentment, because Patricia was a nice girl, and she hated herself for being envious of her. 'That's a kind thought, Tish, but

I wouldn't let you anyway.'

'You do it.'

'It's my life, I'm used to it. Your life is different. When you leave here, you'll forget I even existed.'

'You're my friend, of course I won't. I shall write to you. Is that your brother, Aaric? He's handsome, isn't he?'

Callie nodded. 'He's clever, too. Would you like to meet him?' But Aaric had taken their mother's arm and they were moving on down the road. She shrugged. 'It'll have to be some other time. I'll see you tomorrow. Mr Lazurus, thank you for thinking of us. I know my mother will feel comforted.'

'You're welcome, my dear. Let me know if there's anything I can do to help.'

Callie caught up with her mother and Aaric and they walked home together. They had left Kitty with a neighbour, so Callie collected her and took her back to her mother, where she got an extra-firm hug.

'I'm going down to the beach,' Callie said. 'There's plenty of coal lying about.'

'I'll come and give you a hand,' Aaric said from the kitchen.

She hugged him. 'I can manage. You stay and keep Ma company. It'll take her mind off Giles.'

It took Callie an hour to fill the cart halfway because the coal was so scattered. Smelling of seaweed and salt, a bitter wind blew off the sea, turning the tears she shed for Giles into rivers of ice, and numbing her to the bone as it cut through her clothing. Dry grains of sand grazed her ankles and cheeks.

Her teeth chattering, she thought of the warm stove in the kitchen. But she could hear the tide creeping across the sands, and if she didn't rake the coal there would be none to burn because it would be washed out to sea again. And if she didn't move with it, the North Sea would soon surround her and take her with it.

This will be my life if I allow it to be, she thought as she took a shovel to the coal mounds she'd made. Callie didn't mind hard work, but the constant grind and the battle to make ends meet was not an appealing thought. She wanted more from this life than hardship.

'And, by heck, somehow I'm going to get it,' she muttered, throwing in the last shovel of coal.

The light had almost gone as she straightened up to ease her aching back. It soon became clear that she was going to have difficulty dragging the cart up through the sand. She picked up a couple of splintered planks that had washed ashore from some wreck to use as tracks.

But as she put her shoulder to the cart a wave washed up the beach and over her ankles.

'Damn!' she said, knowing she'd have to empty out half of the contents. But the wheels had sunk into the wet sand and the cart was too heavy to tip. The next wave hissed over her feet, ran up the beach and was sucked back down again.

Somebody shouldered her roughly aside. The voice was Sam Brown's. 'Tek the handle. You pull and I'll shove before yon tide teks cart and all awa'.'

Reluctantly, Callie did as she was told. She didn't want to be beholden to Sam, but her ma needed the coal and they couldn't afford to lose the cart. But still it wouldn't budge.

Cursing, Sam managed to get the planks under the wheels and joined her at the dragging end. Together they hauled the cart up the beach and on to the road, where Sam's horse and cart waited with his brother at the reins.

'Thanks,' she said grudgingly.

'It's not a job for a girl by herself. Don't fill the cart if you can't manage it.'

'Aye, well, I didn't think, did I? Our Giles used to help.'

He shuffled back and forth. 'I'm sorry about Giles. He was a little 'un, but game.'

'Giles couldn't help being small.'

'I didna say he could. He was a feisty little sod, all the same. All you Ingrams are. I heard your da has been thrown out the house.'

'Mind your own business, Sam Brown, 'less you want a good clout around the ear for your trouble.'

He grinned. 'The last time you clouted me I couldna hear for a week.'

'The next time you won't be able to hear for a month.'

'Get away wiyyer.' Sam chuckled. 'Can you manage the cart by yerself, Callie girl?'

'Yes.'

'Good. It'll save me the bother of helping out.

When are you gannin' out wi' me?'

'Never. I don't go out with boys. I've got better things to do.'

As he climbed up on his cart he turned and said, 'You're growing a nice pair of tits. I wouldn't mind a feel of them for helping you out.'

'Don't you talk dirty to me, else I'll tell my da and he'll give you what for.'

'Your da wouldna lift a soddin' finger.' Sam and his brother burst into raucous laughter and the horse moved off with its load.

As she trudged home through the darkness, slowly pushing the heavy cart, Callie began to wonder how they'd manage if her da didn't come home. He'd spend her wages on drink if her mother wasn't there to keep him under control.

Tom had told them that Ebeneezer hadn't been near his boat since the storm, and they'd had to clean the rotting fish from the net, repair the damage and make her tidy.

'His heart is weighed down with sorrow, Ma,' Chad had said, somewhat poetically.

Her mother had carried on with what she was doing, as if she hadn't heard him.

Already there had been fewer fish to sell this week without her da's input, and Callie could only rake enough coal at weekends to supply their immediate needs – which left none over to sell.

Callie found that the gate to the yard was open. Sam Brown's cart was further up the lane, and she could hear the sound of the coal being shovelled.

As she went in, arms came round her from behind and her breasts were roughly fondled. She gave a loud yelp, heeled her attacker in the shin, then picked up a lump of coal and swung round to thump him. When he grunted with pain, she hissed at him, 'You dirty pig, Sam Brown. Keep away from me.'

The door opened and light shone through from the kitchen. Aaric called out, 'Is everything alreet, our Callie?'

She couldn't tell Aaric; it was too embarrassing. Slamming the door on the escaping Sam, she said, 'Aye, I tripped on one of the flagstones, that's all.' Face burning with fury, she began to shovel the coal from the cart into the bunker.

Aaric held out a hand for the shovel. 'I'll do that.'

'You'll dirty your clothes, Aaric. Besides,' she teased, 'you're the delicate one in the family.'

'That's all in the past. I've been going to a gymnasium twice a week in the evening, learning to box. Just for the exercise, mind. But don't tell Ma, else she'll have a fit. It's not as if I'm going to enter any boxing tournaments. And I'm wearing an old pair of trousers now, so it doesn't matter if they get dirty.' He kissed her cheek, then took the shovel from her. 'Who was that in the yard?'

'You don't miss much, do you? It was Sam Brown, but I didn't invite him, if that's what you're thinking.'

'I wasn't thinking that. He's a sly one, is Sam Brown. Did he bother you?'

'He tried to. I thumped him with a piece of coal.'

'You're only a slip of a girl, Callie. Sam Brown is a strapping lad who's three years your senior. You'll let me know if you can't handle him, won't you?'

'Aye.'

'I saw Mr Tupper the other day. He taught me, tha knows, and he thinks highly of you.'

A smile crossed her face at the thought of the astute old man who tutored herself and Patricia. 'I like him. He makes everything he teaches us sound so interesting. I'll be sorry when I have to stop my schooling.'

'It doesn't mean you have to stop learning.'

'But you know what will happen. I'll probably have to wed some lad Da chooses for me – Sam Brown, I suspect, since he's begun to think he owns me – and I'll stay at home, have babies and work like a slave for him ... just like Ma and Verna.'

'Don't you want a husband and babies, then?'

'Of course. Only I don't want babies I can't afford to feed and educate ... And I want to marry a man I can love and respect, and one who treats me the same way. I'd like to travel and see other places, and have the chance to make something of myself.'

'Most of us want that, Callie.'

'But it's easier for men to do what they want, isn't it?'

'D'you think it's easy for Da, or Chad and Tom?'

'I know it's not, Aaric. But Da and the boys are happy doing what they do because it's their choice. Even if it wasn't, they could walk away from it tomorrow, like Joe did. But I can't. I feel trapped!'

'I'm sure Da has your welfare at heart.'

'Just like he had Giles's welfare at heart?' she said. 'You know, Da won't budge an inch once he's made up his mind about something. I don't think I'll ever forget the expression in Giles's eyes. Dad didn't close them; he said he thought Giles was still alive. He was scared, all alone under that cold ocean and struggling in the net like a fish when he died. His fingernails were torn off where he struggled to get himself free.'

'Aye! He would have been scared. He was only a little lad.'

'Ma begged him not to take Giles. Da just told her to shut up.' Passionately she cried out, 'I wish it was Da who'd died instead!'

'I imagine he feels the same way.'

She nodded. 'Yes, he would, wouldn't he? And he'd expect everyone to feel sorry for him for feeling like that.'

'You're being unfair, Callie.'

'I know. One day I've got to get away from here ... I've just *got* to, Aaric.'

Silence stretched between them for a moment, then Aaric gently touched her cheek. 'I hear you, Callie. Get away in and help your ma now. I'll be raking coal at weekends as well, from now on. At least until we get enough in to see us through winter.'

The next day Callie left her mother sitting in the rocking chair.

'I'll be back this evening,' she said. 'I'm sure Mr Lazurus won't mind if I don't sleep there.'

'You don't have to keep an eye on me,' Mary said. 'It's wash day, and I've got plenty to be getting on with. Aaric is with me at night.'

But Callie worried about her mother. She'd lost children before, but Callie had never seen her so down.

'Disease is different,' she'd said once. 'You expect it to end in grief, so you're prepared.'

Chad and Tom were wed to the William sisters in the church one Saturday, and without fanfare. Ebeneezer knelt in prayer next to his wife, but it was as if he didn't exist to her. Ma didn't look at him once, or acknowledge him in any way.

Agatha cornered Mary after the ceremony. 'You'd better take my brother back soon,' she warned. 'I can't afford to keep him.'

'Then throw him out on the street,' Mary said. 'Besides, he's got my Callie's wage to live on. Have that off him.'

'That's his house you're living in. Be careful it's not you who gets thrown out on the street.'

'Leave her alone,' Callie hissed.

They stayed for a short time at the Williams' house, eating sandwiches and wishing the couples well. Afterwards, they walked home.

Their father had given the boys a deposit to buy a house as a wedding gift, and they'd moved out to set up their own households.

'Your father's a dark horse. He kept that money quiet,' Mary said bitterly.

They were then left with only Aaric's wage to live on. Callie decided to take matters into her own hands. She requested a meeting with Mr Lazurus, and said simply, 'My mother's in need of my wage, Mr Lazurus.'

'I've paid it to your father in advance, my dear.'

'Oh, I see.' Dejectedly she turned away, remembering that Patricia had told her so at Giles's funeral.

'Wait,' he said. 'There's no reason why you shouldn't have your Christmas gift in advance. He drew an envelope out of his desk drawer. It contained five shillings.

Callie's relief was written on her face in the smile she gave him. 'Thank you so much, Mr Lazurus.'

'What are your plans for Christmas?'

Usually, the turkey would be hanging from a hook in the kitchen, a looped rope tied around its feet. There would also be a row of plum puddings hanging there at this time of year.

'Aren't we going to have Christmas?' she'd already asked her mother.

'Aaric's wage doesn't stretch that far,' had been the answer. 'Besides, the family is going to spend the day at your aunt's.'

Callie shrugged as she gazed at her employer.

'We have no plans. Things are a little difficult at home at the moment.'

'Your parents are still living apart?'

'Aye. There's only myself, Aaric and Kitty left at home.'

He nodded. 'Then I have a favour to ask your mother. If I write to her, perhaps you could deliver the letter for me.'

When Callie got home she was eager to tell her mother the news. 'Da's already had my wages in advance, but here's the five shillings Mr Lazurus was going to give me for Christmas. And here's a letter from him too.'

'Open it and tell us what it says, Callie. I hope you haven't been a trouble to him.'

Dear Mrs Ingram,

I promised my great-niece that I'd do my best for her at Christmas, for she'll miss her brother and cousin.

Patricia remembers with enjoyment the dinner she shared with you. My housekeeper will be absent over Christmas and, although she has kindly offered me a pudding, we look forward only to a cold and dismal meal.

What better way to celebrate than with congenial acquaintances? If you are not otherwise engaged, you, your son Aaric, and your two lovely daughters are invited to celebrate the Christmas season with Patricia and myself, with a traditional festive meal. Needless to say, I'm prevailing upon you to help me cook it!

On the assumption that you will agree, please supply me with a list of purchases I need to make for said meal.

Yours sincerely, and extremely hopefully,

Harold Lazurus

For the first time since Giles's death, Callie heard her ma laugh. 'Harold Lazurus has all the charm in the world in him. No wonder you like him.'

'He's a lovely man. Shall we go?'

'Aye, I'd like to, though I can't speak for you or Aaric,' Mary said comfortably.

'What if Aunt Agatha invites us? She's asked all the others.'

'Agatha's trying to make herself the head of the family now, but it won't be long before she wants her brother out from under her feet. She'll leave any invitation to the last stroke of Christmas Eve, so I'll know she begrudged asking us. Callie, love, you must know that I won't go anywhere near your da, unless I have to. I don't expect you to side with me, though. If you want to go to Agatha's and spend Christmas Day with your father, brothers and sisters, you can.'

'I can visit them any time. I'd rather spend Christmas with you. Tell me, so it's clear in my mind, will you never ask Da to come back home?'

'No. But this is his house. I'm afeared of what

he'll do when Agatha starts nagging at him...'

'That fancy wife of yours isn't coming,' Agatha said as she pulled the gizzards from the turkey and threw them into a pan to flavour the gravy. 'Left it to the last minute to let me know, she did. There's manners for you. Obviously she hasn't got those she was born with. A fat lot she cares about her children. She favours that Aaric and Callie above the others. That girl has got ideas above her station, too.'

'Let it up, wiyyer, Aggie. Pass me over that bottle.'

'You're drinking too much, just like our da did.'

'Shut yer yap.'

'Don't you talk to me like that, Ebeneezer. This is my house. If you don't like it here, you can go home.'

He did want to go home, but he couldn't stand the silence from Mary. By God, he missed the comfort of his woman, though, and Agatha's cooking was nowhere near as good as his wife's. Anger burned in his cheeks as he thought of the way Mary had split the family down the middle. She needed a good crack to bring her to her senses.

He'd got Callie's wage off her employer in advance, so Mary must be managing on Aaric's wage. That wouldn't go far, and the boy didn't have the wind in him to do a second job. Ebeneezer would starve them out if need be. Mary would soon ask him back when there was nowt in the larder, no coal to keep them warm, and the young 'un was mithering with hunger.

Only the week before, from the window of the public house, he'd watched his woman gathering cockles to sell door to door. He'd ignored the lump in his throat at the sight of her. The bloody woman should have learned who was boss by now. *By heck, though, Mary's turned out to be a worker*, he'd thought. She'd been useless when they'd first wed, but she'd learned to survive. Now she needed to be taught another lesson. He'd be buggered if he was going to beg to be allowed back into his own home.

'We'll see how good you are without a man to look after thee, woman,' he'd muttered darkly, before turning back to the landlord. Throwing some coins on the bar, he'd said, 'I'll have me another pot of ale to sup; I've got a reet wicked thirst on me.'

Nine

Callie and her mother had been to the early Christmas service at church, leaving Aaric to look after Kitty. Callie had hoped that her da would be there, but he wasn't. Only Tom and Chad were, looking uncomfortable in their Sunday suits. They were seated with their new wives, both of whom had smug looks on their faces.

'That'll change before too long,' her mother said caustically.

'I've left a fish for you by Giles's grave,' Chad whispered as he pecked her on the cheek. 'I'll try and put another there next week.'

'It's a nice size,' her mother said of the cod when they arrived home and tore off the newspaper wrapped around it. 'We'll get two meals out of it – and a feed of fish cakes as well, I shouldn't wonder. The head and bones will make some tasty soup stock. It was nice of Chad to think of us.'

'And why shouldn't he? We're his family too.'

'Things change when you marry, especially when you have kids. The family you were born into has to come second. Put the fish in the larder; I'll see to it when I get back. Fetch that basket of fruit pies while you're there. It's a gift for Patricia and her uncle. It's not much, but better than nothing.'

Escorted by Aaric, Callie and her mother walked the two miles along the sea front towards Harold Lazurus's house, her mother pushing Kitty in the old perambulator that all her children had used. If Mary was nervous, she didn't show it, and she didn't mind wearing the ugly brown and cream outfit she'd bought for Callie to wear. Over it she wore a warm fringed shawl of blue-checked wool, a gift from Aaric.

'I'll feel like a queen in this,' she'd whispered, stroking it when she'd unwrapped the parcel.

Aaric had kissed her. 'You are a queen, Ma.'

Callie had fashioned her mother a drawstring purse from some shiny material Patricia had given her, lining it with a strip of linen cut from her petticoat to give it strength. After all, nobody would look under her skirt and see the hole. She embroidered the purse with a rose, and placed the money she'd saved from her salary inside it. There would be no more to save now, she thought sadly, since her wage had been taken in advance by her da.

Her mother's eyes had filled with tears and she'd hugged her. 'Eh, that's a good, caring girl you are, Callie. No thought for yourself. You and Aaric have always been the best of my children.'

'Except for Kitty over there, and Verna,' she teased. 'Then there's our Jane, Tom, Chad and Joe. I bet you'd say the same thing to all of them, and to your grandchildren.'

Her mother smiled. 'Aye, you're right, Callie. I wouldn't know which to choose between you if I had to. Kitty's the last of my babies, and she's the most even-tempered of you all. I remember when Giles was a baby...' She stopped short. 'But it's no use thinking on it, since it won't bring him back. Come along, let's go; the turkey will need time to cook.'

The village was almost deserted as they set out. The village green was rimed in thick frost, and each breath they expelled was a cloud of steam. There was a lonely figure walking along the edge of the water, a dog at his heels. Her father hadn't been near the house since her mother had thrown him out. Callie wondered if he missed them all.

Patricia gazed out from behind the curtain when Callie knocked, as if she'd been keeping a lookout for them, and a smile sped across her face.

The door was decorated with a holly wreath. She had the door open in a couple of seconds, and burst out. 'You'll never guess. A big parcel came on the train yesterday. It's from Theron and James, and there are gifts for all of us, even you, Mrs Ingram. I've put them under the tree.'

'Goodness,' her mother said. 'This is unexpected. How on earth did your guardian know I'd be here?'

'Great-uncle Harold telephoned him in London from his office a couple of weeks ago.' She hugged Callie, whispering in her ear, 'Don't forget to introduce me to your brother.'

'Aaric. This is Miss Lazurus.'

Patricia beamed a smile at him. 'I've heard so much about you. Callie says you're an expert at adding up numbers. How incredibly daunting.' She held out her hand. 'Welcome to the Lazurus home. You can call me Tish, if you wish. Most of my friends do.'

Aaric looked bemused. 'I'm pleased to meet you, lass. I understand you've been ill. I hope you soon get well.'

Patricia made a dismissive face. 'Thank you, but I'm really much better now. Nearly back to my old self. The doctor said if I don't catch a cold, I should be completely over it by spring.' She gazed at the sleeping Kitty and smiled. 'She's so sweet. I quite adore her. I wish I had a baby sister.'

'You might have a daughter of your own one day.'

Patricia gurgled with laughter. 'I imagine I'd make an awful mother. I'll go and fetch Uncle, shall I? We thought we might make an early start with our assistance. We've been in the kitchen, peeling vegetables. We've made a terrible mess, I'm afraid. My uncle is trying to tidy it up. He's scared that you'll turn around and go home if it's too messy; then he won't get his proper Christmas dinner after all!'

'Don't listen to her nonsense,' Harold said, a smile on his face as he advanced into the room and extended a hand towards Aaric. The introductions were made all over again.

'Right, I've made up a list of duties. Mrs Ingram and myself will be the chefs – although you'll be in charge, of course, Mrs Ingram. Callie and Patricia can set the table, and look after young Kitty.'

'What shall I do?' Aaric asked.

'You're appointed as general foreman. Make sure the girls behave themselves, and keep the fires burning in the drawing room, dining room and library, if you would, young sir. And, of course, serve your mother and me a small glass of sherry every now and again. Oh yes, and perhaps you could look after Mr Tupper when he arrives, Aaric. I didn't like to think of him left alone today when I have the fortune of good company, so I invited him along. Callie, perhaps you'd show your brother where everything is kept.' He held out an arm to their mother. 'Shall we go then, Mrs Ingram? The turkey awaits its fate.'

'Thank you, Mr Lazurus,' she said, getting into the spirit of the day.

'Do call me Harold,' he said as they walked away together.

Harold Lazurus had spared no effort. It was a wonderful dinner and a perfect day, with a sing-song around the piano at the end.

Stomachs filled to the brim, the Ingrams walked home in a warm glow of contentment. Kitty, who was almost buried under a pile of parcels, cuddled a toy cat made from rabbit fur against her cheek. Aaric wore a warm grey scarf with matching gloves.

The smiles they wore faded when they reached the house and saw that the door to the lane was swinging wide open. The back door was splintered around the lock, where it had been kicked open.

Flour drifted in the air and was settling over everything. There were scuff marks and footprints tramped everywhere.

'I'll go in and have a look around first,' Aaric said. He was back in seconds. 'Whoever did this has gone, but they've messed the place up reet good.'

Mary sighed when she saw the pickle her kitchen was in. 'I think we all know who did this. His filleting knife has gone off the mantelpiece, and I can't see anything else that's missing. We'd best get the place cleaned up.'

It was cold inside the house. In every room the furniture had been turned over, crockery had been smashed, and a chair was tipped over so it leaned against the stove. *Thank God the stove had been damped down, else it might have caught fire and set alight the whole row of terraced houses*, Callie thought.

The fish Chad had given them had been cut to pieces and trodden into the flagstones on the kitchen floor. Its blood and guts had been smeared over the walls, and the head stuck on a hook where Ma usually hung the soup ladle.

Tears came into her mother's eyes. 'Eh, what a wicked waste of a good fish.'

'I'll see if Chad or Tom can give us another

one,' Aaric said.

'Stoke the fire up, then help Callie right the furniture. See if you can do something with that door, Aaric. I don't want someone coming in and murdering us in our beds tonight. I'll give our Kitty a feed and put her down to bed before I give you a hand.'

Callie could hear her mother quietly sobbing to herself while she fed Kitty. Placing the tin tub on the hob she filled it with water to heat.

'Why would Da do such a nasty thing to us, Aaric?' Callie said, near to tears herself. 'You, Kitty and I have got no quarrel with him.'

'We can't be sure it was him.'

'Because he's my da I try to make excuses for him, too. But what about the filleting knife? Who else would have done it?'

'I don't know. As soon as the furniture's righted I'm off to Aunt Agatha's to see what I can find out.'

'What about the door?'

'There's a bolt in the drawer, I can screw that on. At least Ma will be able to secure it from the inside for now.'

When they'd finished tidying the place and had picked up the pieces, Aaric installed the bolt. Callie fetched a pail, scrubbing soap, and a brush from the yard. 'You go on now, Aaric. I'll take Ma up a cup of tea, then start on the floor, else that fish will begin to stink to high heaven when the house warms up.'

When Callie went upstairs with the tea, and to change into her old work skirt, she touched a fingertip against her mother's tears. 'You rest, Ma. I can manage by myself.'

'No, I'll drink this and come down. I don't usually feel sorry for myself, but we had such a lovely day and it was a shock to come home to this. I'm good and angry; it will add grease to my elbow.'

'Well, the kitchen floor is going to need two scrubs to get that fish out of the flags, so I'll do that first. Once that's done the rest is not so urgent, though we're going to be a bit short of crockery.'

'Oh, so that's why you've given me this old enamel mug. I was going to throw them out.'

'Good job you didn't then, because that's all we've got to drink out of for the moment. And we'll have to eat off the enamel pie plates.'

'We haven't got much food left to put on them anyway. From the mess I saw, he seemed to have tipped most of the stuff out of the larder.'

'We'll manage. Aaric has gone to see our brothers. They won't let us starve. And I'll dig some cockles out of the sand for us tomorrow, and rake enough coal to last you the week. And there's that hamper Theron Grace sent for you.'

Her mother snorted. 'Fancy stuff from a fancy London shop. The man's got more money than sense. A body needs a solid meal inside it.'

'There's a piece of smoked ham in it that will last us a week or so. Stop scolding the poor man, Ma. It was nice of him to think of us at all. He could hardly send you a hamper with a side of mutton, a cabbage and a pound of potatoes in it.

What sort of Christmas gift would that be?'

'Aye, you're right.' Her mother was laughing at the thought as Callie went downstairs.

Callie managed to save most of the flour and oats, which were still in the bins. It looked as though the intruder had been disturbed on the job and had nipped out through the front door, otherwise he'd have tipped it all out. The jug of milk and the dripping hadn't been touched.

Heaving a sigh of relief, Callie began to wash the mess from the walls. It was a tedious business. She then tucked her skirt into her waistband and started on the floor. The water quickly dirtied, and she had to go to the pump often to refill the bucket.

Gradually the slimy mess was lifted from the floor, though some greasy marks remained where the fish had been ground in so hard. Callie scrubbed hard at them, her hands reddening and growing numb from the cold water. She found a metal button in a crack between the flagstones, a tiny piece of dirty blue material attached to it, as though it had been ripped from a shirt. She shoved it into her apron pocket. Something odd lodged elusively at the back of her mind, but she couldn't say quite what it was or bring it to the fore.

When Callie crept upstairs, it was to discover that her mother had fallen asleep, so she gave the floor a second scrub, then tipped some of the hot water on it to rinse it, sweeping the diluted suds out through the door with the broom. Finally, she dried the puddles as best she could, wringing out the cloth into the bucket. The heat from the stove would quickly dry the rest.

She smelled of fish and soap when she finished, and her knees hurt from the hard stone floor. *What a way to spend the end of Christmas Day*, she thought with a wry grin.

Suddenly she remembered that she hadn't opened her gift from Theron Grace. From its shape, she'd thought it was a book. But when she unwrapped it she discovered a rose-decorated, lacquered box. She'd never seen anything quite so pretty. Inside, wrapped in tissue, was a delicate silver and turquoise brooch in the shape of a peacock.

Her hand trembled as she picked it up. 'How fine a gift it is,' she whispered, and tears pricked at her eyes, for she knew she could never wear it – at least, not where her father could see it. Even so, she pinned it to her ragged bodice for a moment, to admire it.

James had sent her a pair of warm and cheerful red gloves and a tin of shortbread. At least he'd been practical. Patricia had given her a box of writing paper with matching envelopes, and a tiny jade elephant hanging from a white ribbon, to which a key could be tied.

'The elephant will bring you good fortune in the years to come, and the compendium is to remind you to keep in touch after I return to London,' Patricia had said. 'You will, won't you?'

'Of course.'

'Promise?'

Resisting the urge to shrug, Callie smiled as she promised. As much as she loved Patricia, their relationship had been born out of loneliness, and she suspected her friend would forget all about her a month or two after she'd returned to London.

Upstairs, her mother began to stir, and was soon up and about again. Aaric returned half an hour later. He placed a fish on the table and a parcel of smoked herring. 'That's from our Tom, and the kippers and loaf of bread is from our Chad's wife. Da hasn't been out all day.'

Their mother's hands went to her hips. 'Just because he said it, that doesn't mean he's telling the truth.'

'He didn't say it, since I didn't ask the question. He's having trouble with his stomach, and has spent the day in the outhouse.'

'Eh, he never. Your father hasn't had a day's sickness in his life.'

'Well, he has now. They reckon he's been trotting back and forth all day.'

Mary grinned. 'It's that sister of his. Some say she poisoned her own husband with her cooking. Now she's trying to get rid of Ebeneezer the very same way – and good luck to her. How bad is he, Aaric?'

'He's doubled up and cussing fit to bust.'

'It would take more than Aunt Agatha's cooking to kill that tough old devil,' Mary said, chuckling at the thought.

Callie grinned at her. 'Why should you care anyway, when you've thrown him out?'

Her mother's expression was one of amusement. 'I wish I'd thought of it myself, that's all. It serves the stubborn brute right. I expect he'll recover in time.'

'He wants to come home,' Aaric said.

'Did he say so?'

'He said nowt at all to me. Tom told me.'

Mary's eyes hardened. 'Tom – and the lot of you, come to that – can keep your noses out. I'll not willingly take him back, not even if he crawls up the street on his hands and knees and begs me. He killed our Giles. I'll not forgive him for that in a hurry.'

'It was an accident.'

'An accident that was brought about by Ebeneezer's nature. He always sets out to have his own way, and he doesn't care who gets hurts in the process.'

'His conscience is troubling him. He's suffering, Ma,' Aaric pleaded.

'Aye,' she said bleakly, 'so it should be. He can learn to live with it as far as I'm concerned. Enough of this now, Aaric. It's not solving the problem of who did *this* to us. If your da wasn't the culprit, who was?'

The three of them gazed blankly at one another.

Queen Victoria died in January and the shops were draped in black crêpe. It was a hard winter. The situation between their parents had split the Ingram family firmly down the middle, because as far as their da was concerned, you were either for him, or against him. Mary, who'd already learned to be economic during the course of her marriage, was now forced to scrape the bottom of the barrel even further. But she was enterprising. With no fish to sell, she found a job in a public house, scrubbing the floors on her hands and knees after the place had closed for the night, knowing Aaric was home for Kitty if she woke. And she took in other people's mending as well. The hardship only strengthened Mary's resolve that those children still living with her should have something better in their lives.

'Aaric, if anything happens to me, you should get Callie away from here. Look after her and Kitty.'

'I'll do my best, but our da might have something to say about that,' he told her gently.

'Aye, no doubt he would,' she said bitterly, 'for he's made plans to wed Callie off to Sam Brown as soon as she's old enough. Then she'll live a life of misery, the same as I did. She's got a brain in her head, has our Callie, and is too good for that sort of life. Take her as far away from here as you can. The pair of you can make something of yourselves.'

'And what about Kitty?'

'She's a good girl who will never be trouble to anyone. Callie's already promised me she'll look after her.'

Aaric hugged her. 'I promise I'll do what you say if you stop talking daft, Ma. You're not going anywhere, yet, so stop worrying about it.'

Callie never suffered real hunger, for she ate plenty at the Lazurus house. But on Sundays she always said she wasn't hungry, and only took a cup of tea. That left a bit more for Aaric and her ma to eat.

Often she'd take home a ham bone from the Lazurus larder, or the peelings, for Mrs Perkins was heavy-handed with the paring knife. She swapped some of the scraps for half a dozen eggs from Mrs Higley's hens every week, but kept the best of them for her mother to make soup with, for Kitty was on solid food now.

Callie spent every weekend raking coal from the beach, and looking for anything of value that the tide had washed up. Not that she could lift anything with weight attached to it, and the scavenging lads snatched up most of the timber, especially Sam Brown and his brother, who loaded them on to his horse and cart.

Sam waylaid her in the lane one day, blocking access to her yard with his cart, and pushing her against the brick wall with one hand, while his sullen brother looked on.

'I'd help you with that if you were nice to me, tha knows.'

'I'd rather eat maggots.'

'Aw, come on, Callie. When are you gannin' out wi' me?'

'You're skewed if you think I'd go out with you. Let me go or I'll fetch you a clout that'll make your lugs ring like church bells.'

Instead, he grabbed her face with both hands, then leaned forward and kissed her, his wet mouth pressing against hers. A shudder ran through her.

'Ugh!' she spluttered when he let her go, and spat at his feet before scrubbing her hand across her mouth. She felt sick.

'Let me have a go, Sam,' his brother said with a high-pitched giggle.

'Don't you touch me, you scabby little rat,' Callie warned.

Her eyes widened when he took a knife from under his jacket. 'Unless you want fettling wi' this, tek that back.'

'Nay, lad.' Sam chopped his brother across the wrist and the knife dropped to the ground. Sam picked it up and gazed at it. 'Where did you get this from?'

'I found it.'

'Liar. He got it from our house, that's where. That's my da's filleting knife. See, it's got his initials cut into the handle.'

Sam gazed at his brother. 'Where did you say you found it?'

'In the lane,' the boy said.

Suddenly Callie remembered the image of the footprints on the floor. They'd been smaller than the usual adult-sized feet, but she hadn't seen it at the time. Sliding her hand into the pocket of her pinny, she fisted the button. The younger brother was wearing a blue shirt.

'He's got a button missing and a rip in his shirt.'

Sam threw her a glance. 'It's an old shirt.'

She drew the button from her pocket and held

it out to him. 'Whoever stole that knife also tipped our house upside down and destroyed our food on Christmas Day. He left this behind, and the floor was covered in footprints where he'd tramped everything into the flagstones.'

'I found the knife in the lane, and that's not my button. Besides, I'm not tall enough to reach up to your mantelpiece.'

'Unless you stood on a chair.' Hands on hips, Callie shrieked, 'See, he's lying. I didn't say the knife was kept on the mantelpiece, and that button's from his shirt.'

'What button?' Sam threw it over the wall into his own yard, then took his brother by the ear. 'Are you daft, or summat? If you took that knife it's stealing. What if they call in the constables? You'll be thrown in jail for doing damage.'

'No I won't. Her da gave me thruppence to do it,' he squealed.

A smile spread slowly across Sam's face. 'There you are then, Callie Ingram. Your da owns the house you live in, so no crime was done. I believe my brother when he said he found the knife in the lane.'

'Well I don't, because I know he didn't. And he threatened to slit my throat with it.'

'Nay, lass. All I saw was my brother tekking it out of his pocket to give it back to you. Then you started screeching, accusing him of all sorts of things. Get away inside wiyyer, girl.' He threw the knife at the gate, where it buried itself in the wood. 'Tek this and all – not that your da has any use for it these days, the ugly old sot.

Thanks for the kiss. I've had better.'

She lashed out at him, but he knocked her arm aside so it grazed along the brick wall, skinning her knuckles. He clicked his tongue and the horse moved forward.

Callie didn't rub salt into the wound by telling her mother. She pushed the knife to the back of the mantelpiece behind the clock, where it could be discovered the next time it was dusted. She confided in Aaric, although she didn't tell him about the forced kiss.

Sam didn't approach her again, or offer to help her with the cart. Unless Aaric was with her, Callie had to make twice as many journeys with lighter loads of coal.

Once or twice she saw her father sitting on the sea wall, his eyes filled with misery, and looking out to sea. If he saw her, he didn't acknowledge her, and she didn't approach him because he was now diminished in her eyes. She was torn between a desire to forgive him, and loyalty to her mother, who she loved with all that was in her.

Chad and Tom took his boat out from time to time, but mostly their father's Coble was beached on its side, blasted by the wind-driven sand.

Patricia's health had improved, and the girls began to enjoy long walks together. Spring came, and with it the day Callie had been dreading: Patricia's departure.

Callie had expected Theron Grace to come up from London to collect his cousin. Instead, Mr

Lazurus had decided to pay a visit to London himself, and travel with her.

The two girls clung to one another, tears in their eyes, while the bags were loaded on to the hired coach carriage.

'Come along, my dear, we don't want to miss the train,' Mr Lazurus said. He helped Patricia into the cab and kissed Callie on the forehead before pressing an envelope in her hand. 'This is to help your mother out a little. When I return, the pair of you must come and take tea with me.'

Patricia blew her a kiss as the cab moved off. 'Don't forget to write to me, Callie,' she shouted. 'You have my London address. I'll try and persuade Theron to allow me to come back in the summer for a holiday.'

'Such a dear child,' Mrs Perkins said, drying her eyes on her apron. 'I don't mind saying that I didn't approve of you coming here, but you've done her the world of good, and no mistake. Come away inside now, girl. I've got a basket of food you can take on home. It will save it having to be thrown away. I've been having a clean out of the cupboards, too. There's some odd dishes and cups too, if your ma can use them. And I'll be sorting out the linen. Some of it never gets used, and Mr Lazurus said to throw it out. It's yellowed from being in the cupboard for such a long time, but I daresay a good boil will bring the whiteness up.'

'Thank you, Mrs Perkins.'

She nodded. 'I'll be giving the house a good spring clean over the month Mr Lazurus is away. It's a lot of work. I told him you might like to give me a hand. He said he was going to suggest it himself, so he's left me some wages to pay you for every week you work.'

Tears came into Callie's eyes and she smiled with relief. 'Mr Lazurus is so kind, Mrs Perkins. And so are you.' Flinging her arms around the woman's waist she hugged her tight. 'Thank you. My mother needs the money.'

'Aye, I know lass, and it's a good girl you are. That's enough tears now. Come away in. We'll have some tea and a slice of cake together before you go home. Eh, but it's going to be quiet without the pair of you. You take Mr Lazurus out of himself, bless him ... I'm going to miss her, you know.'

'So am I,' Callie said as she slid the envelope into her pocket.

Ten

Ebeneezer had been drinking steadily all night.

He weaved through the streets, his feet taking him where they would. He soon found himself standing outside his own house.

'Mary,' he shouted out. 'It's piddling down with rain. Fer pity's sake, let me in.'

The curtain in the upstairs window twitched.

'I know you're in there,' he shouted.

The window of the next house was thrust open and a man said belligerently, 'Bugger off, Ebeneezer. Let a body have his sleep. Yer old lady's out scrubbing, so she can put food in your kids' bellies.'

'This is my house.'

'Mebbe, but this here is my piss pot, and if you don't move on I'll empty it over your head.'

Ebeneezer moved off, keeping a careful hold on the half-empty bottle of rum he carried. He didn't want to drop it, since the landlord had told him there was no more until he'd paid off his slate.

'Ungrateful bugger, after all the money I spent there,' Ebeneezer muttered to himself.

Across the road, hidden in the entrance to a lane, Mary stood in the rain, her eyes straining into the darkness as her husband weaved off. Her dislike of him was a knotted fist of tension in her chest. As soon as he turned the corner she was across the road, slipped her key into the lock, and hurried inside.

'Has he gone?' Callie whispered from the darkness.

'Aye,' her mother said. 'But I know Ebeneezer. One of these days he's not going to take the hint, then we can look out.'

Ebeneezer got the same treatment at his sister's house.

'You're drunk,' Agatha stated. 'I told you last time that I wasn't putting up with it again. Besides, I'll need your room for my summer visitors. I've had enough. You can get your things packed and get out.'

'I've got nowhere to go, Aggie. Mary won't have me back.'

'That house used to belong to our family. It's yours now, not hers. Go and show her who's in charge. I'm sick of keeping you, and sick of hearing you whine about how hard done by you are.'

'You're a hard-hearted, nagging old cow, Aggie, just like our mother was. It's a pity your husband didn't survive. A good slap now and again would have kept you in line.'

'Like you keep your wife under your thumb? Look at you, you old sot, snivelling at the thought of her. She's made a laughing stock of you, I can tell you. Poor old Ebeneezer Ingram hasn't got the guts to handle his own wife, or keep her happy, they're saying. He's a failure. What's more, I heard that wife of yours is getting friendly with that Lazurus chap.'

'Is she hell as like! I'll have to see about that.' The blood in his veins began to boil, and his head thumped. 'Let me in, Aggie. I'm your brother.'

'You're a pathetic, snivelling rum-gut, that's what you are. No wonder Mary wants rid of you.'

'Ah, I'll get my bonny lass back. She just needs a bit of persuading. But I need a good night's sleep first.'

'You're not coming in. Got it?'

'Alreet, alreet, I'm not deef, woman,' he said. 'If my own sister won't have me I'll go and sleep under my boat.'

'You do that. Come back for your things in the morning, when you're sober.' She shut the door in his face.

'Bitch,' was all he said.

Ebeneezer sat on his boat in the rain, taking sips from his bottle and muttering to himself. Towards dawn the rain stopped. He was soaked through, and cold.

'I'm cold too. I'm all alone down here, and I'm scared, Da,' a voice called across the water.

His heart thumping, for it had sounded like Giles's voice, Ebeneezer looked around him into the gloom. 'Who is that?'

There was no answer, just the sound of the sea creeping across the sand towards him. On the horizon, a yellow dawn smudged the underbelly of a bank of low cloud. The fishermen would be out there, beyond the horizon, hauling in the nets and packing the fish tightly in the bottom of the boats, ready for the wind and tide to bring them safely to the shore. He wished he was out there with them, where he wasn't quite alone.

Soon Verna's husband would be down with his cart to get the fish on the train for the London market while it was still fresh. Ebeneezer didn't want Robbie Wilkinson laying down the law to him. The man was too big for his boots now he had a bit of money in the bank. But Verna did all right by him. She was a good, steady girl who knew her place – not like that Callie of his, who knew too much for her own good, and was filled with fancy ideas by her mother. It would take a strong man to settle Callie down to marriage, but Sam Brown was the one to do it, when the time came.

'Da, help me!'

He threw the empty bottle away from him and lumbered to his feet, thinking he must be turning into a barmpot if he was hearing the voices of the dead.

'Shuddup, it's not you, Giles,' he shouted. 'I took you home to your ma. God knows, I'd have given my own life to save yours, but it was too late.'

Tears slid down his cheeks. He'd go and see Mary. She'd be up now, still in her nightdress, her long hair hanging down her back in a braid. The kettle would be steaming on the hob. She'd been a good wife and mother, had bred well for him, even though they'd lost their fair share to disease. Ebeneezer couldn't remember their faces or names. He couldn't understand why Mary had taken him to task over Giles, when he was just one of many. It wasn't fair.

He'd tell her it was an accident, make her understand. It wasn't right, a man not being allowed into his own house and his wife's bed. By God, he had the right to her. The ring on her finger said so. And if that Lazurus chap came calling on her, he'd give him a few clouts before he sent him packing. That would teach him not to go sniffing after another man's woman.

He went in through the lane, being careful not to scrape the door over the pebbles. The kitchen was in darkness; the door wouldn't budge. Things had changed. If Mary now worked at night, she probably slept in later in the mornings. He'd wait.

Before too long Aaric came into the kitchen and lit a candle. He ate a slice of bread and dripping while waiting for the kettle to boil, then drank a cup of tea, leaving the pot on the hob to keep warm.

Ebeneezer crouched into a corner when his son unlocked the door and came into the yard to use the outhouse. When the outhouse door closed behind him, Ebeneezer slid into the house and into the parlour, shutting the door quietly. Eh, but it was lovely being in his own home, away from Agatha's constant clacking. Taking a seat in his favourite chair, he rested his head against a cushion and fell asleep, thinking he'd make things right this time.

The rest of the house stirred. Aaric left for his job at the wood yard, then Callie came downstairs to clatter about the kitchen before going off to the beach.

As Mary fed Kitty her breakfast, she wished Callie didn't have to go out to rake coal. She ran a finger over one of the plates the girl had brought from the Lazurus house. It was so pretty, with a flower pattern circling the rim. The china was of different patterns, but Mary didn't care. It was nice to have lovely things about her.

She dressed Kitty and set her on a quilt in the wooden pen against the wall to play with her toy cat, some spoons and enamel bowls. She'd make a racket, but it kept her out from underfoot. She'd probably fall asleep there after a while, and then Mary intended to boil up the linen Callie had brought home.

Callie hadn't yet realized that the goods were a charitable act on behalf of Mr Lazurus. The linen was perfectly serviceable, and Mrs Perkins would probably have kept them for her own family or sold them at the market place if she hadn't been instructed otherwise. But the woman hadn't seemed to resent it, and Mary had accepted the gift for what it was. She'd long run out of false pride. With a family to clothe and feed, she couldn't afford such scruples.

Her daughter came back with the coal and a

medium-sized cod. 'The boats have just come in. Chad gave me a fish.'

'Good, he's taken the scales off and gutted it for us. Guess what I found when I was cleaning the other day. That filleting knife I thought had been taken. It was behind the clock, but be damned if I know how it got there. We still don't know who turned the house over though...'

'I don't suppose we'll ever find out now.'

'I still think your da had something to do with it.'

Callie avoided the issue. 'I'll go and put the coal in the bunker, shall I?'

'Nay, Callie, love, I'll do it. You get yourself cleaned up and get on off to work. That extra money coming into the house is handy. I can put a bit away for a rainy day. Perhaps that Mrs Perkins will give you a reference when you've finished there. Then you can write to our Jane and ask her if she can get you a job in London now you've left school. That reminds me, you can post my letter to her on the way.'

'Da said I mustn't go to London. He'll be cross.'

'Well, we won't tell him till after you've gone. He didn't go after Jane and bring her back, so he won't go after you. He's got no right to try and prevent you from bettering yourself. Nobody has.'

A few minutes earlier Ebeneezer had been woken from sleep by the sound of talking. His head thumped against the inside of his skull something cruel, his mouth was stale and his eyes dry and sore.

The voices came clearly to him, and the euphoric mood he'd gone to sleep on had been vanquished by a depressive blackness. He groaned as he moved his head. How dare his woman undermine him with his own children!

'What was that noise?' he heard Callie ask.

'I didn't hear anything. Probably someone in the street. Your da hasn't got a key, since he never used the door to the street, and the back door was bolted last night. Thank Mrs Perkins for the linen, won't you? It will last a long time. When is Harold Lazurus coming home?'

'Not for a couple of weeks. He's invited us for tea when he gets back. He said he'll be lonely without Patricia and me there.'

'A pity his wife died. He's the type of man who would thrive with a woman to look after. He'd respect a woman, would that one. Not like your da. Bye, love. I'll see you later.'

'Lock the door. Seeing da out there last night rattled me. Not that I'm frightened for myself, since he's never laid a finger on me before, accept for the odd whack with the strap.'

There's always a first time, maiden, Ebeneezer thought sourly as the door closed behind her.

Mary began to sing softly as he walked up the passage towards the kitchen. The lid on the kettle was rattling. Good, he could do with a cup of hot tea.

Kitty stopped her chuckling to stare at him with her mouth open. Mary had her back to him.

Her hair hadn't been braided, and it hung to her waist in ripples.

'Hello, Mary,' he said.

She spun round, her hand going to her heart. The fright in her eyes was immediately replaced by wariness. 'What are you doing here, Ebeneezer?'

'It's my house, remember? I live here.'

'Not any more, you don't.'

'Aye, I do, bonny lass. I've decided to come home to where I belong.'

She dragged in a breath. 'You can get out.'

Behind him, Kitty had started banging a spoon against a dish. He turned to snarl at her. 'Shuddup, I've got a headache.'

'Don't take it out on our Kitty. It's not her fault that you were on the bottle last night.'

Bang ... bang ... bang...

His skull nearly split in two when he bent to snatch the spoon from the child's hand. Kitty began to cry, and Mary darted round the table. Thrusting him away, she put herself between him and the child, saying bitterly, 'You've already killed one child; you can leave this one alone.'

By heck she looks good, he thought, *despite bearing all those children*. Her breasts were round and full and she smelled of carbolic soap. He hadn't touched another woman since he'd met her, and now he felt the need to bury himself inside her for comfort. That would cure his headache.

'Upstairs,' he said, grinning at the thought of

satisfying his new-found lust.

'Go to hell!'

He should have known she'd resist. Well, he wasn't having any more of it from her. Ebeneezer backhanded her before twisting her hair in his hand and pushing her in front of him. He'd have this woman under his control one way or the other, even if he used force.

Callie had forgotten to take her mother's letter to post to Jane, and returned to the house to retrieve it. But it was driven from her mind as soon as she walked into the kitchen and heard the sounds of a struggle. Her father was cussing, her mother's cries ringing out above it.

Kitty was in her pen, bawling, and held out her arms when she set eyes on her. Swinging the infant up on to her hip, Callie took off at a run to fetch her brothers from the boat harbour.

Chad and Tom managed to subdue their father between them. Callie tended to her mother's injuries, weeping over her bruises and swellings, her blackened eyes and loosened teeth. Her da had been savage in his punishment, and any sympathy she'd felt for him fled.

She raged at him. 'There was no need to be so cruel. You're a damned bully and a drunk, and I hate you.'

'Hold your lip, girl; you're getting too big for your britches.'

'Nay, Da, Callie's reet,' Chad told him. 'You had no call to thump Ma like that. She needs a doctor. If you lay a finger on her again, I'll bluidy well tek thee apart.'

'And after our Chad's finished I'll do the same,' Tom growled. 'Now, tek a sodding grip on yerself, man.'

Despite all their protests, Ebeneezer moved back in. But it was no triumph for him to find his wife cringing away from him every time he so much as looked at her. It hurt more that he had to suffer such dislike in the eyes of his children. Consumed by guilt, he slunk around, shoulders hunched, and couldn't bring himself to meet anybody's eyes. He spent long hours fishing, and not a drop of liquor passed his lips. When he was home the house was filled with tension.

Callie continued to dig for cockles, sold fish door to door, and raked coal from the beach, as well as giving her mother a helping hand about the house. She called in on Mr Lazurus once but, although happy to see her, he was going out to a meeting.

The weeks passed, but eventually Patricia wrote. Her letter was full of the social events she'd been to, the parties, the play she'd attended. *Dearest Callie*, she wrote. *You must write and tell me every exciting event that's been happening in your life, so I can picture it in my mind.*

'Aye,' Callie said softly. 'Which exciting event do you want? The ha'penny I found on the beach? My mother having the stuffing punched out of her, or the fact that the womanly cramps have visited me? Our Verna tells me that I can now grow babies inside me, so I've got to be careful not to let any lad under my skirt...'

What's the point of answering, she wondered. It wasn't as though she could leave her mother now.

It took a long time for Mary physically to recover from the beating Ebeneezer had inflicted on her, although eventually the swelling went down and her bruises faded. But she hugged her side now and again, and no longer had much of an appetite.

When Callie asked what ailed her, she shrugged. 'It's nothing much, just a bit of blood in my water, and an ache in my side sometimes. And I feel tired.'

'You need some blood tonic.'

'Aye, but I can't afford any. Your da has to pay off the debts he ran up.'

Some inner spark had gone from her mother, Callie noticed. She went about her duties lethargically, and the light had gone from her eyes, as if the incident had robbed her of a sense of worth. She rarely spoke when her husband was home.

One morning, about four months later, Callie found her mother crying soundlessly into her apron. She wrapped her arms around her and hugged her tight. 'What is it, Ma?'

'I have an infant inside me again.'

'Oh, Ma.'

'I have a bad feeling about it, Callie.'

Frightened by her words, Callie said, 'Hush,

Ma. It'll be all right. I'll help you.'

Her mother patted her hand, saying tiredly, 'Aye lass, I reckon you'll have to.'

Two months later, her mother called her up the stairs. Her pale face was covered in a sheen of perspiration. 'Callie, love, I'm bleeding. Likely I'm losing the infant, but it doesn't feel right. Best you go and fetch the midwife.'

'Summat's wrong,' the woman said when she arrived. 'Your ma needs a doctor.'

But the doctor was out on a call, and by the time he got to the house Mary was unconscious. 'Her liver's swollen and bleeding,' the doctor said to the frantic Callie after examining her. 'She must have fallen and damaged it at some time. The infant's dead inside her, too.'

'Can't you take it from her?'

'It wouldn't make any difference. I can't heal her liver. It's just a matter of time, and she has precious little of that left. There's nothing I can do, I'm afraid.'

Except issue a death certificate, Callie thought bitterly only a little while later as she and Verna washed her mother's body ready for the undertaker. Kitty played quietly in the corner, unaware of the tragedy.

'I've left my babies with Aunt Agatha,' Verna said. 'When the boats come in you'll go and tell Da and the boys, won't you?'

'The doctor said he'd send his boy with a message to Aaric. He'll do it.' Verna eyed the blue outfit hanging on the chair, one of the two that Theron Grace had bought for Callie. 'Is that what we're going to dress her in?'

'Aye. It's mine, and I want her to have something nice to wear.'

'It's too fancy to put to waste in the grave.'

'Nothing's too good for our mother, and I want her to look like the lady she was before she married Da,' Callie said passionately. 'She was good-hearted, brave and hardworking. Da didn't deserve her. He set out to spoil everything that was beautiful in her, and to destroy her pride and spirit. And he did. Ma finally realized she'd never escape him, and has been dying piece by piece since that beating he gave her. I hope he'll be satisfied now. He's killed her and I'll never forgive him.'

'Hush, Callie, you shouldn't say such things. It's wrong.'

'It's what I feel, Verna. I despise him.'

'Best to keep such things to yourself.'

When their mother was dressed, Callie brushed her long hair and neatly braided it. She kissed her pale cheek before placing pennies on her eyelids. 'There won't be an angel in heaven that can touch you, Ma. You look lovely.'

'Aye, peaceful like, as if she hasn't got a care in the world,' Verna said with a catch in her voice.

'Now don't you start me off crying, Verna. I've got things to do on her behalf.'

Kitty stood on her plump legs and took a couple of staggering steps towards the bed. She pulled at her mother's skirt and smiled. 'Mama.'

'Did you see that, Ma, she just took her first

steps.' Picking her sister up, Callie smiled at her. 'That's a clever lass, you are. Your ma's gone to sleep for a long, long time. Give her a kiss goodbye.'

Kitty giggled at the pennies keeping her mother's eyes closed and reached out a plump little fist for them.

'No, love, you can't have those. And from now on, you'll have me to look after you instead of Ma. That's what she wanted.'

There was relief in Verna's voice. 'Our Kitty's used to you being here. She hardly knows me, and I couldn't have her anyway, I've got another on the way myself.'

The funeral was over. Her father was in a state. Tears filled his eyes and his voice shook.

Harold Lazurus offered his condolences. 'I'm so sorry, Mr Ingram. Callie, is there anything I can do to help?'

Ebeneezer said in a low, savage voice, 'Aye. You hung off my woman's skirt when she was alive, encouraging her to stray from her lawful husband. Now, you can stay away from my lass. I don't want her head filled with what she can't have. Gerrit?'

Harold looked taken aback. 'You dishonour your wife, sir. It was friendship, nothing more. I'm acquainted with Mrs Ingram's family, and was once at school with her brother.'

'Look around you, mister. Can you see any of the Brightman family here? We're Mary's family. She had no other. Be warned, now. I won't tell you again.'

'I'm so sorry,' Callie said, her eyes filling with tears, for Mr Lazurus had been good to them.

Her father planted his hand on her back and gave her a push. 'Gerroff home with you, maiden. You've nowt to be sorry for.'

'Mebbe not, but *you* have,' she said, tears rolling down her cheeks as she stumbled away.

Eleven

Callie took her mother's place in the household. She was expected to do Mary's work as well as her own, and even though the family had tragically shrunk in size over the past few months the work was still constant. Kitty needed looking after. Now she was walking, she got herself into all sorts of mischief.

Her da was a silent, authoritative figure, who criticized her efforts and sometimes mistook her for her mother, calling her Mary. He drank steadily, though not enough to get roaring drunk. Callie was thankful for that.

'He's suffering,' Aaric said.

'Aye, and so he should be. I don't feel sorry for him, only for the lives he's ruined. And he intends to ruin mine, Aaric.'

Aaric helped with the coal raking as much as he could, but his working hours didn't coincide with the tides. Callie was constantly weary. She longed for her mother to talk to, and whenever she felt down, she visited her grave and spoke of her troubles. It made her feel better.

'I don't know what to do, Ma. I feel so trapped. I despise Da as much as you did. I hate myself for that and the feeling sits like a sticky black lump inside my chest.' She placed her fist against her heart and whispered, 'I want to cry, but I can't.'

She'd been forbidden to visit Mr Lazurus, but somehow her feet took her towards the road that led to the railway station where the posh folk lived in their big houses. There, she easily sold the catch of fish, and dawdled in the hope that she might run into him. But she never did.

No matter how hard she tried to avoid them, wherever she went she seemed to run into either Sam Brown or his brother, Alf. It was as if they'd deliberately laid in wait for her so they could torment her. She thought they might be following her, but then dismissed the idea. Why would they do such a thing?

But the feeling persisted. Also persisting was the need to talk to Mr Lazurus, to thank him for his help.

One day she found herself outside his house. She took a quick look around to make sure that nobody who knew her was about, and then she slipped inside the gate.

Mr Lazurus had opened the front door before she had time to ring the doorbell, already dressed in jacket and hat, his cane grasped in his hand. A smile came to his face, though the look in his eyes said he was in a hurry.

'Ah ... Callie ... how very unexpected.'

'You're going out?'

'As you can see. I'm late for a meeting. Rather an inopportune moment for you to visit, actually. Will you walk with me? We can talk on the way.'

'No, I'd better not. Someone might see us and tell my da.'

He looked sad, but said gently before he walked off, 'Come and have tea with me one day. Sunday is the best day to catch me in.'

Having given in to impulse, Callie wondered if there was any point in trying to maintain such a friendship now Patricia was gone.

She received a short condolence letter from her friend, one so full of affection that it made her cry all over again. At least she'd known the love of her mother, while Patricia had hardly ever experienced it.

Yet their lives were too far apart for friendship to be maintained long term. What did Patricia know of real hardship? Nothing. She threw the letter into the stove, then was filled with guilt because of the envy she felt towards her friend.

Summer was fast approaching when one night her father said, 'I'll be wanting to talk to you after dinner.'

Unease filled her. Her father ate his dinner slowly, chewing noisily, then scraping the gravy up with his knife, so the blade screeched along the fine patterned glaze, setting her teeth on edge. He waited until he'd finished his pudding then sucked the crumbs from his teeth with his tongue while she made the tea and placed a mug of it in front of him.

'Yer a good cook, reet enough.'

The tension became too much to bear. 'What do you want to say to me, Da?' she asked when he raised the cup to his lips.

'I'm going to wed the widder next door.'

That was the last thing she'd expected to hear. 'Tilly Brown?'

'Aye.'

'But Ma's hardly cold in her grave.'

'Dead is dead, Callie; your ma's nay coming back. Tilly and I have sorted it out between us.'

Callie's eyes narrowed as a kind of dread grew inside her. 'Sorted what out?'

'Sam will be coming fishing wi' me. You'll wed him and live next door. Tilly will move in here since she needs someone to father a bairn or two on her before she gets too old. And that Alf of hers needs a da.'

Very convenient for all concerned, she thought. Except herself! Callie kept the anger from her voice though, waiting to see what else he had in mind. 'What about our Kitty and Aaric?'

'Tilly will mother Kitty. As for Aaric, he's earning a wage and is old enough to fend for himself. Likely Agatha will tek him as a paying boarder.'

Callie's hands went to her hips. 'I promised Ma *I'd* look after Kitty.'

'Aye, lass, I know, but she hasn't got a voice in the matter since she upped and died on us.'

'I'm not going to marry Sam Brown.'

'Aye you are, so mek yer mind up to it. Sam's a good, hard-working lad. He's looked after his ma, and he'll look after you. The banns will be called and you'll be wed in the church in six weeks' time.'

Her temper flared up. 'I can look after myself, too. Sam Brown can go to hell, and be damned to him, and to you, too.'

'When you raise the devil in this house remember it's your father you're talking to.' The slap that stung her face had enough force to nearly knock her off the chair, and she tasted blood in her mouth. 'I've had enough of your lip, maiden. You'll do as I bluidy well tell yer.'

'You can't make me marry him,' she said passionately, her face flaming.

Her da gave a mirthless grin. 'Aye, I can.' He stood, scraping his chair back. 'I'm gannin' out. Get on with the housework, and when yon lad from next door calls on you, you treat him wi' respect.'

'I'd spit in his eye first.'

'A word of warning: be careful he doesn't spit back.'

'Hah!' she flung at him when he took his jacket from the hook behind the door and headed out of the yard.

But she couldn't convince herself she'd have the courage to oppose him, even with the defiant gesture. Married to Sam Brown in six weeks? The thought was too horrible to contemplate. She desperately needed to talk to somebody, and she could only think of one person.

By the time Sam came calling she'd locked the back door and had hidden upstairs, reading the book Patricia had given her when they first met. How Callie wished it was Mr Bingham calling on her. Not that she craved riches, for she'd happily marry a beggar if she loved him and was loved in return.

Her fingertip traced over the inscription when she heard the gate to the lane scuff the ground, as if somebody had shut it. Good, Sam had gone.

To Miss Calandra Ingram from Patricia Lazurus ... a token of my friendship.

Miss Calandra Ingram. She imagined being announced at a party, with her hair up in an elegant bun and wearing a gown trimmed with lace, sweeping into a London drawing room on the arm of Theron Grace. She'd dance, too. Patricia and James had taught her how to waltz, and had told her that Theron was a wonderful dancer...

But now none of that would ever happen. She felt a strong surge of remorse at throwing away her friendship with Patricia and James. And Theron, of course, though he wasn't really a friend ... more like a distant uncle who was often in her thoughts. He had too much presence to be completely forgotten, she thought with a smile.

Her glance went to Kitty, who was lying on her back, cuddling the furry toy cat Theron had sent her for Christmas. Her sister had been grizzly for a while after their mother had died, but now she seemed to have forgotten about her, though she clung to Callie and sometimes called her ma. Her spiky baby hair had been replaced by dark ringlets, and her face was filled with the innocent vulnerability of sleep. What plans did her father have for Kitty? Would he marry Kitty off at seventeen to Alf Brown, so he could keep them all in the family and under his control? She shuddered.

Both Jane and Joseph had run away to lead their own lives. Apart from a photograph of Joe in his uniform that he'd sent with a letter saying he was well, nothing had been heard from either of them for quite a while. Aaric had written to them both when their mother had died, but neither had answered, or come to the funeral.

'Joe is probably at sea, and might not have got the letter, but I would have expected our Jane to come,' Verna had said. 'I suppose she's too good to want to know the likes of us now.'

Gently kissing her baby sister's downy cheek, Callie went downstairs to wash the dishes and tidy the kitchen.

Come Sunday afternoon, when the fishing fleet had put to sea, Callie headed for the house of Harold Lazurus with Kitty supported in a sling astride her hip. It was a fair day, still, with a touch of humidity. The sea was an expanse of milky glass as it receded gently towards the sky, where a smudge of smoke on the horizon traced the passage of a ship.

She should be gathering coal, she thought, but today her mind was filled with a restless type of rebellion as her thoughts turned to how she could escape Seafield. She had no money, no income, and was completely at the mercy of her father. Not that he showed her much.

The feeling of being followed was still persistent. Callie stopped and looked around her, at the shadowed hedges and trees that filled the gardens of the houses. There were only a few houses built at the village end of the wide lane. They were large and belonged to the more prosperous families. Beyond, behind and around them stretched the fields and the allotments. Mr Lazurus's house was in the finest position, with a good view over the sea. It was a pity he had no family to fill it.

Callie couldn't see anyone she recognized amongst the people out about their business. As for her, in her scarf and shawl she was indistinguishable from the other cockle women and coal gatherers, not worth a second glance. She shook her head, thinking she really must stop imagining things.

Mr Lazurus gave her a wide smile as he opened the door. 'Ah, I was hoping you'd come today. I asked Mrs Perkins to make us a cake.'

Callie grinned. 'She always makes you a cake for the weekend.'

'So she does,' he said gently, 'but this is your favourite, the sticky gingerbread.'

Callie was touched that he'd remembered it was her favourite, but then remembered it was *his* favourite too. She laughed. 'And yours.'

He chuckled and turned to Kitty. 'Look at you, young lady. You've grown since I last saw you.'

Kitty aimed a dribbly smile towards him. Callie wiped her chin, saying proudly, 'She's walking well now, and gets into all sorts of mischief.

I'd better lift the ornaments up out of her way.'

'We'll have tea in the library, since the tray is already in there. There's not much in there that she can damage. Fetch yourself a cup and a plate. Callie. And better bring a cup for Kitty. In the meantime I'll find her something to play with. I believe Mrs Perkins found a Noah's Ark in one of the upstairs cupboards.'

He was gone for a few moments, and then came into the library carrying a wooden ark, which he set down on the rug. The top lifted off, revealing many brightly painted wooden animals and Noah with his wife. Kitty was fascinated by it and played happily.

'I spoke to Patricia on the telephone yesterday,' he said, pouring tea into the cups.

'How is she?' Callie asked, eager for news.

'She was upset because you haven't answered her letter.'

A blush stole across Callie's cheeks and she mumbled, 'Things have been difficult.'

'Yes, I know, but wouldn't a short note telling her so be good manners? Surely it wouldn't take up too much of your time.'

She drew in a deep breath. 'To be quite honest I don't see the point. I doubt if we'll see each other again, Mr Lazurus.'

'I'm sorry you should think that, when Patricia treated you all with respect and kindness.'

'It's nothing to do with the way I was treated. You made me feel like a princess. And that's part of the trouble. I'm a fisherman's daughter and Patricia is too far above me.'

'You were treated as an equal in my house, and were also regarded as one by Theron Grace. Do you think the hand of friendship has no value? Would you willingly hurt Patricia's feelings by using her, then turn away from her without a word of explanation?'

Mortified, tears filled Callie's eyes. 'You don't understand, Mr Lazurus. I wouldn't do anything to hurt Patricia, but staying friends will soon become impossible.'

'Come, dear,' he said when she had dried her eyes on her apron. 'I didn't mean to upset you. Tell me what has happened to make you feel this way.'

'That's why I visited today ... I wanted to ask your advice.'

'And instead of listening, I chided you. I'll help if I can. What's troubling you?'

'My father has arranged that I should marry in just over five weeks. I don't want to. Can he make me?'

His eyes widened. 'Good gracious, that was unexpected. If you're unwilling, no clergyman would sanctify such a union. Perhaps you'd better tell me the whole story.'

While she did, Kitty was lifted on to his lap and a napkin tucked under her chin. Blissfully, she ate the small pieces of cake Mr Lazurus fed her, and washed them down with half a cup of milk before being set down again to play.

Callie stumbled over her words because just saying them aloud made her realize how little her opinion meant to her father, and that made her angry.

Harold's forehead had creased in a frown while she talked. When she finally ran out of words, he said, 'Normally, I wouldn't advise anyone of your tender age to disobey their parent or legal guardian. In this case though, I cannot sanction such a scheme. You shouldn't be forced to wed against your will just to accommodate your father's future plans. All you need to do is say no, and keep saying no. Would you like me to talk to your father on your behalf? Perhaps I can find you employment, where you can support yourself.'

Her heart quaked at the thought of what her father would say or do to that. 'Please don't. He'd be furious. I think he's using Kitty to keep me here. I need to get away and take her with me.'

Her host suddenly looked agitated. 'I'll hear no more of this, and I strongly advise you to put such a scheme out of your head. Conspiring to remove your sister from her home would ruin me. We'd both end up in jail.'

'But my mother asked me to look after her. She made me promise.'

'That wouldn't hold up in a court of law. Your father is Kitty's parent. In fact, you're both under his care.' He stood, placing his hands on the table, and looking quite stern. 'You should ask that brother of yours to act as your spokesman. Aaric struck me as being a rational, sensible young man. Now you must go, Callie. I need some quiet time to absorb what you've said and think it through. I'll see you out.'

'I'm sorry,' she said, near to tears when they reached the porch. 'You've been kind to me, and I wouldn't do anything to upset you. Thank you for the tea.'

When they stood on the porch he kissed her gently on the forehead. 'Goodbye, Callie dear. I'll try and think of some lawful way I can be of help to you, I promise. Just keep saying no to the marriage. And don't forget to write to Patricia.'

'Aye, I will.' *Even if only to say she couldn't remain friends with her*, she thought.

Callie's smile faded as the door closed behind her, and she wondered how much Mr Lazurus's promise had been worth. *Just keep saying no*, he'd said. Fingering the bruise on her cheek, she shrugged. Look where saying no had got her so far!

She was too absorbed with her troubles to notice Alf Brown speeding off across the fields.

Harold watched Callie go. He felt sorry for her; she had too many burdens for one so young.

The affair surrounding her mother's family came into his mind. To all intents and purposes, Mary Brightman seemed to have fallen off the ends of the earth when she married, and was soon forgotten. But her name had brought it back to Harold. With it came distaste, for he'd met Callie's grandmother, Sally Brightman, and a nicer, more compassionate woman he couldn't wish to meet. He couldn't imagine her willingly throwing her daughter out in the street. She was one of Theron's clients and the family resemblance to Aaric and Callie was strong.

Thinking of the connection, he wondered if Callie's problem could be approached from a different angle. For a moment or two he struggled between his need to help the girl, and his good sense telling him it wasn't any of his business.

But two heads were better than one, he thought. He went through to his office and placed the trumpet-shaped telephone receiver to his ear. This was a wonderful invention, he thought, going through the motions to place his call to London.

'Theron Grace speaking.'

Theron's voice was so clear that Harold almost looked around to see if he was standing behind him.

'Hello, who's there?' Theron repeated, impatiently now.

'Theron, it's Harold Lazurus.'

'Ah ... to what do I owe the pleasure of this phone call?'

They exchanged pleasantries, then Harold said, 'I have a problem I'd like to talk over with you.'

'It must be a knotty one if you can't solve it by yourself.'

'Oh, I could easily solve it. All I need to do is walk away and do nothing – allow events to take their course.'

Theron gave a sigh. 'What's stopping you?'

'Conscience.'

'The name of the problem wouldn't be Miss Callie Ingram, would it?'

'As a matter of fact, it would.'

'A delightful, spirited girl.' Theron chuckled. 'You haven't taken it into your head to propose marriage to her, have you?'

'Lord, no, it's not that sort of problem,' Harold said hastily. 'Callie is hardly out of childhood, though she has a remarkably mature head on her shoulders, at times. However, you're not too far off the mark. Someone is about to make a wife of her. She's being forced to the altar in just a few weeks.'

'The devil she is!' Theron spluttered.

Harold leaned back in his chair and put his feet up on the desk, settling in for a long talk now Theron's interest was fully engaged. 'Callie has turned to me for help. Unfortunately, her suggestion as to a solution to the problem was an unlawful one – one that would have ruined me – so I sent her packing. I'd still like to help her in some way, but without being directly involved. I remembered your habit of approaching problems from different angles and coming up with several solutions.'

'I simply mix and match the variables until something other than the most obvious route suggests itself. Tish tells me I do this because I can't stand being out-manoeuvered.'

Harold chuckled at that. 'An astute observation on her part. Do you have the time to discuss this now, since time is fairly short?'

'Tish is out visiting and I'm not expecting

anyone to call, so yes, now is an excellent time to indulge in hypothesis. One thing I must know, Harold: what's stopping Callie from running away from Seafield, like her sister did?'

'Callie promised her mother she'd look after Kitty.'

There was silence for a moment, then Theron said softly, 'Ah, yes, I see ... there are obviously two sacrificial lambs here.'

'And one is being played off against the other. Either Callie leaves Seafield without Kitty, or she stays and looks after her, like she promised her mother.'

'And since to take Kitty with her would mean trouble for all concerned, we both know which way she will jump.'

'I wouldn't expect anything else from her, and although I've told her she can say no to the marriage, she's being pulled in all directions. I fear that events might be arranged to make refusal impossible.'

Theron sucked in a breath. 'Like what happened to her mother?'

'Exactly.'

'I'm seeing Sally Brightman next week.'

'Business or pleasure?'

'Seeing her is always a pleasure, but it's business as well. I'm thinking that it might be a good time to make her aware of the relationship between my family and her granddaughter. Would you object to that?'

'Mrs Brightman is *your* client, Theron. You must do as you think best.'

'I'll take that as a sign of approval. Now, about the rest of Callie's family. Would it be too far-fetched to suppose that any of them might assist her?'

'Aaric, perhaps. They're fairly close. He works at the sawmill as a clerk. His boss is constantly bragging about how much work the young man does for his wage. He practically runs the accounting side.'

'Yes, I remember Aaric. He returned my contract with Callie and negotiated a new clause – that should her employment be terminated prematurely, unless misconduct could be proved, the girl should be awarded her wages up to the contract termination date.'

'The sad thing is, she saw very little of that wage since it went directly into her father's pocket. Aaric is a quiet, pleasant young man.'

'Yes, I thought so too. And it so happens that I'll be needing a new clerk in a few weeks' time, since my current one is just about to move on. Suppose Aaric Ingram was offered the position, wouldn't it present an opportunity for him to make something of himself? And suppose Callie saw the way clear to accompany her sensible young brother to London? I would be pleased to offer the girl her former position as companion to my ward, of course. I wonder, too, if these things were to come about, would Aaric convince Callie of the wisdom of leaving the infant with her family – albeit, at the last moment...'

Harold smiled to himself as Theron began to pull together the threads of his thoughts.

Twelve

Callie had managed to avoid Sam Brown for a while, but now he sat at the kitchen table with his mother and brother, and watched as she dashed back and forth, trying to get the Sunday dinner on the table. Her father was in his chair, sucking on his pipe.

'Lovely plates, Ebeneezer,' Tilly Brown said, turning them over and examining the maker's marks.

The woman was large boned with thick, straight brows over small muddy eyes. Her hair was pulled back into a bun at the nape of her neck.

'They were a gift to my mother from Mr Lazurus, after somebody broke the door down and smashed everything we owned,' Callie said.

It was a reminder to Alf Brown, who gazed nervously at her father and said, 'Callie went to his house last week. I saw the old man kiss her.'

Her father's eyes honed in on her. 'Is that true, our Callie?'

Callie's heart thumped, but she realized it was her word against Alf's. 'He's lying.'

Tilly gave her a hard look. 'You should put the plates on to warm, then the food won't get cold.

And you need to make the batter for the pudding.'

'I intend to.' She was forced to squeeze past Sam to open the larder door. When he squeezed her thigh, she slapped his hand away and, exasperated, snapped, 'Touch me again, Sam, and you'll wish you hadn't. Go into the parlour so I've got room to move.'

'We're used to sitting in the kitchen,' Sam said, flushing to his ears at the slap and the reprimand in front of his mother.

Kitty was in her pen. Giving her a couple of spoons, Callie smiled when her sister began to bang on the bars of her wooden pen. A pained look came into Tilly's eyes. 'Can you stop the child doing that, Ebeneezer; it's giving me a headache.'

'Shuddup, Kitty,' her father grumbled.

Kitty kept on banging, but in his usual fashion, her da ignored the noise; he was used to it.

'Well, if you won't stop her, I will.' Tilly ripped the spoons from Kitty's grasp with such force that Kitty fell backwards and banged her head. The child burst into tears.

'Nay, what did you do that for? She wasn't doing any harm,' Ebeneezer said.

Pushing past the woman, Callie gathered her sister up and cuddled her. She kissed her plump fists. 'Look at her fingers; you've scraped the skin off.'

'It's nothing. It's about time the child learned to do as she's told.'

'It's about time yours did, and they're much

older.'

Alf sniggered.

Ebeneezer rose from his chair, a scowl on his face. 'Can't you wimmin do anything wi'out squabbling? I'm gannin' out while you settle yer differences. You lads can come wi' me, all reet.'

After they'd gone Callie put Kitty back in her pen and faced Tilly over the table. Tilly put her hands on her hips and glared at her. 'If you want to get on wi' me you can stop being so snippy, miss.'

'What makes you think I want to get on with you?'

Tilly looked taken aback. 'Well, aren't you the little madam. You're just like your ma. She thought she was too good for the likes of us, too.'

'She *was* too good for you. And I'm proud of the fact that I'm like her.'

Tilly gave harsh laugh. 'It won't do you any good. My Sam will soon knock that out of you.'

'Your Sam can go to the devil. I'm not marrying him.'

'Don't think you're living here wi' your da and me. I won't have it.'

'If my da decided I was to stay, you'd have no say in the matter. Now, kindly get out of my way while I get the dinner cooked.'

'I'll wait in my own house, thank you,' Tilly said with a sniff.

'No need to thank me, you're more than welcome to wait there,' Callie called out after the woman as she stomped off.

However, Tilly came back just after the men arrived, an aggrieved look on her face.

'Aaric's not here yet,' Callie said when they had all seated themselves and waited to be served.

Her da picked up the carving knife and sharpened it against the steel. 'Pass the meat over, our Callie. If Aaric's not here on time he can go wi'out.'

Tilly Brown took it upon herself to criticize everything Callie had cooked. The meat was too tough, the gravy too thin, the greens watery.

'This batter pudding is soggy in the middle,' she announced.

Alf, who was shovelling food into his mouth, mumbled, 'I like it like that.'

Ebeneezer stared steadily at Tilly. 'Get away wiyyer. Callie was taught to cook by her ma, and there's nowt wrong wi' it.'

'It's tastes alreet to me,' Sam said, coming to her defence too. 'I like my food and at least I'll have a wife that can cook. Give us some more of those mashed spuds, would yer, luv.'

As if she was already wed to him! A silent scream gathered inside Callie as she saw in her mind what would be the pattern of the years to come. And she'd hardly lived yet. *She must escape. She must!* Perhaps Aaric would help her. He might give her the train fare ... But where would she go?

She jumped when Sam, concealed by the tablecloth, pinched her private part and said, 'It'll go cold if you keep me waiting much longer, lass.'

'Keep your hands off me, Sam Brown. We're not wed yet, nor likely to be.' She dolloped a spoonful of mash hard into his gravy, splattering him.

'Did you see that?' Tilly shrieked.

'For God's sake, shut your carping, woman, you're giving me a belly ache,' Ebeneezer said with an irritable sigh.

And that was the last word out of Tilly Brown that day. But she didn't need to talk. Her thin, pursed mouth and the hard-done-by look on her face said it all.

Her da wouldn't stand that from her for long, Callie thought, gazing from one to the other. Her own mother had learned to handle him from a young age, but Tilly Brown had been on her own for a long time and was used to having her own way.

When the fishing fleet was out at sea the tension in the house eased. But the days were passing quickly and Callie was still no nearer to finding a solution to her dilemma.

'I don't know what to do,' she said to Aaric, after taking him into her confidence. 'The banns were called for the first time today, and although I was going to speak up, I was too scared even to squeak in front of everyone. If you would give me the money for the train I could just leave and go to London.'

'By yourself? Don't be daft, Callie. You've never been out of Seafield. Besides, I haven't got any savings left.'

'Aye, you're right, and I can't leave Kitty behind, even though Mr Lazurus told me I could go to jail if I took her. I think Da's counting on me staying because of her.'

'Aye. Da might not have much learning, but he's astute and as sly as they come. He doesn't say much, but a lot goes on in his head.'

Callie laid her head against her brother's arm. 'What will become of us, Aaric?'

He caressed her face. 'You already know that. I'll try and talk to Da about Sam Brown to start with. Even if I could get him to postpone the wedding, that would give you a little time. And I'll go and see Mr Lazurus tomorrow after work, see if he will advise me.'

'D'you think he'll listen?'

Aaric just shrugged.

Aaric's talk with his father didn't go well.

'If I were you I'd keep your nose out, Aaric. You might think you're a canny lad, but you haven't got summat to say worth a scrap. The girl will do as she's told. As fer you, you can do what you bluidy well like. Go to hell for all I care.'

Aaric had expected no less from him.

'Yer ma pandered to you all your life. You tek after the Brightmans – weaklings, the lot of them, fancy shopkeepers and the like. None of them dirtied their hands by doing a hard day's work.

'Except for my mother, and you made sure *she*

dirtied hers. You had to spoil her and then she upped and died on you. Now you want to spoil our Callie, because she looks like her mother. Sam Brown will make her life a misery, and you know it.'

Ebeneezer stood, his face mottled with rage. 'Leave your ma out of this, lad. She were a fine woman.'

'Aye, she was,' he said softly. 'So why did you use her as a punching bag? You broke her spirit and gave her one child too many to carry. It killed her.'

When his father swung at him Aaric ducked under the punch, then put his hand flat against his father's chest and pushed him back in his chair. 'Don't try it, Da,' he warned. 'I'm not some woman who can be pushed around, and I'm no longer a child to be thrashed.'

'Did Callie put you up to this?'

'She's my sister. I promised Ma I'd looked out for her, and I'm going to.'

'Aye, and your ma made *her* promise to look after Kitty. Do your best, bonny lad.' The smile he gave was almost a sneer. 'By heck, you're a fool if you think I don't know which way our Callie will jump when pushed to it. If the pair of you think you're going to outsmart me you can think twice. Now piss off, and stop putting thoughts in the girl's head. They'll come to nowt, tha knows. I'll mek sure of it.'

Aaric didn't have to go to see Mr Lazurus in the end. He found the man waiting for him outside the sawmill at close of business the next evening.

They exchanged handshakes before Harold Lazurus stated, 'I have some business to discuss with you, Mr Ingram.'

Aaric gave a wry smile. 'Aye, I imagined that was why you were here. Does this business concern Callie?'

'Only if you choose that it should, young man. Will you walk with me to my rig?'

They started out. Aaric said nothing while the man gathered his thoughts together. Then his companion said, 'I've long been of the mind that your skills are wasted here, and have taken the liberty of discussing the matter with Theron Grace.'

'Thank you for your interest, sir,' Aaric said politely.

'Theron Grace is in need of a clerk in London. The work is of a legal nature, and varied. But I think you'd find it interesting, and there will be opportunity for advancement. Mr Grace is willing to offer you the position. If you are interested, I have the contract right here.' He took an envelope from his pocket and handed it to him. 'You will, of course, wish to read it before you decide. The contract is not negotiable.'

Aaric gave a little grin. 'All contracts are negotiable, sir.' He scanned the document quickly, grasping the benefits of it immediately. The salary was considerably more than he presently earned, but so would his living expenses be. The offer couldn't have come at a better time, though. There was accommodation, too. He nodded and gazed at the man. 'I appreciate that this is fair dealing, and think we could come to agreement with twenty per cent added to the salary.'

'I'm not that much of a fool. Ten per cent, Mr Ingram,' the lawyer said with a chuckle.

Aaric nodded. He would have taken five.

Mr Lazurus took a smaller envelope from inside his waistcoat. 'Mr Grace has written to your father, requesting that Callie resume her former position as companion to Patricia. The letter is to be delivered at your discretion.'

Aaric gazed sharply at the man for a second or two. What on earth was he suggesting? That he'd encourage Callie to leave with him, then deliver the letter afterwards? He gave a slight grin. Harold Lazurus was as canny as a cartload of monkeys, and he was being manipulative.

He said nothing more about the letter, but slid it into his pocket. 'Will Mr Grace require a reference? My present employer can be difficult.'

'Although he doesn't know it, your present employer has furnished you with a verbal recommendation on several occasions. You're being offered well-paid employment with prospects on that basis, and it's something that might never come your way again.'

'Aye, I know that, and I'm grateful, Mr Lazurus. If you have a fountain pen on you I'll sign the contract here and now, so I can hand a letter of resignation to my employer in the morning with the knowledge that I have a secure position to go to.'

The pen Mr Lazurus placed in his hand was silver-plated and solid. Aaric neatly made the alteration. Witnessing his signature, the older man smiled, saying softly, 'You'll go far, Mr Ingram.'

'I do hope so. But Callie won't want to leave Kitty, you know.'

'It would be kinder if an older and wiser head made that decision for her.'

Aaric nodded. 'I think we understand each other, Mr Lazurus.'

'Exactly, Mr Ingram.' Harold Lazurus climbed up on to his rig and smiled. 'One other thing, young man. Do you have the means to pay your fare to London? If not, Mr Grace has asked me to offer you an advance.'

'I'd rather not start work owing a debt, sir. My needs are few. I have a few shillings put by and a fortnight's wages in hand to come.'

'I'll say good day then, Mr Ingram.' He flicked the whip over the horse's head and was off.

'I'll be dammed,' Aaric said as a smile spread across his face. Making sure nobody was about he headed in the opposite direction, dancing down the lane and turning in circles. He slowed down when he thought of Callie. He must take her into his confidence. It wouldn't take long for news of his resignation to reach his father's ears so he'd do him the courtesy of telling him tonight.

* * *

Ebeneezer's reaction was exactly as Aaric had expected. He filled his pipe, and when the smoke had settled he took a few small sucks. 'So, you're gannin' to London.'

'Aye. I've been offered a job with better prospects.'

His father nodded and his eyes sharpened. 'You'll be tekking the train, then. When are you off?'

The question was too casual. 'I haven't thought that far ahead. I'll have to work out my notice first. Don't you want to know who I'll be working for?'

'I'm not soddin' daft, tha knows. It'll be that sly lawyer feller.' He gazed at Callie, whose eyes were filled with hope. 'This talk doesn't concern thee, since you're going nowhere. Finish those dishes, then go and rake some coal.'

'What about Kitty?'

'She's asleep, and I'm not gannin' anywhere. Tilly is coming over for a visit. Happen Sam might be on the sands, and happen he might help you if you're nice to him, maiden.'

'I wouldn't be nice to him if he was being sucked head first into the quicksand,' she retorted, and turned away, tears trembling on her lashes when her father laughed.

'I'll help Callie myself,' Aaric said.

His father looked suspiciously at him. 'I thought you were going to that fancy sporting club you belong to, the one full of pampered lads who'd fetch up their dinners if faced with the sight of blood.' He gave a short, harsh laugh. 'Boxing – hah, that's a gudden. I poked my head round the door once and it looked more like a dancing class. I doubt if you could punch your way out of a sack of sprats.'

Aaric's eyes glistened. 'I doubt if I'll ever have to, and the reason I'm not gannin' there tonight is because I need my money for my train fare to London.'

'Ay, well, you'll get nowt from me.'

'I don't want nowt.' He watched Callie dry the last plate and set it on the dresser. 'Come on, Callie, let's go while there's still some light.'

It was a balmy evening with a slight breeze. The sand was a cool, damp expanse. Most of the holidaymakers were back in their boarding houses eating their dinners. A couple of donkeys were heading for home, their heads hanging wearily after plodding up and down all day carrying visitors on their backs. Their owner shouted out a cheery goodnight to them.

No wonder he's cheerful, Aaric thought. You could almost hear the cash jingling in the donkey man's pockets.

Sam was sitting on the rock further up the beach with his horse and cart. Callie pretended not to see him when he waved, and Aaric barely acknowledged him. Sam took his place on the cart and clicked his tongue. The horse ambled off towards the road.

Aaric drew the coal line in the sand and raked the first lot into a pile. Callie took up the rake while he shovelled. They worked fast. When

Callie tired, Aaric took over and the cart was soon overflowing. They pushed the cart up to the road and sat on a strip of grass, their faces beaded with perspiration and their hands and faces streaked with black.

Aaric pushed his hair back from his eyes and smiled at his sister. 'I'll be glad not to have to do this any more.'

Callie took a shilling from her pocket and handed it to him. 'I raked it up from the sand. You can put it towards our train fares.' She looked anxious for a moment. 'You are taking me, aren't you? Mr Lazurus did arrange something for me?'

'Aye, there's a job for you with Theron Grace, the same as before.'

'It will be nice to see Tish again, and exciting to be in London. We can call on Jane, too. I'm so glad you've been offered employment.' A grin flitted across her face, blossoming into a fully fledged smile that slowly faded. 'If Da finds out I'm going he'll stop me.'

'He didn't go after Jane, and he won't go after you. He won't find out if you don't tell anyone.'

'When will we be leaving? The marriage is only three weeks away.'

'I'm not sure yet. I'll have to work two weeks' notice to get what I'm entitled to. Trust me.' Aaric didn't want Callie to know of any plans he made in case she gave them away. 'Callie, do be very careful. Da's shrewd by nature, and is clever at figuring things out. He's already suspicious. Just go about your business as usual.'

'There's a sack I can put Kitty's things in,' she said happily. 'My bits and pieces will fit into my basket.'

He felt his heart lurch. Perhaps he was a coward, but now was not the time to tell her that Kitty had to be left behind. He stood up, guilt flooding through him because he didn't like deceiving her. 'We'd better go.'

Two boys and their father had come down to the sand and were building a sandcastle. 'Did Da ever build castles with you?' she asked.

'Never ... he was always too busy working, trying to support the family.'

'D'you think he loved us?'

Aaric drew in a deep breath. He'd always been made to feel like an outsider by his father, mainly because, like Callie, he hadn't fitted into the Ingram mould. He'd grown out of the weak chest that had plagued him through childhood, but that weakness had placed him firmly amongst the least worthy of the family in his father's eyes. He just wasn't manly enough by his standards.

'You have to remember that Da had a hard life. He was brought up to be tough, and to not show his true feelings.'

'When I was a child I used to love him, because he made me laugh, especially when he was cross and his face crumpled up. Since Giles died I've grown to despise him. He killed our mother and I told him so. Every time he looks at me he sees her, and he wants to punish me for reminding him of what he did to her. That scares me. Sometimes he calls me by her name, especially when he's been drinking.'

Placing his arm around her, Aaric pulled her against his shoulder. 'He suffered over Giles, and he's suffering over our mother. He just doesn't know how to show it.'

'Can we sit here a while longer, Aaric? I don't want to go home while Tilly Brown is there. She snoops into everything and I get annoyed.'

'You need to stop setting yourself up against everyone and everything, Callie love. You can't change their behaviour, only your own. If you treat people well they're more likely to treat you in the same way.'

'You're nice, Aaric. Much nicer than I am.' She placed a hand over her heart. 'Sometimes I feel Ma inside me, right here. I know what she'd say to Tilly Brown if she was still here, and to Da. So I say it for her.'

Aaric laughed, mostly because his sister's face was so solemn. 'Are you telling me she advises you?'

Callie grinned. 'You wouldn't believe me if I said she did.'

A thought sneaked into his head as they sat there together, enjoying the peace of the golden evening. This was something he might be able to use to his advantage.

Thirteen

Time seemed suddenly to slow down.

Callie went about her chores, trying to remain inconspicuous, though inside she was a churn of nerves. She knew she'd miss Seafield, with its uncluttered beach and the sea and sky with its many moods.

She had no real wish for wealth, though it would be nice to live life without the constant grind of trying to earn enough to make ends meet. Although she didn't mind gathering the coal and selling the fish her father caught, it would be nice if she could have a day off. The sketching block James had given her for Christmas remained largely unused, except for a few quick sketches of her ma and Kitty. She laid those, along with her copy of *Pride and Prejudice* and the pretty box Theron had given her, in the bottom of her basket.

If she wasn't being pressured into marrying someone she loathed then she wouldn't have minded staying, allowing matters to take their natural course, for there were other young men in town who'd looked at her more than once. But her father had branded her as Sam's girl, and now the others kept their distance. To do otherwise would fetch them a thumping from Sam Brown. Not that she had ever encouraged Sam, and most of the time was able to avoid him. But she still had the feeling she was being followed.

Alternating between excitement and despair, Callie listened to the banns being called in church for the second time. Luckily Aaric had seated himself between herself and Sam. After the service she gave Sam the slip and visited her ma's grave.

'I've brought Kitty to visit, but I can't stay long,' she said, setting her sister down and pulling up a couple of weeds that had taken root. 'I've got some news, Ma. We're leaving Seafield and going to London.'

Kitty suddenly began to cry. Callie caught a movement in the corner of her eye, and turned round in time to see Alf Brown duck down behind a gravestone. Four strides and she had him by the collar. She gave him a good shaking. 'You sneaking little rat. What are you doing, coming round here and frightening my sister?'

'I'll tell my ma you did that,' Alf squeaked, kicking out at her and catching her on the shin.

She pushed him backwards and scooped up a stick. 'Come any nearer and I'll give you one across your backside, and I don't care what you tell your ma. Who told you to sneak after me, Sam?'

'Your da.'

She should have known. 'Well, you can go and

tell my da I'm having a private talk with my ma.'

'She's dead.'

'I speak to her ghost.'

Alf's eyes widened. He shivered and looked around him, whispering, 'I can't see any ghost.'

'There are lots here. I'll ask some of them to visit you while you're in your bed, shall I? I can see one behind you now. It's that sailor who drowned ten years ago. He's so horrible, all black and bloated and the crabs have eaten his eyes. Can you feel his hand against the back of your neck, where the hairs are standing on end...'

Giving a yelp, Alf took off, tripped over a tuft, scrambled up again and began to run.

Callie chuckled as she picked Kitty up, soothing her and saying to her mother, 'That's got rid of Alf Brown for a while. I'll try to come and see you during the week, in case I don't get the chance again.'

As she walked away it reminded her that she should go and say goodbye to Mr Lazurus. He might let her have a rose from his garden for her mother's grave. But during the week she didn't get a chance. A storm came in and it took two days to blow itself out, which put her behind with the washing.

Her father sat in his chair in a cloud of stinking smoke, watching her every move. They didn't talk, except when necessary. Callie had absolutely nothing left to say to him. She was jumpy with nerves and bit her fingernails down to the quick.

When the fishing fleet was able to put to sea again it was a relief. It was nice being alone with Aaric and Kitty in the house.

Tilly Brown came round the next day while Callie was struggling to get a sheet on the line in the wind. Hands on hips, she said, 'Have you been putting wicked ideas inside my Alf's head, girl?'

'I've got better things to do, and he's got plenty of wicked ideas of his own.'

'Don't you get smart wi' me. He told me you saw a ghost at his back in the cemetery. Now he's too frightened to go to sleep.'

'Serves him right for following me all the time.'

'Your da wants an eye kept on you. If I told him all that Alf tells me he'd give you a good thrashing.'

'Told him what?'

'That he saw that lawyer fellow kissin' yer, as bold as brass, standin' on his doorstep.'

Callie's heart leapt. 'Don't go making nowt out of a kiss on the forehead. He's an old man. Besides, Alf has already told Da that particular lie, remember?'

'The lawyer's not that old. My Sam wouldn't like it if I told him the man had his hands all over yer.'

'What do I care what your Sam likes? Alf made it up because he likes to make trouble.' She remembered Aaric telling her not to keep setting herself up against people, and shrugged.

'Here, tek the other end of this sheet and peg it to the line. I'm sorry if I frightened Alf. I was talking to my ma, in private like. I miss her. He hid behind a gravestone and scared our Kitty half to death.'

She nodded. 'I reckon he deserved it then.' Her eyes went to the expanse of white sheet. 'Your da has some good linen.'

'Aye,' Callie said, but she wasn't going to tell Tilly where it had come from, in case she got the wrong idea.

'I'll leave you mine when I move in here. You know, Callie, we could be friends, with me marrying your da and you marrying our Sam. I always wanted a daughter. Now I'll have two, what with young Kitty and all. I could help you with the wedding, too. Have you got a nice dress to wear?'

Tilly Brown was trying hard, but her eyes were calculating. Callie was suspicious, thinking her da might have put Tilly up to this. 'Aye,' she said. 'I've got my best outfit, and that will do for a wedding.' But would it heck as like be worn for any wedding to Sam Brown. They'd have to drag her to the altar by her hair – and if she didn't get away with Aaric she was going to see the reverend, tell him so and put a stop to it.

'That'll save a bit of money then. He's a hardworking lad, is our Sam. As soon as he puts a ring on your finger he'll be going fishing with your da. There are plenty of other girls who would be glad to tek him, but he set his cap at you a couple of years ago. Besides, they wouldn't be able to manage a home as well as you can. Your ma taught you well.'

Callie cringed at the thought of being at Sam's beck and call, but she bit down on the retort she'd been about to make. 'Aye, she did,' was all she said.

Life went on as usual, but the days crawled now she knew she was leaving. After she caught up with the housework she went to the beach, which was littered with coal and other debris. Kitty played on the sand while she and Aaric gathered the available coal and talked of London.

The bunker was filled now and the coal spilled over into the yard. There was enough to feed the stove for quite a while – and some to sell, if need be.

The fishing boats were out for two days, coming back with a big catch. Boats were unloaded. Verna's husband was there with his cart, picking the best of them, sorting and packing them in wooden crates to get on the train to London. 'Tell Aaric the lads are giving him a send-off at the Seven Moons on Friday,' he shouted to her.

Afterwards there were nets to be mended and boats to be caulked, to stop the water leaking through the seams.

Friday saw Callie almost on a knife edge. Aaric still hadn't told her when they were leaving, but it must be soon. She was ready. She'd packed most of Kitty's stuff in the sack, hiding it under her bed with her own basket.

'I'll try and be back in time to put Kitty to bed,' she told her father as she lifted the heavy basket of fish on to her arm.

'It's Friday. It shouldn't tek yer too long to sell them, lass. I'll be visiting Tilly as soon as our Aaric gets home.'

And it didn't take long. The boarding houses paid well for good quality fish, and her basket was soon light on her arm. When she reached the house of Harold Lazurus, she looked behind her for signs of Alf, who was still dogging her heels despite her warning. Not that it mattered now, since they'd soon be gone.

The road was fairly busy. A group of three men stood talking around a horse and cart. Children played with hoops and women stood and gossiped. A man had stopped to tie his boot laces. His cap shaded his eyes as he bent over, but he was facing in the opposite direction. When a man and a woman with a child crossed the road and came between them, the man straightened up and strolled off towards the sea front.

Satisfied she wasn't being watched, Callie slipped through the gate belonging to Harold Lazurus and made her way to the back door.

'Callie, what a lovely surprise,' Mrs Perkins said. 'I was just about to take the tea tray into Mr Lazurus before I go home. I like to get away before it's dark with all these strangers on holiday in the village.' She added another cup and a piece of cake to the tray. 'I daresay he'll be pleased to see you. He's in his office. You can take the tray through for me, and tell him I'm off home now.'

Mr Lazurus didn't look up from the paper he was reading. 'Put it over on the table, please, Mrs Perkins.'

'It isn't Mrs Perkins. It's me, Mr Lazurus. Callie Ingram.'

He looked up, the concentration on his face relieved by a smile. 'Callie, my dear. Just the person to cheer me up. How are you?'

'Well, sir.'

'Good ... perhaps you'd pour the tea while I finish reading this. I'll only be a minute or two.' Picking up a pencil he scribbled words in the margin as he read, then smiled and put the paper aside. He took the seat opposite her.

'I'm sorry I disturbed you,' she said.

'I'm not, there's nothing more delightful than entertaining a young lady. To what do I owe the honour of this visit?'

'I wanted to thank you for being so kind to me.'

'It was my pleasure. I heard from James today, you know. The boy's not enjoying university at all, I'm afraid.'

'He wanted to study art in Paris.'

'An uncertain profession, unfortunately. Very few artists can make a good living. I remember when I was a boy...'

The conversation proceeded along quite different lines than Callie had wanted to take it on. It became obvious that he didn't want to discuss anything that might implicate him in any way with her flight from Seafield.

The shadows were beginning to lengthen outside, and she still had to visit her mother. 'Please can I have a rose from your garden to put on my ma's grave on the way home?'

'Of course you may. There's a nice red one under the kitchen window.'

'If I stick it in the ground, will it grow into a bush? Ma liked roses.'

'Quite possibly.' If it didn't, Harold decided he'd plant a rose bush on Mary Ingram's grave, just for Callie.

She said goodbye sadly, giving him a hug before she left.

Harold watched her go from the upstairs window, the basket over her arm containing a perfect red rose amongst the fish scales. She headed for the shortcut over the fields and allotments, hurrying along. A man sauntered up the road and took the same route. It was a popular one with the locals.

Harold hoped her brother would manage to get her away safely in the next day or two. Aaric Ingram was the son he'd like to have had. Harold had great faith in the young man.

Callie stuck the rose in the earth over her mother's grave. The churchyard was full of long, mournful shadows, and the air about her was soft, warm and purple. 'I haven't got much to say, Ma, and might not visit you again. I just want you to know how much I love you, and I always will. Now, I must get home.'

She stood, and headed for a row of trees that formed the boundary, then came to a sudden halt when Sam Brown stepped out from behind a tree.

'Where've you been?' he said.

'Selling fish, where else? Not that it's got anything to do with you.'

'Yer wrong, lass. It has everything to do wi' me. You're my woman.'

'No I'm not. I'll never marry you.'

He put out an arm when she tried to push past him. 'Aye, you will, girl. I'll mek sure of it.'

'All I have to say is no, and the clergyman won't perform the ceremony.'

'That might be so, but nobody else will want you after I've finished wi' you.'

Her mouth dried up. 'What are you talking about, Sam Brown? Lay one finger on me and my da will kill you.'

'Nay, lass, he'll likely stick a shotgun up my arse and march me down the aisle, laughing all the way. And it'll be worth a beating from your brothers, though neither of them could tek me on singly.'

He cracked the knuckles on his hands, which were large and meaty. The same hands grabbed her by the bodice and ripped it open. He smiled at the sight of her naked breasts. 'Look at them, so pretty and neat. Just how I like them.'

'Then grow a pair on your own chest.'

When he placed a hand over one of her breasts, she kicked him. He cursed and, hooking his foot behind her ankle, pushed her to the ground. She tried to hit him with her basket, but it was ripped from her grasp and thrown aside.

Straddling her, he played with her breasts, pinching and fondling them. When she screamed he stuffed the skirt of her apron in her mouth.

Planting a hand in her midriff he rolled off her and thrust his hand up under her skirt and roughly fondled her. His breath was heavy against her ear as she tried to fight him off. She could neither scream nor escape as his hardness grew against her skirt.

When he loosened his grip to undo his trousers she spat the apron from her mouth and kicked out at him, catching him when he exposed himself. But there wasn't much force behind the kick and she was almost spent as she tried to crawl away, shouting for help.

'Little bitch, you're trying to ruin me,' he said, dragging her back by her ankles. He punched her in the midriff, then the face, and pulled her upright. She stood there swaying and the fight went out of her as she gasped for breath.

He turned away and relief flooded through her. He was going. Then something lashed across her back. It felt like fire. She turned. Sam stood there, his belt in his hand.

'Stop it!' she screamed, and dropped to the ground, coiling in on her pain.

'It's about time you learned who's the boss, Callie Ingram.' He set about her with the belt, ignoring her pleas to stop, even when he caught her across the breasts and face. When he did stop, she was too weak to even whimper.

He threw her skirt up and knelt across her body, his grossness nudging against her bare thigh. Her outstretched arm clawed into the dirt. Instinctively she took up a handful and ground it into his eyes.

He swore and rolled off her, rubbing at the dirt. Staggering to her feet, Callie clutched her bodice over her nakedness and began to stumble towards her home, glad of the darkness to hide her, and stopping only to vomit a couple of times.

She'd lost her basket, and the money she'd collected for the fish had been scattered from her apron pocket. Her da would be furious.

Staggering through the back door, she locked it behind her, collapsed into a chair and burst into tears.

It wasn't her father who came into the kitchen first, it was Aaric. The blood ebbed from his face when he set eyes on her bleeding nose, swollen mouth and bruises.

'It was Sam Brown,' she said, answering the question in his eyes. 'He took a belt to me when I fought him off.' Slipping the remains of her bodice from her shoulder she exposed the welts.

'Did he...?'

'No,' she said vehemently. 'I ground dirt into his eyes and managed to get away. I've lost the money for the fish. Da will be furious.'

'Sod Da,' Aaric said, surprising her. He filled a bowl with warm water from the kettle and gently bathed her face and her back, smoothing arnica into the welts afterwards. He handed her the flannel, saying gruffly, 'You can do the rest yourself. I'm going out now, but be ready to leave early in the morning.'

'You're going after Sam?'

'Aye. The bluidy coward's not getting away wi' this.'

Her blood ran cold. 'Be careful, Aaric. He's tough.'

'Aye, I will. Don't worry. My brothers will be there to look after me.'

That made her feel better.

After she'd cleaned herself up she packed the rest of Kitty's things and fetched her mother's neatly darned old bodice to change into. She climbed on the bed fully clothed, her body aching from the beating. She wanted to stay awake until Aaric returned safely to her. Tears trickled down her cheeks at the thought of him being hurt. But the shock of the beating brought tiredness with it, and she fell into the deep escape of sleep.

The bar was crowded, and a raucous shout came from his brothers. 'What took you so long, Aaric?'

'Callie did. She ran into Sam Brown in the cemetery on her way home and the bugger gave her a thrashing.'

'Nay, he never!' Tom said.

'Aye. He took a belt to her, too, because he couldn't have his way wi' her. Is the coward in here? I intend to tek him apart.'

Chad put a hand on his arm. 'He's in the corner. But you don't want to mix it wi' him, our Aaric. His blood is up.'

'Aye, but so is mine, as it happens. Someone's got to watch out for our sister. She doesn't want to wed the bullying bastard, and I'm not going to stand by and see her pushed into it.'

'You get yerself on that train, lad. Let Chad and me sort it out for Callie,' Tom said.

'I'm taking her with me, and that's that.' He raised his voice. 'Sam Brown, come outside. You and I have got summat to settle.'

'Sod off, wiyyer?' Sam roared. 'I'm having mesself an ale. Mess wi' me, bonny lad, and I'll knock your bleedin' head off your shoulders.'

'Will you heck as like.' Aaric pushed through the crowd, picked up the pot of ale and threw it in Sam's face. 'There's yer ale. Now, gerrout.'

Sam spat on his hands and sneered, 'You asked fer it.'

The landlord pushed between them. 'Not in here, you don't. Down on the beach, the bluidy lot of you.'

'My money's on Sam,' somebody said as the crowd of drinkers moved as one across the road and spilled on to the sand. 'What are the odds on the pen-pusher, landlord?'

'Practically nil. But I'll offer ten to one to anyone who wants to tek a bet on him.'

'I'll put a shilling on him,' Tom said loyally.

'Aye, me an' all,' Chad said in a resigned voice.

The crowd fell silent when Ebeneezer walked

into the circle and gazed around him. 'What's gannin' on here, Tom?'

'Aaric is taking on Sam. He gave our Callie a thrashing.'

'How badly did you hurt the maiden, Sam?'

Sam shrugged. 'It weren't nuthin' much. She called me names and I gave her a slap or two. Next thing I know your Aaric comes storming into the pub threatening me.' He grinned. 'Still, he offered me a fair fight.'

'More fool him.' Ebeneezer spat into the sand and turned to him, amusement in his eyes. 'You're barmy, Aaric. He'll slaughter you. My money's going on Sam. Alreet?'

'Please yourself. I'll wager a pound on myself, landlord.'

The landlord chuckled. 'Let's see the colour of your money before you die, lad.'

Calmly, Aaric handed his jacket over to Chad. 'There's money in the pocket. Look after my jacket, will you?'

'I hope you know what you're doing, Aaric.'

'Last bets,' the landlord called out as Sam and Aaric stripped down to their vests.

Sam was the shorter man; he was stocky and had broad, powerful shoulders. Tom and Chad hadn't seen Aaric stripped down for a while. He was tall and well muscled, without any spare fat, and had long arms and a solid wall of muscle on his stomach.

'You've got the longer reach,' Tom whispered. 'Keep out of his grasp. If he gets you in a bear hug, you're gone.'

'Go easy on him, Sam,' Ebeneezer taunted.

Sam grinned, spat on his hands and beckoned, showing off. 'Come on then, Aaric. Let's be havin' yer.'

Aaric smiled. Stepping forward into the circle of men he raised his fists in a boxing stance.

Sam laughed. 'Will you look at him now, just like a proper boxer.'

The two men circled, then Sam rushed forward like a bull, his shoulders down and his arms outstretched. The uppercut Aaric dealt him snapped his head up, and his nose began to bleed. Shaking his head, Sam came rushing forward again.

Aaric jerked Sam's head back with a right hook, then stepped in and pummelled his stomach.

When Sam started to gasp for air a series of punches put him on his back. A disbelieving jeer came from the crowd and a couple of the men began to walk off back towards the bar. Sam staggered to his feet and was floored again. He picked up a handful of sand.

'Watch out,' somebody shouted.

The sand went wide as Aaric turned gracefully on his feet. A punch to the midriff and Sam was down for the third time. He stayed down.

Aaric gazed at his father. He understood that the fight was between them, not himself and Sam. 'Is that good enough for you, you old devil?'

His father didn't answer, just turned on his heel and walked away.

They left Sam on the sand. Aaric was hoisted on to his brother's shoulders and borne up to the pub. A drink was placed in his hand.

Tom clapped him on the back. 'That was a bluidy surprise. Sam didn't even get a punch in. I'm proud of yer.'

'That's not the last of it,' Chad said soberly. 'You've made a fool of Da and he won't be crossed. He'll be at the train station in the morning with Sam and half the fishermen in tow, and he'll probably skin you alive.'

'I'm his son,' Aaric said.

'Not any more. And he'll have all routes out of the village covered within an hour. He's made up his mind. He won't let you tek Callie, and will expect Tom and me to back him.'

'He'll use Kitty to prevent Callie from leaving. I'm thinking of walking across the sands into West Hartlepool.'

'Don't be daft, you'll never mek it in the dark, and will fall into quicksand or summat. Besides, the tide will be up within the hour.'

Chad sighed. 'I'll get your winnings. You go home and soak those hands in cold water. Be at the fishing harbour just afore dawn with our Callie. We'll get the pair of you away. You can pick up the train in West Hartlepool.'

Aaric bowed to the inevitable. He'd have to take Kitty, and somehow they'd manage.

Callie was woken by Aaric's touch. He had a candle. She rose quietly. 'Thank God you're all right, Aaric.'

‘We’re not out of the village yet. Let’s get going. You needn’t be quiet. Da was out when I came home, and he didn’t come back during the night.’

Callie groped under the bed for the sack, but found only the basket. Gazing at Kitty’s bed she sighed with relief at the hump under the cover. The sack must have slid further under the bed. But when she pulled the cover back they revealed only a cushion and Kitty’s fur cat.

Her heart plummeted. ‘He’s taken Kitty. He must have sneaked in when I was asleep, and before you came in. Her clothes are gone, too.’

‘We’ll have to leave her.’

‘I promised Ma...’

‘And I promised Ma that I’d look after you. Kitty’s not going to come to any harm, and Verna will keep an eye on her.’

Callie hesitated. Aaric was talking sense.

‘What’s it to be, Callie? Either you leave Kitty behind, or you can stay here and marry Sam Brown. Have no doubt about it. That’s what will happen. They’ll try and prevent us leaving, and I can’t fight them all off.’

Tears filled her eyes.

‘What would Ma think was best for you to do?’ Aaric said softly.

She knew what her ma would say, and her aching body told her it was madness to stay around and live the same sort of life her mother had. She picked up Kitty’s fur cat and placed it in her basket to remember her sister by.

Aaric placed Theron Grace’s letter flat on the

mantelpiece behind the clock, though his father was too short to see it there. Perhaps he'd find it one day.

They slipped out of the house and headed for the boat harbour. There was no moon. Tom and Chad's Coble was waiting for them at the fisherman's harbour. They set sail, and a short time later were put ashore on the beach in West Hartlepool. There was enough light now for Callie's brothers to see her bruised and swollen face.

'Look at yer, our Callie. My God! No wonder Aaric went after Sam.'

'And the sod said he'd only given her a slap or two.'

'He took a belt to her and she's covered in welts,' Aaric said.

'And Da expected me to wed the thug,' Callie said. 'I wish I'd seen Aaric thrash him.'

'Strikes me that our lad knew a thing or two 'cause he hasn't got a bruise on him – ain't that reet, Aaric?'

'Aye. I've been taking lessons.'

'We best be gannin' off before it gets too light, Chad,' Tom said nervously.

'Which way is the railway station?' Callie thought to ask.

Chad said, 'Tek the bridge over the railway lines and keep going till you come to Mansforth. Turn right, then left into Reed Street, then keep zig-zagging right and left across to Church Square. The railway station's on the other side of it.'

Callie hugged them both. Aaric shook his brother's hands, wincing at the pressure on his own.

'I nearly forgot.' Chad fumbled in his pocket, grinning as he handed over some money. 'Here's your winnings; you deserve them. We must go before we're missed. Good luck, you two.'

There was a lump in Callie's throat as the boat sailed off into the darkness.

Aaric said. 'No regrets now, Callie?'

Shakily, she smiled. 'Aye, no regrets. Let's get going.'

But she couldn't help wondering how Kitty would fare, and knew that one day she'd come back to find her.

Fourteen

The excitement of the train journey soon wore off, as did the novelty of the different scenery passing by.

Callie's battered face drew pitying stares. Aaric, with his swollen hands, invited glares, as though he'd inflicted the bruises on her personally. Aaric was tired after a night without sleep. Fatigue and worry was etched into his fine features. Both were hungry, they hadn't eaten or drunk anything since the day before.

Aaric managed to buy a couple of current buns at one of the stops. Although they were stale, washed down with ginger beer the buns swelled in their stomachs, and the two fell asleep in opposite corners of the carriage.

They woke in time to change trains and were faced with an even longer journey ahead. At York they swallowed down a mug of strong tea and a sandwich. Aaric bought some apples to eat on the train later. At least the carriage had a corridor down one side, and conveniences, one for ladies and one for gents, where they could make themselves comfortable when needed.

But the train was crowded, the corridors packed with travellers who hadn't been lucky enough to get a seat and were sitting on their luggage. Aaric gave up his seat to a tired-looking woman with a child, and brother and sister swapped seats now and again, so one could rest while the other stretched.

This train hurled itself through town and countryside at an exciting pace, the landscape a blur, the wheels clacking over the rails and the tunnels a dense and noisy black rush that dulled the ears and made Callie jump. Towards the end of the day, when everyone around them looked weary, the swaying carriage began to slow and they pulled into a station.

'This must be Kings Cross,' Aaric said, lifting their bundles down from the overhead luggage rack.

With the station solid under her feet, Callie gazed in awe at the great expanse of glass curving above them. 'I wouldn't like to clean *those* windows.'

The engine that had pulled them was further up the platform. It hissed spouts of steam and panted like a great black dog. The air had a sooty smell to it. Callie grinned widely at her brother as the passengers pushed and shoved around them. 'I bet Da has got steam coming from his ears, too.'

Aaric's laugh held a sense of disbelief. 'Well, it seems that we're in London at long last. Now we have to find the address.'

'No we don't. There's Theron Grace at the barrier – and Tish is with him.' She jumped up and down above the heads in the crowd and frantically waved, finally catching Patricia's eye. Grabbing Aaric's hand she pulled him after her.

The girls hugged, then Patricia gazed at her, her eyes widening. 'You look absolutely *pummelled*. What happened to you?'

'She probably butted heads with a goat, but detailed explanations can wait until we get home.' Theron smiled at her. 'Hello, Calandra Ingram. Welcome to London.'

She grinned at him. 'How did you know we were on this train?'

Patricia answered for him. 'Great-uncle Harold telephoned Theron this morning just as he was going out. Mrs Perkins had told him that she'd heard that you'd left Seafield, and he thought it likely you'd be on this train.'

'So Tish insisted on meeting it, just in case,' Theron said, and he thrust a hand out. 'Welcome to London, Aaric. I'm pleased you decided to accept the position.'

'Aye, well it was a step up for me, tha knows.' Aaron winced at the pressure on his hand. Theron gazed at them and raised an eyebrow. Her brother shrugged. 'They'll mend.'

'Aaric gave Sam Brown a thumping after he attacked me,' Callie said fiercely.

There was a sudden silence, into which Patricia threw a giggle. 'Remind me not to argue with him, then.'

Aaric said gently, 'Nay, lass, I'd not thump anyone unless it was for a very good reason.'

Straight-faced, Patricia retorted, 'Aye, well

you'd better not, else I'll fetch you a gudden with my umbrella, tha knows.'

'Of course, if you happened to tease me too often about the way I talk I could possibly change my mind,' Aaric added with a smile.

Theron, who'd been examining with some curiosity Callie's black eye, and by doing so making her self-conscious, now chuckled. 'Behave yourself, Patricia. Shall we go? Both of you look tired, and are hungry I should imagine. You can stay at my home tonight, Aaric. Tomorrow, I'll show you where your rooms are situated and introduce you to your predecessor, who will ease you into the position over the following week. Where is your luggage?'

'We're carrying it,' Aaric said wryly. 'I have my Sunday suit in the bundle.'

'Ah ... of course. Come along then. We'll pick up a hackney outside the station. One of us will have to sit up with the driver, Aaric. I'd prefer it to be me, so I don't have to listen to the female chatter.'

It was only a short ride along Euston Road and Gower Street before they turned into Bedford Square and came to a halt outside a house in Charlotte Street.

How pretty the park opposite was. Three steps up from the street to the front door and they were standing in the hallway of a comfortable and elegant house. There was a spacious hall, dark wooden doors leading off and a staircase going up the side. The house smelled faintly of tobacco, leather, beeswax polish and gas lights.

It was exactly the sort of home Callie had imagined Theron Grace would have.

'You're sharing my room with me,' Patricia said, pulling her towards the stairs. 'It was Theron's idea. He said it will save us having to dash back and forth between bedrooms every time we think of something important to say about the latest fashion in the middle of the night.'

'Very thoughtful of him,' Callie said drily.

The room was pretty, the walls covered in cream paper scattered with bunches of pink rosebuds and yellow butterflies. A bed of incredible softness was covered in a dark pink brocade spread. Callie had been given a wardrobe and dressing table of her own.

She claimed the dressing table straight away, giving her enamelled box pride of place on top. She placed her drawing block and change of underwear inside a drawer, then she stroked her fingers gently over Kitty's toy cat before placing it in the drawer, too. She wished she hadn't brought it. Kitty loved the cat and would miss it.

'We have a private room, where we can wash or take a bath, and it has a WC in it. Downstairs there's a cloakroom with a WC in it as well, but I leave that for the men.'

'What's a WC?'

'A water closet.'

'Ah,' said Callie, none the wiser, though she discovered what it was a little while later and marvelled at the novelty of using such a modern outhouse, but indoors.

Patricia asked one of the maids to bring up a jug of hot water. Callie washed the staleness of the journey from her body and changed into her other outfit, one of the two Theron had bought for her.

Patricia wept over the bruises on her body, then said fiercely, 'I wish Aaric had killed Sam Brown.'

'I'm glad he didn't, else he'd be in jail.'

'Stop being so practical.' Eyeing the grey outfit as Callie tried in vain to button the bodice, Patricia said, 'What happened to the blue dress? It was much prettier, and bigger.'

'I buried my ma in it. I wanted her to look nice when she met her maker. And I put that handkerchief you embroidered for her in the pocket. She was fond of you, Tish, and treasured it.'

Patricia hugged her tight. 'I was so sorry to hear about her death.'

'Aye. I miss her. But we have to go on living as best we can, Tish. When I'm older and married, I'm going back for Kitty, because I promised Ma I'd look after her. This doesn't fit any more.' Callie threw the bodice aside and picked up the old one.

'I thought you didn't want to get married.'

'Not to Sam Brown.' Callie shuddered. 'But I might meet a young man of means when I'm older.'

Patricia took a blue checked blouse with puffed sleeves from her wardrobe and handed it to her. 'Here, you can have this if you like it.

Don't you want to be in love?'

'Of course I do, but I'll make sure I fall in love with someone with means,' she said, slipping into the blouse. She gave her host a kiss. 'It's pretty, thank you.'

'You could marry my brother. He's going to have means when Theron thinks he's old enough to handle it.'

Opening her jewellery box, Callie took the peacock brooch from it and pinned it to the neck. 'And you could marry *my* brother, except he's as poor as a church mouse.'

'Oh, I wouldn't mind that.'

'Aaric would though. He wants to get ahead. He wouldn't marry unless he could afford to keep a wife and family.'

'That means I'd have to wait ages. How dreadfully boring men are over money. I shall also have to find someone who's already made his fortune.'

The pair dissolved into loud laughter at the thought. Downstairs, Aaric and Theron exchanged a smile.

Aaric settled himself into his new accommodation, a pair of cramped and sparsely furnished rooms in Temple Bar. Business was conducted in an outer chamber. Having once slept in a smaller space with three brothers for company, Aaric appreciated his privacy and solitude.

His predecessor had decided he was not cut out for the law. He intended to accompany his sister and her husband to Australia, to dig for gold. He was a chirpy fellow.

'I would have stayed, except I see no future working for Mr Grace, though he's a fine gentleman who does a lot to help the poor. He intends to bring that young cousin of his into the firm. So if you're looking to take up articles, you should look elsewhere.'

Such an idea hadn't entered Aaric's head. Like everything he saw or heard, he stored the idea tidily in his brain, to be examined when he'd taken his bearings. He glanced around the untidy office. He'd sort out this place for a start.

For a small charge the woman downstairs cooked him a large breakfast, which carried him through until the evening meal, when an equally large dinner took him through to breakfast. For an additional fee she would also do his laundry. Her husband cleaned the stairs and windows and the chambers within the building. Aaric felt entirely at home there, surrounded by law books. His nights were spent studying, his days writing briefs for his employer and dealing with the public.

Theron said to him one day, 'I can't take on all cases, but if I'm convinced the accused is innocent, I'll do what I can. I usually call on my wealthier clients, and I consult with others in my home. My poorer ones will come here. Most of them are illiterate, and some are inarticulate. It's up to you to get details from them, to evaluate any evidence they might have, and interview witnesses. Be thorough, Aaric. Keep an open mind. Sometimes a case can turn on one point or a scrap of paper. And remember, what would be a minor nuisance to us might be of great importance to them. If they come to you with a petty dispute you can advise them on, or settle, then do so. Sometimes all it takes is a letter. You can contact me on the telephone if you need to.'

'I'll do my best.'

Theron had a book under his arm, and placed it on the desk. It looked exactly like the others, with worn brown leather binding and gold lettering on the spine. 'You might find this useful. It's a cash box, which you can hide on the bookshelf inside your accommodations. Sometimes witnesses will ask for something to loosen their tongues. The contents of the box are replenished every so often. No receipting or record keeping is required.'

When Aaric raised an eyebrow, Theron smiled.

'I only consider cases where I think the person charged is innocent, and often the witness will lose a day's wage by coming to court. Sometimes I'm guided by instinct alone. Some of the people I represent are facing the death penalty for crimes they didn't commit. They are wretchedly poor. The evidence of a witness and the way it's delivered might sway a jury. So would you let a man state his truth on an empty stomach and the loss of his pay, when the price of a meal would ensure his goodwill?'

'Of course not. Do you fund the poor yourself?'

'Not entirely. Although I'm a wealthy man and

contribute to it, the fund is flexible, and maintained by a group of people who are accountable to their own consciences, and who support charitable causes. Helping me represent the poor is one of them. There are others who do this, too.'

'And what of the pride of the poor?'

Quite gently, Theron said, 'When a life, or that of a loved one, is at stake, none of us can afford pride. Sometimes you have to close your eyes to certain things, as you will learn.'

'Yes, sir.'

'And Aaric, talking of pride ... appearance goes a long way in commanding confidence and respect from clients and magistrates alike. Remember always that you are representing my firm.' He flicked a card on the table. 'To that end I'd be obliged if you'd visit this gentleman's outfitter as soon as possible. They know what's required and you'll not be billed. And get rid of the flat cap, it's out of place here.'

'Yes, sir.'

When Aaric looked uncomfortable, Theron smiled. 'You'll feel more confident in a week or two, I promise.'

Within a few days, Aaric had a decent wardrobe, including a dinner suit. He felt comfortable working for Theron Grace and with the trust invested in him. The work was absorbing, and he was grateful for the opportunity to use his own initiative. For the first time in his life, Aaric felt useful, and appreciated.

* * *

Theron laughed when he saw Patricia's name written in his appointment book one morning. She was nothing if not enterprising.

'What is it, Tish? I can't spare you much time this morning.'

'Then I'll come straight to the point. Callie needs a complete new wardrobe.'

'Is this coming from her?'

'Lord, no. She wouldn't ask for anything. But you once said you didn't like to see her wearing my clothes, and I can't take her out visiting dressed in rags.'

'You have charge accounts scattered all over the place, don't you? Use them.'

'You wouldn't object if I bought Callie some clothes, then? She has absolutely nothing to wear.'

'My dear, of course not. We can't have her running around in public with her bare bottom showing. People will talk.'

Patricia giggled. 'Theron Grace, you're shocking. I'm sure you're not a fit person to be my guardian.'

'Oh, don't be such a prude, Tish. I don't see why you even needed to ask me.'

'I didn't want you to froth at the mouth when the bills arrive.'

'Ah, I see, it's my health you're thinking of. Just a moment,' he said as she turned to walk away. 'How much are you thinking of spending?'

'Quite a lot, but I'll try and economize. Is there a limit?'

'Not this week, so make the most of it.' Grinning at the thought of Patricia economizing, or even being able to bankrupt him, Theron rose to his feet and kissed her forehead. He gazed at her and smiled. 'You really like having Callie here, don't you?'

'Oh, yes. You like her too, don't you?'

'Of course I do. She's a nice child, if a bit contrary. Buy her something for when we entertain as well. Nothing fussy. The girl is too lovely to needs frills.'

Theron revised his comment about Callie Ingram being a child after a week of the doorbell ringing and parcels being delivered. Maids constantly seemed to be dashing upstairs with packages.

Bills piled up on his desk, forcing him to revise his opinion that Patricia wouldn't send him bankrupt. But there was an air of excitement about the house, and he enjoyed it.

Patricia came down to the drawing room one evening and said, 'We want your opinion on a ball gown.'

'I'm sure I can manage an opinion.'

'So am I,' she said darkly, and kissed the top of his head to take the sting from her words. 'You may come in now, Callie.'

Theron's eyes widened when he saw her. She'd emerged from her drab disguise and was self-conscious in a cream dress fashioned from some soft, opaque material. Buttoned up to the neck, it was trimmed with lace. Her hair was swept up and decorated with flowers.

'Parade up and down,' Patricia told her, looking smugly pleased with herself.

'I can't. I feel too embarrassed.'

Theron stared at Callie, slightly shocked. 'My God! You're absolutely exquisite. I hadn't realized you were quite so grown up.' *Or quite so perfect*, he thought, taking in her narrow waist and the slight exaggeration of her hips at the back – enhanced by the fashionable bum roll, no doubt. As for her pert breasts, they needed no enhancing. 'A vision of beauty.'

His announcement brought a blush to tint her cheeks a delicate pink, then she gave a shy smile. 'Thank you, Mr Grace.'

'Do call me Theron.'

'There, I told you he'd like it,' Patricia said.

'I must arrange a little dinner party so I can show you both off,' he said, his voice as dry as his throat. 'Doesn't James have a birthday soon?'

Some days later, Sally Brightman was delighted to meet with Theron Grace. 'Will you take some refreshment, Theron?'

'Unfortunately, I can stay only a few minutes. I just wanted you to know that your grandchildren have arrived, and are now settled in.'

'What are they like?'

'Aaric is a quiet young man, a thinker. He'll do well for himself if he's given the opportunity.'

'And Calandra?'

A smile touched his mouth. 'A lively girl, if a bit on the defensive side. She's trying to improve herself, but Tish tells me she's worried in case her father comes after her. Callie looks very much like her mother.'

Sadness came into Sally's blue eyes. 'It's been such a long time. I can hardly remember what my daughter Mary looked like.'

Gently, he said, 'You only have to look in the mirror, Mrs Brightman. You could visit Callie, you know, and make yourself known. I'll pave the way for you if that's your wish.'

'I must think about it. I'd like to see her first, without her knowing who I am. Then I could make up my mind whether an approach would be wise. I'd have to inform my sons, of course. They might not wish me to pursue this course of action.'

'Of course, you must consult them. But I cannot guarantee that Callie might not take it into her head to approach you directly, since she knows of your existence.'

'You must counsel her against it.'

Theron sighed, for Sally Brightman was proving to be a difficult nut to crack. 'If I do she'll be aware that we're in touch, and that will pique her interest even more. The girls usually walk in the park in the mornings.'

'Alone?'

'They're modern young women who are almost eighteen years of age. Several of the ladies who live in the square take their exercise there, and the park is just across the road. Be careful though; if you want to take that approach don't get too close. Callie's a straightforward though passionate little thing at times, and she loved her mother dearly. Now, I must go.'

She nodded. 'Thank you, Theron. I know I'm being difficult. I'm afraid she might blame me for what happened to her mother.'

'I cannot guarantee that she won't. But sometimes it's better to get these things out in the open. I'll be arranging a small dinner party soon to introduce her to social occasions. James will be home for his birthday the week after next, so I have a good excuse. I intend to invite you. You know, Mrs Brightman, I'm sure Callie feels dreadfully out of place. She looked as though she might bolt down the nearest rabbit hole at the thought of being seen at a dinner party. She needs a woman to talk to, to be advised by. They both do.'

'You have a persuasive tongue, but you're as transparent as glass, my dear.' Sally Brightman chuckled. 'Perhaps it's time you took a wife. Being a bachelor becomes a habit.'

'I'm rarely home and although I am never without a pleasant companion to take to the theatre –' *or to bed on occasion*, he thought – 'love doesn't enter into it. I'd like to get Tish safely married and off my hands before I think seriously of marriage myself.'

'You'll fall in love without trying one day.'

Not too soon, Theron thought. There were enough complications in his life. He'd just received a letter from James's professor.

* * *

Callie and Patricia slowly traversed the path round the square. It was nearing the end of September and the trees were a blaze of autumn colour.

Callie's fear that her father might come to London to take her home had lessened, and the constant tension she'd lived under in Seafield had fled.

She found that living a life of leisure and filling the empty hours with something productive was quite hard work. Theron's house was fully staffed, so she didn't even have to make her own bed. And although she was employed as Patricia's companion, Patricia treated her like a sister. Callie wanted more in her life.

Her efforts to find her sister Jane had been set aside by Theron, who told her that Aaric had made enquiries at the domestic agency. 'Your sister has left her position as nursery maid. She told the agency that she was about to marry. She didn't leave a forwarding address, but they think her husband was a baker, since she told them they were going to open a bread and pie shop. I'm making further enquiries.' Those enquiries were made through the eyes and ears of a lad who ran messages for several legal gentlemen. Theron wasn't expecting too much from him.

Theron had news of their brother, Joe, however. 'He's part of the crew of HMS *Victoria*, which is in the Mediterranean Sea. Aaric is going to write to him via the admiralty. If you'd like to send a message to him as well he'll place it in the envelope with his.'

'Thank you for letting me know.'

'You should write to your father, Callie. Let him know you're well. He'll probably be worrying about you.'

'He'll be angry because I defied him. I doubt if he'll ever speak one good word about me again.'

Theron took her hands in his. 'That may be so, but it's nice to let people know you still think of them. You do have time to write, don't you?'

'Too much time. I'm used to every minute of my day being accounted for,' she told him.

Theron had been concerned about this. 'It hadn't occurred to me that you might be bored.'

'Oh, I'm not bored. I didn't mean to give you that impression. We're going to famous buildings once a week. We went to the museum yesterday. And we've got Buckingham Palace on the list for next week. If we're lucky we might see King Edward.'

'Well, run like the dickens if he sees you first. His Majesty is partial to lovely young ladies,' he said drily. 'And lovely mature ones as well, come to that.'

Callie had smiled.

'You've not listened to a word I've said. What are you grinning at?' Patricia demanded to know.

'I was just remembering something Theron said about the King.'

Patricia made a face. 'I imagine it was something uncomplimentary. He is shocking sometimes. I'm so looking forward to seeing James next weekend,' Patricia said with a grin. 'I'm going to wear my new pink dress for his birthday dinner; what about you?'

Callie's stomach lurched at the thought of going to her first social occasion. She had so many new garments that she felt overwhelmed by them. 'I haven't yet decided what to wear.'

'Wear the dark blue brocade; it matches your eyes. We'll ask Betty to put our hair up.'

They'd neared a woman sitting on a bench. As they were about to pass her she gave a gasp and the book she had on her lap slid to the ground.

When Patricia bent to retrieve it, Callie caught the woman's eyes, and started. They were the same colour as her own. The colour ebbed from the woman's face – and that face was totally familiar to her.

Shocked, Callie stared at her and the word *ma* formed on her lips.

'Are you ill?' Patricia asked the woman.

'No ... I'm fine, thank you, dear. You must be Patricia. And you, young lady, must be Calandra Ingram. Perhaps I'd better introduce myself— '

'I know who you are,' Callie said harshly. 'Did Mr Grace tell you we walked here?'

'Yes, but...'

She felt as though she'd been walloped in the stomach. How could Theron have done this to her?

Patricia was gazing from one woman to the other, the perplexity in her expression being replaced by understanding, because the likeness was so great.

'Oh, Lord,' she whispered, 'you must be Mrs Brightman, Callie's grandmother.'

'I haven't got a grandmother, at least not one I want to know.' Turning, Callie walked rapidly away from them.

'Callie, wait,' Patricia called after her.

But Callie couldn't bring herself to stay and be nice to this woman who'd denied her own daughter, grandmother or not. She picked up speed and was soon out through the park entrance and across the road. She pushed past the startled maid who opened the door, and scrambled up the stairs. Gaining the safety of her room she threw herself on the bed and burst into tears.

Fifteen

Callie felt a fool for reacting the way she had. The next morning she was summoned to Theron Grace's den. It was a room that glowed with wood panelling and brass lamps and it had a large fireplace. He always looked so at home there, so in command of himself, she thought.

What if he sent her home to Seafield?

She scowled. That didn't mean she had to go back there. But then, he might want the money back that he'd spent on her, and she didn't have it, so he'd have to have the clothes instead. 'Did he say why he wanted to see me?'

'Theron's hackles are bristling because you insulted one of his clients,' Patricia said irreverently and picked up her hairbrush. 'Why on earth did you run off? Here, you'd better brush your hair before you go there.'

'It's not dry yet, and I'm not afraid of him.' Callie shook her head and tousled her hair even more, despite knowing it was a childish gesture. 'He had no right to arrange a meeting with my grandmother without asking me, and I'm going to tell him so.'

Leaving Patricia with her mouth open, Callie clumped off down the stairs and slid into

Theron's office, closing the door behind her. Leaning against the panel she said, 'You wanted to see me, so here I am.'

He glanced up from what he was doing, his face stern. His dark eyes glinted as he took in the disarray of her hair. She felt suddenly nervous. 'I've just washed it; it's still damp.'

'So it is. Come here, Callie.'

Her heart quaked as she crossed the blue carpeted space to his desk, and said fiercely before she ran out of courage, 'Before you say owt, I want to tell you that you had no right to arrange that meeting without the courtesy of telling me first.'

Resting his chin on his knuckled fingers he looked at her, a slight frown forking across his forehead. 'I thought you'd stopped saying "owt".'

'I have. Sometimes it slips out when I'm nervous.'

'Are you nervous?'

'Of course I am. Wouldn't you be if you were standing here in front of Theron Grace? It's like going to the scaffold.'

'I fail to see any comparison. I'm not a hangman.'

'But you're going to lay down the law to me, so this must be as bad as being a prisoner in the dock.'

'I doubt it, else I'd have scowled at you and said, "What is your excuse for your bad behaviour, Miss Ingram?"'

'I don't want to play games, Theron. I'd prefer

to get this over with. I do want to say this first, though: if you dismiss me, please don't do the same to Aaric. What happened is not his fault, and it wouldn't be fair. You should have told me. I was unaware that my ... that Mrs Brightman is your client.'

'Your grandmother is a very good client, which is why I'm upset with you. I'd like you to apologize to her, Callie.'

'Why didn't you tell me about her?'

'Mrs Brightman didn't want me to, and any business between us is confidential. I counselled her against going to the park, even though she didn't intend to introduce herself. I knew you'd see the family resemblance if you met at close quarters.'

He rose, came round the desk and seated himself on the edge, his long legs extended in front of him. His nearness was threatening and she wanted to take a step back, but his eyes were level with hers and they were compelling. His kept his voice soft. 'You were extremely rude to her, you know.'

'Why should I be nice to her when she threw my mother out?'

'I imagine she didn't have a choice. It took a great deal of courage for your grandmother to go to that park today. She wanted to see what you looked like before she took the matter up with her sons. Does that sound like someone who doesn't care?'

Dumbly, she shook her head.

'Now, what to do with you ... What was it you

suggested? That I should dismiss you?'

Her heart sank.

'That would be a problem, since I don't consider you to be an employee. You are a guest I happen to support, a companion to my ward. To that end you have certain privileges, but also obligations. One of those obligations is to refrain from making yourself disagreeable to myself, my family, friends or acquaintances.'

Her face began to burn but she stood her ground. 'I don't recall being rude to you, or to your family.'

He raised an eyebrow. 'You've just suggested I'd dismiss Aaric for something you did. Why did you think that?'

'I didn't think that. Well, yes ... I did think that, I suppose. But at the same time I didn't really. I just said it in case you thought it might be a good idea to punish Aaric to punish me. I didn't actually think you would – in fact I'm sure you wouldn't.'

He chuckled. 'The first four words would have done. You *are* nervous.'

Her nose narrowed as she sucked in a long breath. He was impossible to argue with, so she brought him back to the point of their meeting. 'Perhaps you'd advise me on the protocol, when your client, friend and acquaintance is also one of my relatives?'

'That's an extremely valid point, Callie, but you're simply being provocative for the sake of it. Let me put a couple of questions to you. Which one is deserving of rudeness when to insult one also insults the other? And what does it achieve?'

All the bravado fled from her. 'A lecture from you, to start with. And hurt feelings are not exclusive. I feel wounded by this, too. I'd also point out that provocation seems to be your middle name.'

His lips twitched. 'Actually, it's Daniel. As for the lecture, that was brought about partly by your own action.'

'It wasn't an action, it was a reaction.' The wind suddenly went from her sails. 'I'm truly sorry, Theron. Meeting Mrs Brightman like that was quite a shock.'

'It was just as much of a shock to Mrs Brightman. She had no idea you were so like your mother, or herself come to that, though I tried to warn her. Your mother was about your age when Mrs Brightman last saw her. She's missed her for all these years. It's unfair to her to take up your mother's cause and make it your own, when you only have one half of the story. Instead, you should try and heal the breach. Wouldn't your mother have preferred that?'

'Yes, she would have. I'll apologize to Mrs Brightman.'

'She'll be coming to James's birthday dinner. She wants to meet both you and Aaric beforehand, in private. Can I tell her you'll be civil, and will not run and hide under your bed like a terrified mouse, since this is just as difficult for her?'

She nodded, knowing she'd be braver with

Aaric there.

'Harold Lazurus is paying us a visit, too. He'll be staying here until spring.'

'I'll be pleased to see him again. I'm sorry I upset you when you've been so kind to me, Theron. I don't want you to be angry with me, even though I know I deserve it.'

'I'm not angry any more, since you put up such a good defence. Come here, let's forget about this and not argue any more.' He took her in his arms and held her against him in a hug. His body was a warm column and she could feel his heart beating against her chest. Gazing up at him, her eyes filled with tears and she felt a moment of warmth, followed by a sudden shock as their eyes fused. Gruffly, he said, 'Don't look at me like that. It will get you into trouble.'

'What sort of trouble?'

'This sort.' When he bunched her hair in his hands, a feeling of excitement spread inside her. And when he sought her mouth and placed a soft kiss there, she was filled with an intensity of pleasure and yearning. This sort of trouble she'd welcome from him.

Panic filled her when there came the sound of voices in the hall. She pulled away from him and they stared at each other. She didn't know what to say ... certainly not what she felt.

'It was nothing. It mustn't happen again,' he said. 'You're too young.'

Nothing – was that what it was to him? The unexpectedly tender kiss had torn her apart, exposed feelings she'd never known existed in her. How could he just dismiss what he'd made her feel?

Eyes blazing with embarrassment, she said scornfully, 'I'm nearly eighteen, and I won't be treated as though I'm nothing, Theron. The next time, I'll likely slap you so hard that your brains will rattle.'

She turned and walked away, feeling more vulnerable than she had when she'd first ventured into his den.

Damn it! What had come over him, Theron wondered after the door closed behind her. One minute he'd been acting the stern guardian, the next moment her lover.

Her eyes had been like drowned bluebells when he'd callously rejected what had happened, the hurt in them almost unbearable. Her hair had been like silk in his hands, and had been fragrant with whatever she'd washed it in. Roses, he thought. A smile played around his mouth. She would soak up love and thrive on it, but was passionate in her anger. So, she'd rattle his brains would she? No doubt he'd deserved it, but just the sight of her was beginning to rattle them already.

He was thirty, she was seventeen – a mere child, he told himself. Nearly eighteen, she'd said, as if a few short weeks would make her more desirable, more available as a woman.

Why was he arguing with himself? A relationship with Calandra Ingram was out of the question. The kiss had been a mistake ... a delicious mistake.

That decided, he poured himself a small whisky, even though it was a bit early in the day. At least he'd got around her with regards to her grandmother. He just hoped everything would progress as it should.

Over dinner that evening, Theron announced, 'The pair of you can plan the details for James's dinner party. It will keep you out of mischief. Consult with the cook. At the moment the numbers are fourteen, including family. There might be a couple more if James has invited his friends, but we have eighteen chairs and the table extends. There's a list of names on my desk and you know where the place cards are kept.'

'Oh, good, I've been dying to do this,' Patricia said, and they were thrown into a flurry of activity. There were flower table decorations to decide on and order, the seating to be arranged, and place cards to write. Patricia found a book in the cupboard explaining the steps to take when a dinner party was in the offing, and advising which wine went with what course. She soon assumed the air of an expert and walked about being unbearably officious.

Callie passed on a message to her from Theron the next day. 'James telephoned to say he'd invited three young men.'

Patricia rearranged the seating. 'We'll have two each.'

Callie complained, but mostly because she'd

been looking forward to sitting next to Mr Lazurus.

'Leave the seating to me,' Patricia said. 'It's best to sit next to people you've never met, so you can get to know them and make them feel welcome. Besides, we don't get the opportunity to talk to young men very often, so I'll surround us with them. You can have brother James, and Anthony Bowling, and I'll have Alex Rossiter and Cedric Gaston.'

'I won't know what to talk to them about.'

'Oh, they won't expect you to be intelligent, because you're a woman. Just look over your fan at them, flutter your eyelashes a bit and ask them polite questions.'

'What sort of questions.'

'Ones that encourage them to talk about themselves. Their ambitions for the future, so we can see if they have prospects or not.'

'How did you get to be such an expert on men?'

'By studying Theron and my brother in social situations. Men love talking about themselves.'

There was a flurry of excitement when James arrived. 'Hello, Tish,' he said and, picking his sister up, swirled her round then set her down on her feet. His gaze slid Callie's way and his smile faded. 'Good Lord, look who was washed in on the tide with the coal, Miss Calandra Ingram. I nearly didn't recognize you.'

She felt uncomfortable when he looked her over in a slightly calculating manner.

'How are you, James? It's lovely to see you.

Happy birthday,' she said and held out her hand.

He walked around her, grinning, then took her hand in his and placed a kiss in the palm. 'So self-assured, and all grown up. Now I've seen you, my birthday is a happy one indeed.'

She laughed, relaxing into his banter. 'Thank you, but I don't feel in the least bit self-assured.'

'Where's the leopard? In his den?'

'He's at the station picking Uncle Harold up,' Patricia told him with a giggle. 'And stop calling Theron a leopard. He'll hear you one day.'

'He'd probably feel flattered.' James grinned. 'I'd better make myself scarce before he comes back.' Hefting his bags in his hands he headed for the stairs.

'You've brought a lot of luggage for a weekend,' Patricia called after him.

James turned, giving them both a rueful smile. 'I might as well tell you. I've decided I'm not going back to the university.'

Patricia gasped. 'Does Theron know?'

'My tutor wrote to him, so I'd be surprised if he didn't, but I doubt very much if he'll deal with the problem today, not in front of everyone. I'm just not cut out to study law. It bores me senseless. I'm going to Paris to study painting after Christmas.'

'Theron won't let you.'

'He can't stop me,' James said gently. 'I've already arranged to share a studio with another artist and paid for my boat ticket.'

'What if he cuts off your allowance?'

'I'll manage for a year on what I can earn from

painting, and I come into my inheritance the year after. Is my studio still intact?'

'I don't think anybody has been in there since you left, except to dust. You might need a fire lit to warm it up a bit. Shall I tell the housekeeper?'

'Tomorrow will do. I just want to visit it before I unpack my bags.'

'We ought to start getting ready,' Patricia said as James disappeared into the gloom of the upstairs landing. 'We'll get some hot water so we can wash.'

Everything was in hand. The kitchen was warm and redolent of roasting beef. The cook's face was pink with her exertions, and a couple of maids were peeling vegetables.

Patricia eyed the large dish of trifle. 'That looks delicious.'

'Thank you, Miss Patricia. There's some fruit in your room in case you young misses are hungry, and a jug of hot water so you can bathe. Don't you go worrying about anything now. It's all in hand, and you did a good job with the menu. Mr Grace said so himself. A roast of beef is everybody's favourite.'

Patricia and Callie exchanged a congratulatory smile.

Aaric was waiting for her in the hall when Callie went downstairs after dressing. He looked relaxed and elegant in his dinner suit, as though he'd been born to the life he now led. As she gave him a hug she wished she could be so self-assured. 'Have you been told of my transgression, Aaric?'

'Aye, I have, lass. Theron told me.'

'He said I must apologize to Mrs Brightman.'

'It's the proper thing to do under the circumstances, Callie.'

'I know, but I don't have to like it.' She sighed and slipped her hand into his. 'I'm glad you'll be with me when I do; she'll probably despise me now.'

'I doubt it.' Aaric knocked at the study door and was told to enter by Theron. Callie tried not to look at him when he introduced Aaric and herself to their grandmother, who wore a lace-trimmed gown of deep rose.

Aaric smiled at their grandmother and said smoothly, 'I'm pleased to meet you at long last. Our mother spoke of you now and again.'

Sally Brightman had a small and delicate figure. Her high cheekbones blended into fine wrinkles at the corners of her eyes and mouth. White hair was fashioned into a bun, and was without ornamentation, though she wore a ruby and gold brooch at her throat.

Sally Brightman's smile deepened. 'I often wished things could have been different. You bear a strong likeness to my sons, you know, Aaric.'

'I look forward to meeting them.'

'And I'll enjoy seeing their faces when you do.' Her eyes went to Callie and she gave her a faint, encouraging smile. 'You have a pretty name.'

'My father saw it on a gravestone and liked it.

I'm also called Mary after my mother. Aaric chose that name, didn't you, Aaric?' She gazed up at her brother. An arrow of misery lodged in her chest as she thought of her father. She wished they hadn't parted on such bad terms. She hadn't written to him yet, but she would, even though she knew she'd never forgive him, and he'd never forgive her.

Aaric squeezed her hand and said, 'Aye, lass, I did choose it. Haven't you got something to say to Mrs Brightman?'

Callie drew in a deep breath. 'Of course. I understand that I caused you distress in the park. I wish I could take back my words, but I can't, and I hope you'll accept my apology and forgive me, because I'm truly sorry I was rude to you.'

'If I'd taken Theron's advice instead of insisting on doing things my own way, it would never have happened,' she said. 'Of course I'll forgive you.'

'Ah ... you have more in common with Callie than I first thought then,' Theron said with a chuckle. 'I'll leave you to talk in private. Perhaps you'd join the rest of our guests in the drawing room at half past the hour.'

When Theron had left the room Callie felt as though she could breathe again. Mrs Brightman indicated the chair beside her and Callie seated herself. Aaric sat on the edge of the desk.

'First, my dears, if you can bring yourself to, I'd like you to call me grandmother.'

Callie exchanged a glance with Aaric, who nodded. 'It's only right that we should.'

'Good. I'd now like to learn a little about my daughter's family. Aaric, perhaps you'd like to begin.'

'We have three older brothers. Tom and Chad are married, and are fishermen like our father. Joe is in the Royal Navy. Then there are four sisters. Verna is the eldest and has a family of her own. Jane is in London somewhere—'

'We think she's married too, only we can't find her,' Callie cut in. 'She has a bread and pie shop somewhere. Then there's Kitty, who is the baby. I promised my mother I'd look after her, but we had to leave her behind when we escaped—'

Her grandmother placed a hand on her wrist to stop her. 'Escaped?'

'My father wanted me to marry Sam Brown, but I refused, so Sam bullied me. Then Aaric had to fight Sam because he hurt me so badly, and our older brothers helped us escape to West Hartlepool, where we caught the train to London.'

'Oh, my dears, how dreadful. So there are eight of you altogether.'

'There would have been nine of us still alive if Giles hadn't drowned two years ago – and many more if the others had survived infancy. The last one killed our mother.'

Aaric said gently, 'Enough lass; you have to let the past go. Our mother wouldn't have wanted you to be bitter, when she made the best of what she had. She wouldn't have expected you to grieve for her forever, when you have a life of your own to lead.'

'How can I not grieve when I loved her so much and miss her so?'

Callie's face was captured between her grandmother's soft hands and she was kissed on each cheek. 'As you grow older you'll discover that men think in a more practical manner than women. We'll talk fully of these things at another time, when you and I are alone together, otherwise we'll make ourselves sad. Now, will you walk with me to the drawing room?'

'Grandmother.' Aaric stood, holding out a hand to help her to her feet. She looked so much like their mother that Callie's heart ached to embrace her. But she wasn't ready to commit herself to an emotional relationship until she knew the truth. She wasn't like Aaric, who seemed able to forgive and forget easily.

'Let's enjoy each other's company at the dinner tonight. Although it's a birthday, for me this will be a celebration of meeting two of my grandchildren for the first time. We shall go on from here and become the best of friends, I'm sure. How charming that dress is, Callie, and how pretty you look in that colour.'

Patricia's plan to seat them both amongst the young men, so to be admired, came to naught when Callie found herself placed between Harold Lazurus and her grandmother. James was seated at one end of the table and Theron at the other.

Spread between was a white damask cloth glittering with crystal glasses, colourful with elegant arrangements of hothouse flowers, and sparkling with silver.

'How beautiful the table looks. I believe we have you to thank for it, Patricia,' Sally Brightman said.

Patricia, who was seated across the table between Aaric and the doctor who lived next door, beamed with pleasure. 'Callie helped me, and she wrote the place names because she has a much neater hand than I do. But the maid must have put them in the wrong places, because this wasn't my seating plan.'

Theron, who was made the recipient of an accusing look, managed an innocent expression and a thin smile. 'I'm afraid it was my fault, Tish. I was looking at the plan when it fell from my hand into the fire and was drawn up the chimney. It's probably floating in the Thames by now. I made up another plan as best as I could remember, but you weren't here to consult. It was a most unfortunate occurrence. I do hope it doesn't ruin your evening.'

'Be sure it won't, Theron,' Patricia said. 'There is still the dancing.'

Sixteen

Theron waited until the girls were visiting Sally Brightman, then made his way to the top of the house, where James had his studio.

'I received a letter from your professor. You're not a child, James. I've been expecting you to come to my study and discuss the problem with me.'

Placing the brush down on his palette, James turned to face him. 'I know you have, Theron. To be honest, I've been trying to pluck up the courage.'

'Surely I'm not that fearsome.'

'You have a tendency to hear only what you want to hear, not what I tell you. And although you've turned my hopes for the future into an issue between us, studying art and earning a living from it doesn't present a problem for me.'

'It's my duty to try and talk some sense into you. I'm your guardian.'

'I'm aware of that, and I appreciated that you have been conscientious. The thing is, Theron, you will never make a lawyer out of me. So why won't you recognize the fact?'

'I need a partner I can trust.'

'Then talk Great-uncle Harold round. I'm sure

he could be persuaded to join you. He told Tish he'd been lonely since she left, and he doesn't have Callie to visit any longer. He's also been having trouble with local louts throwing stones at the windows. He could live in the house my father left me.'

'It's tenanted.'

'But the lease will run out in a year's time when I come of age.'

'I do hope you don't intend to throw away your education and dispose of your assets, James. One day you'll have a family to support. You must have a profession.'

'I have. It's painting. As for disposing of my assets, I'm really not that empty-headed. I don't want to argue with you, Theron. I intend to do what my heart dictates, and would rather have you respect my choice. Either way, I'm going to paint.' He stood to one side. 'Take a look at this and tell me if you really think I'm throwing away my education.'

The canvas on the easel was a painting of barges on the river. The water in the evening light looked cold, and there was a hint of fog to diffuse the gas lamps lining the embankment. Light spilled across the river. Under one of the lamps a solitary figure stood at a rail, looking down into the water. Although unfinished, the emerging picture was evocative.

'I'll concede that you have talent. How much would something like that sell for?'

'At the moment, whatever someone will pay me. I'm working to cover the cost of materials.

To build up a reputation you have to study the great painters, constantly improve your technique and find a patron willing to exhibit you. And to have an exhibition you need to build up a stack of canvasses. A successful exhibition can really launch an artist's career. You're right in one respect though, Theron. I probably won't make ends meet for a long while. But this is what I must do.'

Hearing the enthusiasm and conviction in James's voice, Theron's heart sank. It was obvious where James's interests were focussed. He'd been wrong to try and deny his talent instead of nurturing it. 'That painting would look good in my study,' he said. I'd be willing to buy it if we can agree on a price.'

'I'm afraid you can't have this one. It's my first commission, from the man who owns the barges. You can just see his premises beyond the lights. And I'm trying to finish it before—'

'You leave for Paris?'

'How did you know that?'

Theron smiled. 'How could I not know, since it's always been your ambition? When do you leave?'

'Early in the new year.' James jerked his head towards a stack of canvasses leaning against a wall. You might find something that appeals to you amongst those, though most are for practice only, and have been painted over several times.'

James turned back to his canvas while Theron looked at the paintings. Odd that he'd never taken the time to come up here and look at what

James had been capable of before. As he slid one of the canvasses out, he was confronted by a painting of Callie. Shock rippled through him. Her naked body was clad in a clinging bit of draped fabric as she posed with an urn on her shoulder.

Disappointed, he pushed the painting back into place. He wouldn't have expected that of Callie. Perhaps she wasn't a suitable companion for Tish after all. He wondered too, was she as innocent as she seemed?

The next one he pulled out was also of Callie. Standing on a rock with an old wooden rake in her hand, she seemed to be gazing at a small, ragged boy at the edge of the water. Her patched check skirt was flattened against her so her small buttocks were outlined, the skirt hitched up at the front. Ankles and feet bare, her lustrous hair blew in the wind. There was a small mound of sea coal at her feet. Along the edge of the canvas was written *The Coal Gatherer.*

A lump filled Theron's throat. James had captured Callie perfectly at the time, right down to the bitten fingernails. What had this coal gatherer been dreaming about? Escape from the trap of her poverty, or of some young man she'd loved? James perhaps!

But no. She would have been too young back then to dream of a young man.

But James wouldn't have been too young. He'd have been like a young stallion, full of vigour and looking for opportunity to expend it.

'I really like this one,' he said.

James came to stand beside him. 'That's how Callie was the first time I set eyes on her, just on the cusp of becoming a woman. She looked as though she'd walked out of the wind with her wild hair, and she smelled of smoked kippers. But I saw something ethereal in her, as though she shouldn't have been born to the hard life she led.'

Theron smiled, wishing he'd been there to picture it, too. He had to know. 'Did you fall in love with her, James?'

James gave him a level look. 'Of course I did. I still do love her, in fact. Callie was an intense and passionate creature, and so vulnerable. She was being bullied, and she needed a friend.'

'And it was never more than that?'

'Good God! What are you suggesting? What man would take advantage of such innocence?'

'Many would be delighted to.' *Including myself*, he thought.

'She was a child,' James said with some disgust.

'No longer.'

James laughed. 'Believe me, I've noticed it. Don't worry, Theron, I'm not about to tie myself to any young woman at the moment, however desirable. I can't afford to. By the way, Alex Rossiter was taken with Tish, and I've got a feeling he may call on her. He's a decent sort. He's just started work at his father's warehouse, and has good prospects. They're wine merchants.'

'I've done business with his father.'

James said awkwardly, 'I'm sorry I'm not meeting your expectations, Theron. But I know I'd disappoint you more if I continued to study law.'

'I'm not disappointed in you. In fact, I'm rather proud of you. You've been honest with me, and I should have listened sooner. Do your art studies; I won't cut off your allowance. And when you're ready to exhibit, let me know and I'll fund it.'

When a smile of relief chased across James's face, Theron said abruptly, 'Will you part with this portrait?'

'There's one of the Seafield fishing fleet you might like better.'

'I like this one; I don't need to look further.'

'Then it's yours, as long as you don't mind me admiring her now and again. I'd also be obliged if you didn't sell it. I'm fond of my funny little coal gatherer. It was the first canvas where I managed to capture the essential spirit of the subject. You should put her in a gilded frame, show her off to advantage. Have them put a plaque on the bottom, with the name of the painting etched on it.'

'I'll never sell it.' Picking up the canvas, Theron walked off with it hugged possessively against his chest.

'Well, well,' James said softly to himself, and grinned. 'How very unexpected. Let's see you talk yourself out of this, Cousin Theron.'

Patricia had fallen in love, and it was obvious

that her mind was on Alex Rossiter as she gazed out of the window at the rain.

'Do you think he'll come?'

'Of course. He said three o'clock, so you have twenty minutes to wait.'

'That's ages.' She rose and walked to the mirror, where she gazed disconsolately at her reflection. 'I wish I'd put something flowery on.'

'You have flowers on your hat, and the velvet basque looks lovely with the fur trim.'

'I wish I was as pretty as you are.'

'Yes ... it's a pity that you're so ugly. Let's hope Alex Rossiter never gets spectacles so he can see your imperfections.'

Patricia laughed. 'You're horrid sometimes. You know perfectly well I was fishing for compliments. Do you think Mrs Rossiter will approve of me?'

'Do mothers ever approve of the women their sons marry?' She thought of her own mother and the caustic remarks she'd made about Tom and Chad's choices in the William girls. They'd turned out to be kind, hard-working young women, and perfect choices for Chad and Tom.

'Alex hasn't asked me to marry him yet. Goodness, we've only just met.'

'But he will eventually. Why else would he take you to visit his parents?'

Patricia gave a bit of a grin. 'Alex is really sweet. I adore him.'

Callie heaved a sigh. 'So you've said a thousand times over. Yes, he is sweet. The next step will be for Alex to make an appointment and ask Theron for your hand in marriage. The engagement can then be announced when you're eighteen at your coming out ball in February. That will give you time to change your mind...'

'But I won't. And it's *our* coming out ball. I expect Theron will try and find you a suitable husband at the same time.'

'Aye, but he'd better not,' she said fiercely. 'I had enough of that from my father.'

'Theron's being kind, that's all.' She smiled happily. 'James has been paying you rather a lot of attention lately.'

Callie burst into laughter. 'James is such fun to be with; he's teaching me to paint and said I can use his studio while he's away. I regard him as a good friend. But there's nothing personal between us, nor is there likely to be. I'll miss him when he's gone though.'

'I wish you would marry him; then you can be part of my family for ever.'

Touched, Callie hugged her. 'You're the nicest person I've ever known, and I love you dearly. We'll always be friends, even when we're apart. And if by chance I ever have to go back to coal raking, then you'll always be in my heart and it will bring me happiness when I think of you.'

Patricia gave a shiver. 'Don't talk of going back.'

'One day I shall, even though it may only be for a visit. I made a promise to my mother about Kitty, and I have to satisfy myself that she's all right. Besides, when you're married and have a home of your own I'll not be needed here.'

There came the sound of a hackney outside. Patricia picked up her gloves and cape and was gone, a smile lighting up her face at the thought of seeing Alex.

After Patricia had gone, Callie had the feeling that this part of her life was coming to a close. She was happy for Patricia that she'd fallen in love, and wondered if she'd do the same one day. At a loose end, she wandered into the kitchen. The tea tray was set, with a cloth over a plate layered with sliced cake. The big black kettle had a trickle of steam coming from the spout.

She liked this house of Theron's; liked the way it wrapped its silence around her in a comforting embrace. Up on the mantelpiece a clock ticked loudly, the cook's ginger cat arched its back, turned round on the cushion and settled down to toast its other side.

Everything worked as it should here. There was respect and love, and she was learning from it – learning to be less aggressive, to trust more. Before she'd come here she'd been a jangle of nerves, and had mistrusted everyone. Now she'd found the peace inside her – and the laughter. It was not always perfect though. Theron was a constant surge of energy within the house, his active mind like a quiet hum of noise in the background.

She heard the telephone ring in his study, heard him answer it. He had a nice voice, deep, but not too loud. It was always calm, despite his personality. She heard James clatter down the stairs. Doors opened and shut with sharp and impatient rattles and bangs.

'What the devil's going on out there?' Theron called out.

'I'm looking for Callie. Is she with you?'

Her slightly melancholy mood shattered, but still she smiled. James was irrepressible ... irresistible. His charm would always get him what he wanted, as it had with Theron. She walked through to the hall. 'I'm here.'

'Ah, there you are, Callie, my love. What were you doing in the kitchen?'

'Listening to the clock tick.'

She saw Theron smile at her answer.

James laughed. 'Well, you can stop listening to it. Go and get your apron on then come up to the studio. I'll give you another painting lesson now Tish has gone out.'

Theron's eyes glinted. 'The painting came back from the framer this morning, James. Come and see it. You too, Callie, though I haven't hung it yet. It will take two of us to lift it on to the hook on the picture rail.'

'I'll help you with it before I go back upstairs. Wait, I want to surprise her. Put your hands over your eyes, and don't look through your fingers,' James said.

Led into Theron's study, Callie was allowed to unmask her eyes. She gave a slight gasp when her glance fell on the painting. How stormy the sky was, like the day Giles had drowned. She shivered.

'I painted it from sketches I made of you when we first met,' James said proudly. 'You do like it, don't you?'

'It's wonderful.' A lump formed in her throat as she reached out to touch the figure of the small boy at the water's edge. 'That's Giles ... my brother.'

There was an awkward moment when she thought she might cry, but it passed as James said, 'Yes, I remember him. He was a nice lad and I felt sad when I heard that he'd drowned.'

'Thank you for making him live again.' She kissed his cheek. 'I'll wait for you in the studio.'

As soon as she got upstairs she allowed herself to shed a few tears for Giles before she dried her eyes. Anger for her father rose to choke her, then she remembered Aaric saying that her father had blamed himself all along.

'Well, so he should,' she said aloud, then wondered what it would be like to be responsible for the death of your own child. Her father wasn't a stupid man, just uneducated. After Giles had died he'd tried to find peace in the bottom of a bottle, and it was that which had caused the death of her mother. He carried an impossible burden. Her anger turned to pity.

Seventeen

Jane Prichard was in the back room when she heard the shop bell tinkle. Taking a batch of cooling pies through to the shop, she laid the tray on the counter and gazed at the lad standing there. She hadn't seen him before.

'If you want a free loaf you'll have to come in when we first open. The others got here before you and I've already given the stale ones away.' She took a meat pie from the tray. 'Here, have this, but don't tell anyone, else every hungry bairn in London will be on my doorstep.'

Grinning, the lad bit a chunk out of the pie. 'I'm making enquiries about a Miss Jane Ingram.'

'Are you, now? In that case you can pay for the pie, lad.'

'You gave it to me.'

'Well, now I'm selling it.'

He placed the pie on the counter. 'I'll only pay for the piece I ate.'

She got between him and the door. 'You came in here pretending to be hungry and took advantage of my good nature. That's a penny pie, so hand it over else I'll give you a clout around the ear.'

The lad's face fell. 'You wouldn't, missus. I didn't beg for the pie, you offered it.'

'Aye, but only because you looked hungry.' She held out her hand for the penny.

'I am hungry. Don't you want to know why I'm making enquiries?'

'Aye, but you can tell me after you've paid.'

'I can only tell you what I know. But it'll cost you that pie. It's not as though you can sell it to anyone else with a piece missing. And it was a right tasty mouthful I had, missus. If I had a penny I'd buy it, and if I got it for nuthin' I'd tell all my business associates in the legal profession about your shop.'

Jane grinned as she picked up the pie, impressed by his enterprise, and knowing that word of mouth was the best form of advertising for their wares. 'First, I want some information. Why are you looking for Jane Ingram?'

'Theron Grace, attorney at law, needs to know of her whereabouts,' he said grandly.

'And what does he want to know that fer?'

'I don't know. He's not about to tell the likes of me, since I just run messages, and he asked me to keep an eye out for you. But he's a fair gentleman all the same, and I reckon he'll tell you that himself.'

'What makes you think I'm her?'

'Aw, come on, lady. You've got to be her. He said she had a pie and bread shop and she'd talk funny. 'Sides, I've looked in every other pie shop in London.'

'I'm Mrs Jane Prichard now, and it isn't me

who talks funny, it's you, you cheeky little bugger. Where does this lawyer live?'

'He has an office in the Temple, and I've got the address.' He pulled out a grubby card, holding out the other hand for the pie. His stomach growled. 'Fair exchange, missus?'

The two objects were exchanged and the lad edged towards the door. 'I've gotta get going now, I've got messages to run and you're in the way. Thanks for the pie.'

Jane opened the door and the lad escaped, going off up the street at a fast clip, taking bites from his pie.

What now? She turned the card over. Aaric and Calandra Ingram was written in pencil on the back. She stared at it and a smile slipped across her face. Then it faded. What did this have to do with a lawyer? She hoped they weren't in any trouble.

Jane hesitated. She'd worked hard since she'd left Seafield, had got herself a husband who treated her right. It hadn't seemed worth keeping in touch with her family after she'd learned that her mother had died. She hadn't received Verna's letter until a few months after the funeral as it had been sent to her former address.

Jane had put her family and their troubles behind her now. She was proud of what she'd achieved. Ben was a good baker and Jane had surprised herself. Discovering she was better than Ben with figures, she kept the books, managed the business side and served the customers. No more selling fish, raking coal or looking after other people's spoiled brats for a pittance and, after growing up in a large family and watching it wear her mother down, she had no craving for children of her own yet.

So, did she want to get involved in this?

'Not if it costs you anything, tha knows,' she whispered to herself. The lawyer fellow had been looking for her for a reason though, and it was something to do with Aaric and Callie. There might be something in it for her, and she was curious. Perhaps her siblings had died. If they had, the parish could bury them, so it was no good asking her for a handout. Still, it would not hurt to see him and find out what it was all about.

Her thumb ran over the embossed letters. Theron Grace and Associates. He had an office in Temple Bar. That wasn't too far away, and she could take the tramway for the most part.

'Ben,' she shouted. 'I'm going out as soon as you've finished baking the bread, so you'll have to mind the shop fer a while.'

Aaric had just finished taking down a deposition from a witness in a murder case. Mrs Nelligan was a rather garrulous woman.

'Are you sure it was Ella Smith's husband who killed her, and not the man she was entertaining?'

Mrs Nelligan's hands went to her hips. 'I'm not blind, even though he'd growed a beard since I last saw him. Dressed in a seafarer's hat, he were, and a navy jacket. He were rolling drunk, sir. He threw that Pelham feller out the door then went inside. Pelham's head banged against the wall and he staggered off down the alley and collapsed in a doorway. Then I heard her give a couple of gurgling screams.' She gave a shudder. 'Cut off, it were, as though he'd cut her throat.'

Which was exactly what had happened. 'Why didn't you come forward before, Mrs Nelligan?'

'I was scared he'd come after me, so I waited till his ship sailed to America with him on it. 'Sides, my old man told me to keep my nose out of it. He said Ella Smith is a no-good tart who deserved what she got. Happen he's right, but that aside I've been thinking it ain't right, allowing a man to hang for something he didn't do.'

'No, it's not right. Are you prepared to stand up in court, take an oath to tell the truth, and be questioned by the prosecution? I must warn you that the questioning will be rigorous, and if you tell a lie it will incur a heavy penalty.'

'I'm willing to swear an oath on the bible. Besides, I've got proof.'

Aaric stared at her, his heart thumping. 'Which is?'

'Desmond Smith's jacket was covered in blood, so he took it off and hid it. He dropped his knife when he heard someone coming, and ran off without finding it. He come back looking for it later, but it were gone.'

'You have these items?'

Her eyes narrowed. 'Would there happen to be a reward, sir?'

'Aye, Mrs Nelligan. There would be.'

Mrs Nelligan took a small parcel wrapped in rag from her voluminous bag and laid it on the table. 'That's the knife. I haven't washed it so it's still got the Smith woman's blood on it. His initials are carved into the handle.'

'And the jacket?'

'Desmond bundled it up and stuffed it down a grating outside the Owl and Mouse.'

Finishing the statement, Aaric gave it to the woman to read, then dipped his pen in the ink pot. 'Sign and date it if you agree that it's a true record of what you told me.'

'What about the reward then?'

'Ah yes, the reward.' Going into the back room, Aaric, who'd devised his own system of rewards, came back with five shillings and said, 'If we find the jacket, and Mr Pelham is acquitted, there will be another five.'

The paper was signed, and Aaric notarized it. After the woman had gone, he put the knife in a safe place then telephoned Theron with the news.

Theron was jubilant. 'Good work, Aaric. Just what we needed to get the case against Pelham dismissed. I'll get on to New Scotland Yard and go and find that jacket with them, so there can be no mistake. And I'll drop in to collect the knife and the deposition. Will you have time to make a copy?'

'Aye, I will. There's nobody waiting.'

As soon as he hung up, a knock came at the door. He sighed. 'Come in.'

A plump young woman entered, dark-eyed like Verna, and with the look of Aunt Agatha about her, except her expression was more pleasant. 'Are you Theron Grace?' she said.

A smile sped across his face. Rising, he came around the desk and stared at her. 'No, I'm not. I'm Aaric Ingram. By heck, Jane, have you been away so long that you don't recognize your own brother when you see him?'

'Aaric? Good God, just look at you! How did you get to be so tall? You look like a real gent. What on earth are you doing in London?'

'As you can see, I work for a lawyer, as a clerk to Theron Grace, and I thoroughly enjoy it. Wait till I tell our Callie you've turned up. We were worried because you didn't come to Ma's funeral.'

'Verna's letter went to the wrong address, and I didn't get it for a few months after. Ben – that's my husband – and I were setting up the bakery and shop at the time and we've been working hard to make it pay. Since then time's just slipped by.' She grinned self-consciously and said fussily, 'By God, it's lovely to see you, our Aaric. You'd better give me a hug then.'

That done, he said, 'How long can you stay?'

'As long as I want. I've left Ben in charge of the shop.'

'Would you go through to my rooms and make us a pot of tea while I copy this statement?' He reached for the telephone again. 'Mr Grace wouldn't have had time to put on his coat yet, so I'll ask him to bring Callie over with him.'

'Callie's married to a London lawyer? How did that come about?'

'No, she's not married. She lives in his house as companion to his ward,' he said with a laugh when her eyes widened. 'Now, let me get on with this. When Theron Grace wants something done, he always wants it done in a hurry.'

Theron ended the phone call to Mrs Brightman, went into the hall and shouted up the stairs, 'Get your coat and hat on, Callie Ingram. You've always wanted to see where Aaric lives and now's your chance. You've got five minutes.'

Patricia popped her head over the bannister. 'Can I come as well?'

'Sorry, Tish,' he said softly. 'Callie's sister has turned up, and I've arranged for them all to meet their grandmother afterwards. It's a surprise, and she needs some private time with them.'

'What if she decides to go and live with her sister?'

He gazed at her, a slight frown on his face, and said gently, 'Surely you're not jealous.'

Her face fell. 'I think I must be. She's my friend and I love her. I don't want to lose her.'

'Once gained, a friendship can never be lost. If Callie needs her family more than she needs us, then we must be happy for her.'

'Would you be happy if she left us, Theron?'

He thought about it for the few seconds it took for him to realize he'd be most *unhappy*. 'I'd hope she wouldn't forget us.'

Footsteps pattered across the floor and a door

opened. 'Have you seen my gloves, Tish?'

'They're on the hallstand.'

'Aren't you coming with us?'

'No. I've seen the office, and thought I might go and annoy James. Have a nice time. I'll see you at dinner.'

'Does this hat look all right?'

'I refuse to stand here while you two discuss your ridiculous hats,' Theron said firmly.

'You'd better go, Theron's champing at the bit about something,' he heard Patricia whisper before she headed off, calling out, 'James, where are you hiding?'

Callie came tripping down the stairs, wearing something blue topped by a hat with a feather that curled over the crown from the back.

'You're wearing that hat at the wrong angle.' He took it from her head and tilted it forward, so the back of the hat sat forward of the bun on her crown, and the feather curl was noticeable from the front. He carefully fixed the object to her hair with the hat pin and looked into eyes that reminded him, at that moment and in that light, of lapis lazuli. 'There, that's better. Yes, it does look all right; in fact, it makes you look like the saucy baggage that you are.'

'Thank you, Theron.'

Her smile was that of a young women who's just become aware of her attractiveness to a man, and whose instinct was to put it to good use. Her eyes were a wide and innocent blue in a sweep of dark lashes, yet a gleam of mischief lurked in their depths. Her mouth was a tender curve. The cream of her cheeks had assumed a rosy radiance now, and he grinned. The sight of her had brought the urge to kiss that trembling mouth of hers, and the realization he was thinking like a callow youth. Damn it, he even felt like one.

'I never kiss a woman before noon,' he murmured.

Theron realized he'd said it out loud when her head cocked to one side like a little bird. 'Sorry, I didn't quite hear you.'

He held himself back. It was mid-morning. It would not be fair to her, or to himself. He cleared his throat but his voice was more brusque than it should have been when he said, 'I told Aaric I'd be with him by noon. We should be able to pick up a cab at the stand around the corner.'

In an instant she was all apology, reaching for the loose seal-plush coat she usually wore. He took it from her and helped her into it, knowing that if he stooped he could kiss the shining tendril of hair that curved against her ear. He resisted the temptation, breathing gently on it instead and delighting in the tiny shiver she gave. Opening the front door he stood there, making impatient growling noises to hide the turmoil of his emotions, while she threaded several long black buttons through the loops.

She laughed after she completed the task, and walked past him. 'You don't frighten me, Theron Grace.'

Picking up her gloves from the hallstand he

followed after her, wondering if she'd left them there on purpose when she accepted them with a smile and a murmur of thanks.

But no, Calandra Ingram didn't have an artful bone in her body, he thought.

They abandoned the cab in Fleet Street and entered Temple Bar through a narrow lane.

Theron knew exactly where he was going as he strode through the throng, explaining that the Temple, where his chambers were situated and where Aaric was installed to look after them, had been home to the Knights Templar in the twelfth century, which was where the name had come from, and that each of the Inns of Court had a separate chapel, library and hall.

'Where did the Knights Templar go?' she asked him.

'They became too wealthy and too arrogant, and were perceived only to owe allegiance to the Pope. This drew down the ire of the crowned heads of Europe. The Templars in France were tortured and burned at the stake. In England the charges against them were proven false, but the Pope abolished the order. Some of them, along with some of their property, joined the brotherhood of St John, who had a better reputation. The rest was handed over to the lawyers, who established themselves here. According to William Shakespeare, a fight between noblemen in one of the temple gardens sparked off the civil war, and the roses that bloomed there became an emblem for the warring sides.'

'There's nothing civil about a war, surely.'

He looked at her and laughed. 'You're right, Callie, there isn't. But men prefer war to be regarded as a noble cause when their bloodlust is roused.'

'D'you think war is noble?'

'I can see nothing honourable in the act of killing a fellow human being. But if I was forced to defend someone I love, I don't think I'd hesitate. There ... you see, I'm just as savage as the next man.'

'No you're not,' she said, and her flesh crawled as Sam Brown came into her mind. Then she recalled her father beating her mother, and she began to despise him again, something she was trying not to do. 'You wouldn't hurt someone because you couldn't have your own way, or just to prove you were stronger than them.'

He stopped in his tracks, turned and took her hands in his. 'You must put the past behind you, Callie.'

'I can't, not yet. I made a promise to my mother, and until I've done as she asked of me I can't forget anything or feel real forgiveness. I feel that by leaving Seafield I've betrayed her ... and Kitty'

'Kitty's your father's responsibility, Callie.'

'He can't be trusted with that responsibility. After Giles drowned, our mother didn't trust Da any more. That's why she made Kitty my responsibility. I can't just abandon my sister without a fight.'

'For what it's worth, my advice is to wait until

the time is right – a time when you have the best chance of achieving success.' He tucked her arm into his and they walked in companionable silence for a few moments, then he gently squeezed her hand and said, 'Here we are.' They turned into a courtyard, where they entered a door and made their way up a flight of stairs to another door. Theron's name was on it.

He knocked, then pushed it open. It was rather a gloomy room, the only light coming from a small window looking over the courtyard.

Aaric was in the act of placing a sheet of paper into an envelope. 'Well timed,' he said with a smile, and stood up.

'Where's—?'

'In the back room,' Aaric said swiftly, and Theron grinned.

'I thought you might like to be in at the end, Aaric. Callie can mind the firm while we're gone.'

'A good idea.' Aaric drew on his coat.

'What will I do if someone comes in, or the telephone rings?' Callie called after the men as they headed for the door.

'Deal with it, or answer it,' Theron said. 'We'll only be an hour.'

Aaric hesitated. 'By the way, lass, there's a woman waiting in my sitting room for me. Tell her I've gone out for a short while, would you?'

A woman! Callie hoped she wasn't one of those street women Patricia had told her about. She wouldn't know what to say to her.

Cautiously she pushed the inner door open.

The woman was seated in the only armchair. She turned her head to gaze at Callie.

Callie returned the gaze. 'Jane?' she said in disbelief, then began to laugh. 'Theron didn't say a word, and neither did Aaric. What a lovely surprise.'

Her sister leaped from the chair and they hugged each other tight.

Later, except for Theron, who stayed only a few minutes to talk to Sally Brightman, they took tea with their grandmother and met their uncles for the first time. Charles and Edward Brightman welcomed them cautiously, but began to thaw as the hour progressed.

They were shown around the Brightman Emporium in Regent Street, a large establishment with several departments through which crowds of shoppers thronged.

'If Theron Grace will allow it, you and your friend Patricia must come and stay with me for a few days in the new year,' her grandmother said to Callie as they parted company.

'Our birthdays are only a few days apart, so we are to have a ball in February when we turn eighteen. Theron said he'd hire somebody to arrange it, but I think he's forgotten. It will be wonderful to have you there. Jane, you must come too.'

'I'll see,' she said cautiously. 'Ben and I are just getting on our feet, and we haven't got much use for ball gowns and the like.'

Sally Brightman offered her a smile. 'You

won't have to worry about that, Jane dear. I'll make sure you're both suitably dressed for the occasion. As for Theron Grace, Callie, he's an extremely busy man. I'll talk to him on the telephone, and offer to take the problem of the ball off his hands. I know people who will do a fine job, and we can plan it together.'

Jane went back to her shop and her husband and Aaric returned to sleep with the ghosts of the Knights Templar. Callie was put in a cab and returned to Bedford Square. Theron met her on the doorstep. He seemed to be in high spirits, smiling because everything had gone right for him that day.

'It's been a wonderful day,' she said. 'Thank you for finding Jane.'

'I didn't do much, and it was my pleasure, Callie.'

She believed it had been exactly that, since he was the most unselfish person she'd ever known – though he hid it well.

As soon as Patricia had borne Callie off upstairs, Theron sought out Harold Lazurus. 'May I speak with you before dinner?'

They went into the study where they could talk without being overheard. Theron poured them both a whisky. It had been an eventful day and they sipped the spirit in silence, appreciating its smoothness for a few reflective moments, and gazing into the flickering firelight.

Eventually, Theron said, 'Mrs Brightman wishes to settle a portion of money on each of the grandchildren born to Mary Ingram. This sort of thing is more in your line, Harold. Would you mind taking it on? It shouldn't take long, and when you return to Seafield you can deal directly with the recipients. Mrs Brightman wants it done quickly, so I've told her you'd call on her tomorrow when I'm in court.'

Harold nodded. 'I'd be delighted to.'

'And, Harold, there's something else I'd like to discuss with you.'

'Which is?'

'As you know, James has decided to go to Paris to study painting.'

'It will be for the best, Theron. He would have made a poor legal representative if forced into the profession. The education he's had will still hold him in good stead.'

'Aaric Ingram is proving to be highly adaptable to the legal profession and has become indispensable to me. He's being noticed by those who matter, has attended several meetings of the friends, is registered, and is well on the way to being convinced. I'm thinking of offering him articles. May I solicit your opinion on that?'

'I'm pleased that you like him as much as I do. He's a conscientious young man, and I doubt if you could find a better apprentice.'

'You've always been a good judge of character, Harold. Also, I badly need a partner I can trust. I would like that partner to be you. Will you consider it?'

Harold didn't look surprised. 'You will have my answer after I've thought it through clearly.

If it's in the affirmative I'll need a month or so in which to settle my affairs in Seafield.'

'I'd compensate you for loss of any income and pay removal expenses if need be. By the way, they're thinking of selling the house next door, and I'm thinking of buying it. We could have offices on the ground floor and I'll get one of those typing machines and a woman to use it. You could live in the rest of the house.'

Harold smiled. 'I must admit that's a far more attractive proposition than living in the Temple chambers at my age.'

'We shall keep the chambers for Aaric. He fits into the Temple perfectly, and since he lacks a formal and rounded education, like others before him it will be an educational rite of passage for him to remember.'

'If I can help you in any way while I'm here please take my services for granted, Theron. I promise I'll consider your offer seriously.'

'You could prepare the articles, if you would. I'll offer them to Aaric as a Christmas gift.'

Harold leaned back in his chair and gazed at the portrait of Callie over his glass. 'I understand from Patricia that Callie attends the Friends meeting with her.'

'Quite often, though she goes to the Anglican service as well. I put no pressure on either of them.'

'That's an exceedingly good portrait,' Harold murmured.

'I must concede that James has considerable talent for painting females. He has captured

Callie perfectly.'

Harold gave a short bark of laughter. 'But I wonder – will Callie remain captured by James?'

Theron stared at him.

'Just thinking out loud.'

Eighteen

Christmas passed by pleasantly for Callie with an exchange of gifts.

James pulled her under the mistletoe in front of everybody to kiss her gently on the mouth before handing her a framed sketch of herself holding an urn over her shoulder.

'Remember that day?' he said.

Blushing from the kiss, she laughed because everyone else was laughing. 'How can I forget? My arms still ache from holding that urn.'

'That's because it was made of bronze,' Harold said. 'You should have given her a teapot to hold, James.'

'I wanted her to look like a Greek goddess, not a domestic servant. Isn't that the profession you once aspired to, Callie, being a maid?'

'Ah, but since then she's changed her mind,' Patricia said with a laugh. 'Now she's hoping to marry a gentleman of means. In fact, James, when Callie first came here we decided we might marry each other's respective brothers, so watch out.'

James laughed. 'I had no idea Callie had designs on me. Perhaps I should take her to Paris with me. Aaric, how do you feel about such a scheme?'

Aaric laughed. 'All I can say is that Tish has broken my heart by choosing Alex, but I daresay I shall survive.'

To which Patricia giggled, 'So why do you sound so horribly relieved?'

Callie's eyes were drawn to Theron when he drawled, 'I had no idea the pair of you were so mercenary. Was that why you posed for James wearing nothing but a wisp of cloth around you, Callie?'

The silence seemed to go on for ever, then Aaric said, 'What's this, Callie?

'I don't know what Theron's talking about,' she whispered.

'Of course you don't, since you haven't seen the painting I used the urn sketch for,' James said. He laughed, making light of Theron's remark. 'Theron's teasing you. He's referring to my classical Greek study.' He gazed at his cousin, a smile on his face. 'You know very well that only Callie's head and arms posed for me. The body was that of Aphrodite.'

'Oh, I remember that day,' Patricia cried out. 'Poor Callie stood there for ages with a sheet draped over her clothes, and didn't complain once. Can we see the painting?'

'I'm afraid not, Tish. It was an absolute disaster,' James said lightly. 'The body was too mature for the youthful innocence of the arms and head, so I've painted over it.'

Afterwards, Theron came to where she stood and said quietly, 'I'm sorry if I embarrassed you.'

Callie wanted to hit him, and briefly wondered if she'd inherited her father's violent tendencies. 'Are you, Theron? I think you achieved what you set out to do, but you embarrassed yourself more in the process, and that's what you're sorry about. I'm surprised you'd think I'd pose in a "wisp of cloth" to entice a gentleman of means, and even more surprised that an intelligent man would take Tish's remark seriously.'

'Let's not spoil the festivities with a quarrel, Callie. Accept my apology in the spirit it was offered. You can take me to task later, if you wish.'

His smile melted her and she sighed. 'You know very well that I won't be angry with you later.'

'I'm counting on it.' He tucked her arm into hers and whispered into her ear, 'You'd look more enticing in a wisp of cloth than Aphrodite ever could. Did you like the ring I gave you?'

Her fingers touched against the surface of the ring she wore. Pearls circled a blue amethyst set in gold. 'It's so pretty. I really don't deserve it.'

'I know you don't.'

'Did you like the scarf I knitted for you?'

He grinned. 'I'll be honest. It's the most ghastly item of clothing I've ever set eyes on. You have appalling taste, and I will most likely give it to the poor.'

She shouldn't have laughed, but she did. 'It's supposed to be the thought that counts.'

'Come on, Aaric is about to open his gift from me, and I want to see his reaction.'

Her brother's reaction was worth watching. Several pieces of paper emerged from the envelope. He gazed at them blank-faced, then turned them over and began to read. Awareness crept into his eyes, and with it came a smile that inched across his mouth, then expanded. She had never seen a smile so wide on him. He gave a huff of unbelieving laughter before gazing at Theron. 'What can I say? I accept, and thank you!'

'What on earth is it?' Patricia said.

'I'm to be articled to your cousin, Theron Grace.'

Patricia laughed. 'Lord, you poor thing, Aaric. Are you sure you know what you're doing?'

'Aye, I know, and I know where my future lies. You won't regret this, Theron.'

'I'm sure I won't. Now, there's something else that needs to be said. Harold, will you tell them, or shall I?'

But Harold was busy pouring champagne into glasses, and handing them round. 'Oh, you do it, Theron.'

'Harold is going to join the firm, and we intend to set up a suite of offices next door for our paying clients. Many things will be changing this coming year. James will go to Paris, and I'd like to wish him success in his chosen career. My dearest Tish will be engaged to Alex next month and looking forward to becoming a wife. I know your parents would be proud of the fine adults you've both grown into.' He gave a chuckle. 'To you all, my family and my dearly beloved friends, many heartfelt good wishes for the coming year.'

The period up to the girls' ball was a succession of parties and theatre visits. Callie grew sad thinking of Kitty, and wondering what sort of Christmas her sister had spent.

She wrote a letter to her father, addressing it to Verna to make sure it would be read to him. She couldn't bring herself to post it, so put it in her top drawer.

The time spent with her grandmother was a joy to her, and they grew close. 'I'm going to settle some money on you all,' Sally Brightman said one day. 'It's money that came down through my family, and would have been left to your mother. Those of my Ingram grandchildren who are married will get a lump sum to do with as they wish. I've included Aaric in this, since he's of age. You will receive an allowance until you reach the age of twenty-one, or marry, Callie. So will Kitty. Harold Lazurus will arrange this.'

'So I won't be beholden to Theron Grace any more.'

'Has that bothered you too much, Callie?'

'Aye. Sometimes I feel like one of his charitable cases.'

'He's a good man, but I doubt if he feels the same way about you. Social status, class or money doesn't impress him much.'

'Probably because he's never known real hardship.'

'Oh, my dear. Theron wasn't born into money. His mother died giving birth to him, and his father disappeared at sea, without even knowing he had a son. Theron was raised by an aunt on his mother's side, a widow of moderate means who was the eldest of three sisters. It was the younger sister of those three who married into the Lazurus family and was the mother of Patricia and James. He was blessed with a good brain – and with that he earns a good living. Theron's no angel, but give him credit for helping those more unfortunate than himself. He's done a good job with his cousins.'

'And now he has me to look after, too. He probably thinks I'm a nuisance and can't wait to get rid of me.'

'Theron would be horrified if he heard you say that. He thinks very highly of you.'

Callie's heart leaped as she gazed at her grandmother. 'Did he say so?'

'Not in so many words. Tell me, Callie. Are your affections involved with Theron Grace?'

Callie felt the blood rush to her face and she said breathlessly, 'Why should you think such a thing? I'm too far beneath him ... Does he think I am? Oh, how embarrassing, when he regards me as a child, if he ever notices me at all.' She placed her hands against her burning cheeks and whispered, 'I think I love him, and I don't know what to do about it.'

'There is nothing you can do about it, my dear. You mustn't encourage him to be familiar with you, especially while you live under his roof.'

'He kissed me once. Then he said it meant nothing and that I was too young for him.'

Her grandmother smiled at that. 'Are you too young?'

'We talk well together and he never makes fun of me if I don't understand; he just rattles on and explains it all. He teaches me things all the time, and without even knowing it. When Theron's mind comes up with a solution to a problem his enthusiasm is such that he sometimes seems younger than me.'

'And what about James Lazurus? He's fond of you too, I understand. Patricia tells me he kissed you under the mistletoe. He's nearer your age.'

'James is fun and we're good friends, and although he kissed me it was in front of everybody, so we all knew he didn't mean anything by it. I'm fond of him, of course, but it's not the same way I feel when I'm with Theron. Sometimes my insides are all of a churn when I'm with him, and when he notices me I feel scared, yet happy at the same time. Then my heart hammers because I think he might see what I feel, and laugh. Otherwise, I'm content to be with him, sharing his life. Am I in love?'

Her grandmother smiled at that. 'It might not be true love. Young girls often have disturbing feelings towards older men, and they can be mistaken for love. Men are aware of this and will sometimes take advantage of the situation. Theron Grace is a handsome man with a charismatic personality and charm, and your feelings towards him are entirely natural. If there is no encouragement, they will fade in time.'

Callie hoped it wouldn't take too long. Being in love, even if it wasn't true love, was painful.

James stayed in London for the ball, which was held halfway through February in the grand ballroom of one of the more fashionable hotels.

Patricia was burning with excitement. 'Your grandmother said if it had been later in the year we would have had difficulty securing a booking, since everyone will be gathering in London for the coronation of Edward the seventh. Oh, I do love London; it's so exciting. I don't know what I would have done without you in Seafield, though ... Stared out of the window all day and died of boredom, I expect.'

'You would have managed.' Talk of Seafield gave Callie a strong urge to see Kitty. She picked up her sister's furry toy and held it against her cheek.

'You miss her a lot, don't you?' Patricia said gently.

'Aye. Losing her was like losing my own child.'

'You should have brought her with you; I'm sure Theron wouldn't have minded.'

'I was going to, then my da got wind of the plan and he took Kitty away while I slept. He would have stopped me too, if he could have. Just as well I didn't bring her. Your uncle said that Aaric and I could have been charged with kidnapping and sent to jail.'

Callie found herself wrapped in a big hug. 'I

wish I was as brave as you.'

'You can be brave by being the first one to get into the corsets my grandmother sent over. She'll be here in a short while to take charge of us.'

An hour later they stood together in front of the mirror. The corset had given them the fashionable flat-fronted look. Patricia's gown was trimmed with rhinestones around the hem and the upper bodice. It flared out at the back in a froth of pink silk.

Callie had decided on a gown of soft cream silk with a chantilly lace bodice sprinkled with pearls. Both wore gloves that reached above their elbows, and white silk flowers in their hair.

If only you could see me now, Ma, Callie thought, all the while knowing she'd swap all the comfort and finery to have her mother back.

There came a knock at the door. It was Theron bearing gifts of an ivory fan apiece. He gazed from one to the other, his eyes filled with admiration. 'How did the pair of you metamorphose into such beautiful butterflies? Every man in London will be lining up to dance with you.'

'Including me,' James drawled from behind him. 'I insist on having the first dance, Callie.'

'I got into line first,' Theron said.

'So you did. Callie, you must choose between us.'

Looking from one to the other, she laughed. 'I'm afraid it will have to be neither, since this afternoon I promised the first dance to Mr Lazurus. See, it's written right here on my dance card.

'The sly old fox,' Theron said with disbelief.
James just laughed.

A week later and the ball was a mere memory. Patricia was officially engaged. Harold had gone back to Seafield to settle his affairs and James was about to leave for Paris.

The cab waited outside, ready to take him to the dock.

Theron had a lump in his throat as he hugged his cousin. 'I'm going to miss you. I still regret that you're not going to be part of the firm.'

'Lord, I don't, Theron. Consider yourself to have had a lucky escape. You have a brilliant substitute in Aaric Ingram.'

'Yes, he suits me perfectly. It was as though it was meant to be.'

James glanced up at the portrait of Callie. 'And it all started with a chance meeting between myself and an adorable little coal gatherer on the beach, so you have me to thank for it. Which reminds me, Theron, I have something to say to Callie in private before I leave.'

'I thought you said goodbye to Tish and Callie last night. They'll still be asleep.'

'Callie won't. She always rises early. It will only take a minute,' he said, and was gone.

Theron hadn't meant to eavesdrop, but James had left the door ajar. His voice carried clearly from the landing.

'Callie, my sweet angel, my heart. Come with me to Paris, be my inspiration ... my muse ... my lover...'

Callie murmured, 'Shush, James, I can't just pack a bag and leave with you...'

'Why not? You left Seafield that way.'

'Only because I had no choice.'

'Come to Paris in the spring, then.'

Theron's heart sank and he pulled the door shut, but he could hear them laughing together.

Theron waited until James thumped down the stairs into the hall before he opened the door again.

James wore a large smile on his face. 'I'm off, then.'

At the top of the stairs, Callie stood, her hair hanging to her waist in shining ripples. Her face was suffused with laughter and her eyes alive with merriment.

James blew her a kiss. 'I'll see you at the wedding.'

She nodded and blew one back to him. 'Good-bye, James dear. I'll miss you. Nobody can make me laugh so much.'

'We'll all miss him,' Theron said. 'James, you'd better go or the boat will leave without you.'

'And that would be a disaster. *Adieu*, every-one. If nothing else I shall return more fluent in French. Don't forget to write to me, Callie.'

'I won't, I promise.'

When the door closed behind James, Theron turned to Callie. 'Whose wedding was he talk-ing about?'

'Patricia's.'

His brow cleared. 'I meant to ask you before,

but have you written to your father yet?'

'Why do you ask?'

'You've been looking pensive and I wondered if it was because he hadn't answered. It's been a while since you said you'd write to him.'

'I've been sad because I've been thinking of Kitty, wondering if she received the parcel I sent to her. I have written to my father, Theron, but I haven't posted it yet.' She'd felt reluctant to send it, but couldn't think why.

'I'll be going out after breakfast; I can post it for you if you'd like.'

She nodded. 'Thank you. I'll fetch it.'

Nineteen

Seated in the window of the Seven Moons, Ebeneezer Ingram swallowed down a tot of rum.

'Thanks, bonny lad. It warms the cockles on a night like this.' Drawing on his pipe he gazed out of the window into an evening slashed with cold rain.

'Aren't you gannin' home, Ebeneezer?'

'Nay, Robbie lad, not yet. The place doesna seem like home now. Her that was Tilly Brown is nowt but a bag of wind. She can't cook, can't clean and won't open her legs, lessen I spend half an hour tickling her up. Then it's not worth the effort. A man wants to get hisself in and out quick sometimes, so he can get some sleep, not stay up half the night trying to get what he's entitled to have by marriage.'

Robbie chuckled. 'There's a letter come from your Callie today. Verna said I'm to read it to you.'

Ebeneezer suddenly grinned. 'You got the best bitch of Mary's litter with our Verna, Robbie. She knows her place, does that one. Not like our Jane, walking away wi' her nose in the air. She would have come to no good.'

'Not from what Callie says. Jane is married

and has her own shop selling pies and bread. She's Jane Prichard now.'

'And too good fer the likes of us, else she would've wrote.'

'Nay, Ebeneezer, you're too hard on your girls. It were a mistake trying to make them marry so young. Callie especially.'

'I don't blame our Callie fer running away from Sam. He's turned into a nasty piece of work. The bugger gave me a thump yesterday, nearly knocked me out of the boat. Callie's like her mother. She's got a bit of mettle to her, has Callie, and would have landed on her feet with Aaric to look after her. Eh, but the lad fettled Sam Brown, tha knows. I'm reet proud of him now, though he made me look like an auld fool, and lost me a fortune 'cause I put my money on the wrong horse.'

'You were never an auld fool, Ebeneezer, jest as stubborn as a dog's pissin' post, so it bluidy well serves you reet.'

Ebeneezer cackled with laughter. 'Get away wiyyer, man.' The rum had settled nicely in his stomach and was relaxing him. He took a swig of his ale, threw some coins on the table and said, 'Fetch us another one – nay, fetch the rest of the bottle, Robbie. It's just the thing to keep the cold out. Have one yersel'.'

When they were settled with their drinks again, he said, 'What does the maiden have to say fer herself then?'

'She said she's safe and well. And she says she was sorry she left, but she couldn't think of anything else to do.'

'Happens she were reet,' Ebeneezer muttered. 'I still think that Chad and Tom helped the pair of them on their way, but they won't admit to it. Thick as thieves, those two, allus have been.'

'The girl says she's been to balls and theatres and suchlike. And she says she forgives you fer what happened to Giles, and doesn't blame you for her ma's death now, and she says...'

Da, I promised my mother before she died that I'd look after Kitty. I know I was wrong to try and take her from you, but I'd like to see her, to satisfy myself that she's well. By now Mr Lazurus would have contacted you about the generous gesture of Grandmother Brightman...

'It were no more than the woman owed us, sending her daughter into marriage with nowt practical about her and wearing what she stood up in. I were lucky to get a new boat out of them fer my trouble. And that Lazurus fellow telling me that Kitty's portion can't be spent, 'cept in little bits, lessen she dies, then it'll be mine as her next of kin.'

'Mr Lazurus said—'

Ebeneezer snatched the letter from Robbie's hand, screwed it up and dashed it down. 'How dare she mention her ma's fancy man? I'll not hear another word. Can she heck as like come swanking here talking about balls and theatres and such, and tell me what to do,' Ebeneezer growled, and downed his rum. 'Our Kitty's all reet where she is, and Tilly teks no nonsense from her. I'm not having her growin' up with fancy ideas like our Callie.'

The rain had stopped. Bladder bursting, Ebeneezer staggered to his feet. 'I'm off out. Likely I'll walk the drink off before I go home, lad. You tell our Verna that I don't want to hear our Callie's name again – and that goes for all of yer. Gerrit?'

Outside, he relieved himself into the nearest shadow and walked into the wind, making his way to the fishing harbour. He sat on the wall and sucked on his empty pipe for a while. The tide was in, and the sea was a ferment of white breakers that curled into each other like an old man's beard.

The wind stung him with sand grains, but it didn't get through the woollen jumper he wore under his jacket. Mary had made it from greasy wool. He could picture her, sitting in the chair on the other side of the stove, knitting it on thick wooden needles while she sang to herself under her breath. She'd had Giles inside her then.

'You were a grand lass, Mary. I miss you,' he mumbled, sucking on his rum bottle.

'*What you did to me was wrong*.'

'Eh, don't say that, lass. I loved you in my fashion, and it was the only way I could have you.'

'*You're incapable of love. You've got no heart, Ebeneezer.*'

Tears ran down his cheeks. 'Nay, don't be so harsh wi' me, Mary ... I'd do anything to get thee back, tha knows.'

'Da ... help me!'

The voice came from beyond the waves. Ebeneezer stood, shading his eyes. The moon came out from behind a cloud, as round and incandescent as a pearl. It shone a path across the water to where Giles floundered beyond the breakers. The lad was struggling to keep his head about the water.

'Da ... help me. Don't let me drown.'

'Nay lad, don't be scared.'

'Save him,' Mary said.

'Aye, happen I could at that, our Mary.' Running for his boat he hoisted the sail and cast off, heading for the spot where he'd last seen Giles. The wind changed direction and he felt uneasy. Along the horizon a bank of dense cloud crept upwards towards the moon. The wind bit into him, and ice formed on his jumper. He paid it no mind.

'I'm down here, Da.'

Ebeneezer leaned over the side of the boat and saw Giles. He was caught in a piece of drifting net. His eyes were wide with panic. Eh, he were only a little lad, too small to work on the fishing boat. He should've listened to Mary. 'I'm coming, Giles.'

Rolling into the water, Ebeneezer swam down and down into the chilling blackness. His arms closed around the boy and the net wrapped snugly around them both like a blanket. 'You're all reet now, bonny lad,' he tried to say but the water filled their mouths.

Above him, the clouds covered the moon, the sea rose in fury and the coble turned about and headed back towards the harbour in an aimless fashion.

The following day Theron received a telephone call from Harold Lazurus.'Ebeneezer Ingram's body was washed up on the beach,' Harold said gently. 'He was bound up in a fishing net with a seal. His boat was dashed to pieces against the sea wall.'

'I'll let Aaric know. He can inform their sisters and they can travel up for the funeral together if they wish.'

Aaric took the news calmly, saying briefly, 'He wouldn't have wanted to die in his bed.'

Callie's reaction was unexpected. She gazed at him, her eyes growing larger and larger. The colour drained from her face.

He poured her a small amount of brandy and made her drink it. She spluttered and coughed, but the colour returned to her face. She didn't cry, just gazed at him, looking tragic. His heart went out to her when she whispered, 'I should not have written to him.'

'Why shouldn't you, Callie? Was there something in the letter that would have upset him?'

Tears trickled down her cheeks. 'I told him I'd forgiven him, when I hadn't forgiven him at all.'

'Surely that's a good thing for your father to know just before he died.'

'He would have known I was lying – that I'd never forgive him and would always hold him responsible for Giles's death and that of my mother.'

'Why did you mention it at all then?'

'To remind him of it, only I didn't realize it until now.'

'You can't blame yourself, Callie. It was me who urged you to write to him.'

'Aye, it was. You can reason things out and make me see things your way, and I wrote it because I wanted to please you.'

When tears trickled down her cheeks he pulled her close. 'Then blame me, Callie.'

'I have to be responsible for my own actions. My da was a good seaman. He'd never have put out to sea in a storm unless he was compelled to, unless it was to save the lives of others.'

Feeling sorry for her, Theron said, 'You're assuming that your father took his own life. I wasn't going to say this, but now I must. Your father had been drinking heavily all evening, as he habitually did by all accounts. Therefore, it's possible that his judgement was impaired by strong spirits and he fell overboard. The wind shifted and the storm blew up suddenly, according to Harold.'

'Aye, it often happens like that up there.'

'Then it's reasonable to think he was caught unawares, isn't it? Your father was found tangled in a net with a dead seal. Let me put this to you: could it be that he set eyes on the seal and thought it was a man struggling in the water? So he tried to rescue him and lost his own life as a consequence. That would have made him a brave man.'

She clutched at the straw he offered her. 'I suppose so. It's possible.'

'It's more than that; it's probable. Wallow in self-pity if you must, Callie. But if you're to hold yourself responsible for your own actions, then you must allow that your father must be held responsible for the consequences of his. It wasn't you who held a bottle to his mouth, and you didn't place him in his boat and send him out to sea in a storm, did you?'

'I suppose not.'

'Then you're coming up with the worst possible scenario, and blaming yourself for nothing. This is typical female thinking.'

She prickled suddenly, and said, 'I am a female. I'm surprised you haven't noticed.'

He pushed her away from him, engaging her eyes when she subsided into a chair. 'My dear Callie, I doubt if it will surprise you when I say that I'm acutely aware of your female attributes.'

Her mouth twisted into a wry grin.

He felt relieved that she'd taken charge of herself when she turned his words back at him. 'I didn't mean to *wallow* in *self-pity*.'

'I know, but you wallowed so beautifully.'

'Hah! You always have an answer for everything.'

'It comes with practice. Now, let's get back to the matter in hand. Aaric is letting your sister Jane know of your father's unfortunate demise. You can travel up for the funeral if you wish, and Harold will put you up.' He then said something guaranteed to make her smile. 'You'll be able to see Kitty, talk to your brothers and sisters about her and perhaps arrange something for her future. You can make a home for her here if you wish. Or perhaps Jane might want to offer her a home, then you could see her quite often.'

Callie rose and came over to where he stood. 'Thank you, Theron.'

When she reached up to kiss him he could have moved his head, and found her lips. But he thought of James, who also loved Callie, and who was in Paris and who'd urged her to join him. James and Tish were the only family he had, and something like this could split them all apart.

Something like what?

Love, of course.

He gazed over her shoulder at the portrait of *The Coal Gatherer*. How tender it was. James's emotions had connected with the essence of her and had laid it bare on the canvas for everyone to see. That troubled him.

But Callie was unaware of James. She was detached, her tender gaze seeking that of the child, her eyes dreaming of other things.

Her kiss was a dry butterfly against his cheek. According to the sixteenth-century essayist John Lyly, the rules of fair play didn't apply to love or war, he thought and smiled at the irony of choosing to believe it as he turned his head a fraction.

Her mouth slid gently over his cheek and there

was an instant of her mouth against his that seemed to go on for ever, so his stomach fell into a void with the anticipation of it. He knew he mustn't force this moment of awakening in her.

But she didn't pull away from him. Her mouth began to pressure his, and she tentatively kissed him until he took advantage of it.

She hit his senses like a bolt of lightning, robbing him of all reason. He'd never encountered such turmoil as the urgent need in him fought with the notion that Callie was still a child. His body told him she wasn't. She was a desirable young woman who needed a man to love her and to care for her.

Then his mouth cooled and he looked into eyes filled with an awareness as acute as his own. But the awareness was replaced by a mixture of uncertainty, then embarrassment. She touched a finger against her mouth and colour rushed to her cheeks. 'I'm sorry, I didn't mean to do that,' she whispered and was gone, the door closing behind her.

Stunned, Theron stood in his office and knew he needed guidance. Harold Lazurus would oblige him. He gazed ruefully at the portrait. 'I'm not sorry,' he said. 'I'm not sorry at all. James will understand.'

Up in Seafield, after the funeral, a small band of people stood around the grave. Sam and Alf Brown were either side of their mother. The widow was dry-eyed, her face angular with determination. Aunt Agatha resembled her dead brother with her sly looks. The two women glared at each other, making it obvious that there was no love lost between them.

Tom, Chad and Verna were together. Jane stood by herself, as independent as she had been all those years ago when she'd defied her father and walked away from the family at her mother's urging.

Callie stood with Aaric and Mr Lazurus. Only Joe and Kitty were missing.

The atmosphere was thick with mistrust. Mary Ingram's family had split apart and the gulf was too wide to cross. Those from London were city folk. They were different in dress, ways and speech now, though they'd only just realized it. Their siblings were in awe of them, uncomfortable in their presence, feeling less than they were.

Their father was buried in the hole dug for him, and the prayers said over him to speed him into heaven. Callie hoped her ma was waiting on the other side to crack him on the head with a rolling pin, so he'd realize the error of his ways.

'Where's Kitty?' she asked Tilly.

The woman's hands went to her hips. 'Who's asking?'

'You know exactly who. I promised Ma I'd look after her.'

'And I promised Ebeneezer the same. I've been her ma for the past year. She's used ter me.'

'Yer a bluidy liar,' Agatha said, her arms

folded on her chest. 'My brother asked me to tek Kitty in if anything happened to him.'

Tilly didn't back down. 'You're just after the money that comes wi' her.'

'Don't tell me you don't want to get your greedy hands on it. You got the family house; you should be satisfied with that.'

Tilly smirked. 'Ebeneezer left everything to me in a will. I've got it in writing.'

'And whose writing was on the will? Yours.'

'Mebbe, but the signature is his.'

'Aye, but I bet the auld sod didn't know what he was signing, since he was pickled in rum fer most of the time,' Chad said.

'And who can wonder at it, married to Tilly. She didn't give him a minute's peace,' Tom added.

Aaric had a look of disgust on his face.

So did Jane. 'I'm going back to London. Good riddance to the lot of you,' she said, and stomped off without looking back.

Callie would have liked to have been able to do the same. Horrified at the thought of abandoning her young sister to the two warring women, she turned to Harold Lazurus. 'I'm not returning to London without Kitty. Can you do anything?'

'I'll try.' He stepped forward. 'May I suggest that this is not the time and place to argue? Callie has no interest in the property. She wishes to see her sister, Kitty. Mrs Ingram, perhaps we could adjourn to your house and satisfy my client that she's all right. And furthermore, she should be allowed to spend some time with her sister.'

Sam stepped forward, his eyes on her. 'Aye, she can, but Callie's not tekking that girl out of town, and I'll make sure of it.'

'If you try and intimidate Miss Ingram, you'll be reported to the police, and charged.'

'I won't hurt the lass, and neither will Alf.'

Alf's face had taken on a thuggish look. He gave her a flat stare that made her shiver.

'And who made you head of the family?' Agatha shrieked. 'I'm seeing one of those legal fellers. Kitty is an Ingram, and she has blood kin to look after her. Besides me, Verna, Chad or Tom might want to offer her a home.'

The three named gazed uneasily at each other but didn't say anything.

Harold tried not to smile. That made things easier. 'Then I'm to assume there are three parties seeking legal custody. Mrs Tilly Ingram, the child's stepmother; Mrs Agatha Herries, the girl's aunt; and her sister, Miss Calandra Ingram. For the child's sake we should set the matter before a magistrate as soon as possible.'

Everyone looked self-consciously from one to the other.

'Reet then,' Agatha finally said. 'That we will.'

Sam said quietly, 'That changes things. If Callie wants to see her sister she can now wait until we go to court.'

Disappointment filled Callie and she wanted to cry with frustration when Harold inclined his head and stated, 'I'll be representing Miss Ingram. You'll be served with papers notifying you that my client intends to apply to the court for custody of Kitty Ingram. We'll inform you of the date of the hearing. If you have any objections you're welcome to turn up in court with your legal representation and state them.'

'Happen I won't need no lawyer with his hand in my purse. Kitty Agatha Ingram, her full name is,' her aunt said. 'That lass were named after me by my brother. I'll tell yon fancy magistrate that, and it will count fer something. You'll see.'

Aaric caught Callie's eye and grinned.

When they were about to leave, Sam whispered as he passed her, 'If you want to see Kitty, come down to the beach in an hour. But you mind me, you'd better be by yerself else you'll never see her again.'

She nodded, and hurried on to catch up with Harold Lazurus, her skin crawling. She'd do anything to see Kitty.

But her sister was not the plump, happy child Callie had known. Kitty was thin. There were bruises on her arms and legs, her hair was matted and her nose ran. She cringed away from Sam on the windy beach.

Callie drew her into the shelter of her body. 'She's been ill-treated.'

Sam shrugged. 'She falls over a lot.'

When Kitty heard her voice she gazed up at her. 'It's me, Callie. I won't hurt you, Kitty love,' she soothed.

Kitty's eyes widened, but she said nothing.

Callie swallowed a lump in her throat. Taking a small brush from her bag she attacked the dark tangled curls. Laying her head against Callie's arm, Kitty began to snivel.

'It's all right, darling,' she whispered.

'You can keep her, tha knows,' Sam said.

Her heart leapt and she hugged Kitty tight. 'Thank you.'

He smiled when she stood up with Kitty in her arms, and tore the child away from her. 'There's a price. All you have to do is wed me, just like your da wanted. You're even more desirable now you've got a bit of money behind yer.'

Kitty looked back at her, held out her arms for her and began to cry as Sam walked off. 'Shud-dup, else I'll thump you,' he growled at her.

Callie watched them go, tears streaming down her face and thinking how cruel Sam Brown must be to be able to do what he'd just done. 'I'll see you in court,' she shouted, her resolve stiffening.

He turned to stare at her. 'Think about it, Callie. Your sister might have a nasty accident before we get there. She might fall down a well, or get kicked in the head by a horse.'

Fear rendered her weak at the knees. Falling to the sand she began to cry.

'Where've you been?' Aaric said when she got home. 'Theron wants me back in London and I'm catching the morning train with Jane.'

'I went to the beach. Sam said I could see Kitty for a few minutes.'

'You should have taken me with you.'

‘Then I wouldn’t have seen her.’

He gazed closely at her. ‘You’ve been crying.’

‘Oh, Aaric, Kitty is so wretched. She didn’t know me – at least, I don’t think so. If I have to leave her again, I don’t think I’ll be able stand it. Sam said if I married him I could have her.’

‘You’re not thinking of doing such a stupid thing, are you?’

‘No ... but what if something happens to Kitty?’

‘It won’t, love. Kitty is their pot of gold. Let Mr Lazurus handle it.’

‘I was disappointed that our brothers and Verna didn’t offer to take her. That would have been better than Tilly or Agatha.’

‘Aye, well, our Verna has enough on her plate, I reckon. And Tom and Chad are scratching by, and intend to buy a bigger house apiece, and a new boat with the Brightman money. They’d take Kitty in out of duty if they had to, I daresay, but it’s best she goes to someone she was close to, and who loves her. Ma made it clear to all of us that it would be you, and they’ll sign a statement saying so.’

Quietly, she told him, ‘I’m not going back to London until this is settled, and that’s that.’

He laughed and kissed her cheek. ‘You sounded just like our ma talking then. I won’t try and change your mind, but stay out of Sam Brown’s way, and whatever you do, don’t confront anyone. Keep Mr Lazurus informed of anything that happens, however small. He won’t want any nasty surprises if this goes to court. Happen he'll be glad of your company, though, and he won't allow you to do anything stupid. You won't, will you, Callie?'

'Of course not,' she lied. Having seen Kitty again, and the consequence of her betrayal, Callie knew she'd do anything to get her sister back now.

If she had to marry Sam she would. Then at the first opportunity, she'd run away and take Kitty with her.

Twenty

Callie haunted the beach over the following two weeks, but although she saw Sam and Alf from a distance, there was no sign of Kitty.

The days dragged slowly by, made worse by grey skies, heavy winds and gusting seas that battered the hull of a wreck that had been carried by the tide on to the sand the previous winter. It sent up spectacular sprays of water.

Harold Lazurus came and went. Callie helped the housekeeper to pack his personal things.

'He was a fine gentleman to work for. I'm going to miss him. Still, the family who bought the house seem nice – and they're keeping me on.'

The date for the hearing was still a week away.

Callie said to Harold when they were eating dinner together one night, 'I was thinking that if I gave them the money Mrs Brightman gave me, then they might let me have Kitty in exchange.'

'If the magistrate hears even a whisper that you tried to buy her, it will go against you. Theodore Bartlett is an honest man, who will have your sister's interests at heart.'

Face troubled, she gazed at him. 'We will win, won't we?'

'You have a strong case, Callie. But so has your father's widow, because she's the girl's stepmother. Kitty already lives with her, so is used to her. She also has the statement your father signed, and the advantage of already raising two children.'

'Aunt Agatha?'

He shrugged. 'She has a good living, and can provide the child with a home so there's no reason why she shouldn't be considered. However, her disposition doesn't endear her to anyone, and I doubt she'll impress the magistrate.'

'What about me?'

'It's possible that your youth will go against you, and the fact that you're an unmarried woman. We do have witnesses, and they will attest to your mother's wishes, which will, no doubt, be taken into account.'

The day before the court hearing, Callie went to visit her mother's grave and was pleased to see that her rose had taken root.'

'I expect you know what's going on, Ma. If you're able to, ask God to perform a miracle. Tell him to whisper in the magistrate's ear and order him to award our Kitty to me. Theron Grace has told me she can live in his house.' She smiled as she whispered, 'Theron has been good to me, and I think I love him, though Grandmother Brightman told me it might not be true love.' She sighed. 'Being in love is hard, whether it be true or false love, but I shall marry Sam Brown if the magistrate awards Kitty to

Tilly. I have to, otherwise I'll never see Kitty again. He threatened me, and told me that Kitty might meet with an accident. I'm that fearful.'

Harold, who'd thought it might be wise to follow Callie from a distance to make sure she wasn't accosted, stepped quickly back behind a monument when he overheard her words. Then he turned tail and headed back towards the house. Agitated, he headed for his office and picked up the receiver.

'Theron, thank God you're at home. The girl intends to marry Sam Brown if the verdict goes against her.'

'And will it?'

'It quite easily could.' He quickly outlined the weaknesses in Callie's case.

Theron swore. 'Put me on the witness list. I'll catch the evening train, and should be able to make the Seafield connection on time.'

'Come straight to the public school. They've set up a temporary court for the hearing.'

'Who's the magistrate?'

'Theodore Bartlett. He's fair, though very thorough, and he'll do what he thinks best for the child. We could have done worse.'

'How's Callie?'

'There's an air of quiet determination about her. I don't like it. It means she's scheming. She's already suggested that I buy Kitty from Mrs Ingram.'

Theron chuckled. 'I like her thinking. Did she tell you she was going to marry Sam Brown?'

'No. She told her dead mother, and she put in

a request that she ask God for a miracle, so the verdict will go her way. And, Theron, perhaps you should be made aware ... Callie told her mother she's in love with you.'

There was a moment of silence in which Harold could almost hear Theron smile. Then he gave a bit of an odd laugh, and said, 'Ah yes, a miracle ... I might be able to manage a small one of those.'

Harold took heart.

Agatha stated her case first, and the magistrate jotted down some notes.

Tilly sat with her two sons.

Callie, feeling calmer than she expected to feel, sat with Harold Lazurus. She held Kitty's toy cat for good luck, just in case the miracle she expected didn't materialize. She could feel Sam's eyes on her but refused to look his way.

'Do you have legal representation, Mrs Ingram?' The magistrate said to Tilly.

'No, I can't afford it now my husband is dead,' she whined. 'My son Sam will say my piece for me.'

'Am I to take it that you suffer from a speech impediment?'

'No ... only Sam is the man of the house now—'

'But the petition was lodged by yourself, and you have chosen not to be represented, so I'd prefer to hear it from your own mouth, Mrs Ingram.'

She sighed heavily as she stood up, letting the

magistrate know she found him a nuisance. 'It's like this, sir. My husband left a will, and in it he asked me to look after Kitty.'

'Kitty being your stepchild, isn't that so?'

'Kitty Agatha were called after me,' Agatha suddenly called out.

'Please be quiet, Mrs Herries. You've already stated your case.'

'I forgot that bit, tha knows.' Agatha subsided back into her chair, her face seething with anger.

The magistrate gave her a stern look and turned back to Tilly. 'Do you have the will?'

She passed it over and he read through it. 'This seems straightforward. One thing, Mrs Ingram. Why was the section about the custody of Kitty Ingram added after the signature?'

'We forgot about it until after.'

'But the ink is much thinner.'

She shrugged. 'We ran out of ink, so I mixed water into it.'

'Are you telling me the truth, Mrs Ingram?'

'She only wants Kitty fer the money she brings in,' Agatha said.

'Be quiet, woman. I won't tell you again.'

Tilly looked the magistrate straight in the eye, though her eyelids flickered and her face turned red. 'As God is my judge, I am telling the truth, sir. And whatever that cat Agatha Herries says, it's nothing to do wi' the money that Kitty's grandmother gave her. The truth is, it's her who's after the money. As fer me, I love that girl as if she were my own blood.'

Harold smiled when he heard the train whistle.

Bartlett was no fool, and this was going better than he'd hoped. He just wished Theron would get here in time.

Bartlett's eyes fell on him. 'Mr Lazurus, I understand you are here to represent the young lady.'

'Yes, sir.'

'Good. What is her interest in the matter?'

'Calandra Ingram promised her mother she'd take care of her sister if anything happened to her. I have several signed statements to this effect from her brothers and sisters.'

'May I have them, please?'

It took several minutes for Bartlett to read through them all. 'This is all very well,' he said, 'but presumably the father was still alive at the time the child's mother died. As he was the custodial parent the deceased mother's wishes didn't apply, and therefore must be disregarded.'

Callie's heart sank, then rose again when the door opened and Theron strolled in with her grandmother and Patricia.

He was wearing the scarf she'd knitted him for Christmas. His presence drew all eyes to him. He smiled at her and inclined his head to the judge. 'I'm sorry we're late. We had to wait at the station for a cab.' He saw the two women settled then slid into the chair next to them.

Her grandmother smiled at her, and Patricia blew her a kiss. How wonderful that they'd come all this way to support her.

The magistrate frowned slightly, then turned to Callie. 'Young lady. Perhaps you'd tell me in your own words why you're applying for custody of your sister.'

'Because my da is now dead, and I made a promise to my ma to look after her. I love Kitty dearly, and she loves me. We belong together.'

Tilly stood up. 'That girl shamed her da. She were promised to my son, Sam, and she ran away to London and tried to tek Kitty wi' her. And what's more, she's living with that man there.' She pointed an accusing finger at Theron.

Callie gasped, and her eyes widened in horror. 'But it was my da who promised me to Sam. Everyone in Seafield knows Sam Brown waylaid me in the churchyard, and beat me up. That's why I ran away to London, to get away from him. I'm frightened he'll hurt Kitty, because he threatened to. As for the rest, it's malicious lies.'

When Sam glared at her and rose to his feet, the magistrate indicated to the bigger of the two constables, who moved to stand in front of the door. 'Sit down, young man. Nobody leaves this court until I say so.'

Sam subsided back into his chair.

The magistrate gazed over his spectacles at her, then said to Harold, 'An accusation has been made which questions the moral integrity of your client. Do you wish to confer with her over the matter?'

Standing, Harold said, 'I have no need to. The gentleman in question wrote to Miss Ingram's father offering his daughter employment, so he was aware that she was going to London to work. It was something Miss Ingram had done before, acting as a companion to his ward. Yes, she did want to take her young sister, but she consulted with me over the matter and I advised her against it.'

'Quite rightly so.'

'It's true that Miss Ingram lives in the gentleman's house, but she shares a room with his cousin and ward, Miss Patricia Lazurus, who will, I'm sure, verbally attest to the fact if necessary. As for the letter to Mr Ingram, I understand it was delivered by his son, Aaric Ingram. As his father wasn't in, he placed it on the mantelpiece. I have a statement from him to that effect.' He handed over a piece of paper.

'Thank you, Mr Lazurus; I see no reason to disbelieve you. I'll take it into account when I consider my verdict.'

'Ebeneezer didn't see no letter, else I would 'ave had to read it to him,' Tilly grumbled. 'He couldn't even write his name, let alone read.'

'So how did his signature get on the will, then?' Agatha shouted, and Tilly looked sharply at Sam.

The magistrate looked round at the court. 'That is a separate matter the constables might wish to investigate.'

The court fell quiet. Theron smiled at Callie and her heart thumped.

Time sped past as the magistrate went over the several statements and questioned the witnesses, then he said, 'I dismiss Mrs Herries' application for custody on the grounds that the woman came into my court to cause dissent rather than having the welfare of the child at heart.' Agatha snorted her disgust at this verdict. 'Mrs Ingram, you have solid grounds, but I'm a little dubious as to your motive, and your integrity has been brought into question. For one such as yourself on a limited income, the child's allowance would be very inviting.'

Tilly said nothing.

'I'm impressed with the young lady's application and believe she is morally sound. The obvious love and concern she expresses for her young sister is laudable, and her behaviour here in court has been dignified and impeccable. But the fact remains that she is a single woman.'

Theron stood up. 'May I say something at this stage of proceedings, sir?'

'By all means, let us leave no stone unturned. State your name first.'

'Theron Grace. I'm Miss Ingram's employer.'

The magistrate's head jerked up and he half smiled. 'So I gathered.'

'And this lady sitting next to me is Kitty Ingram's grandmother. Sally Brightman has travelled up from London in support of Calandra Ingram's petition.'

Theodore Bartlett smiled at her, then said, 'What do you have to say to the court, Mr Grace?'

'I'd like to state that, although Miss Ingram is currently a spinster, I have every intention of proposing marriage to her. Kitty would be welcomed into my household and I'm willing to assume parental duties.'

Her grandmother gasped. Patricia's eyes widened, then she grinned.

'You're assuming that the young lady will accept your proposal, when, in fact, Miss Ingram looks rather shocked. Do you intend to propose, or are you actually proposing to her at the moment, Mr Grace? I would like to hear her thoughts on the matter.'

'I'm actually proposing. Will you marry me, Miss Ingram?'

'Do you love me then, Theron?'

'Absolutely, would I have asked, otherwise?'

'And what is your answer, young lady?' the magistrate asked.

'Yes, of course I'll marry you.' A smile sped across Callie's face and she whispered under her breath, 'Thank you, Ma. This is truly a miracle – even better than I expected.'

'Before I make my mind up about custody, I'd like to see the child in question. Is she in court?'

'We left her at home, sir, with a minder. We didn't want to upset her by bringing her here,' Tilly said in an ingratiating voice.

'Very laudable,' he said drily. 'Then I'll consider my verdict while you fetch her. Constable, accompany Mrs Ingram to her home and bring the child here to me. I want to satisfy myself she's being properly looked after before I announce my verdict. And see if you can find that letter Mr Grace wrote to the girl's father...'

They were back in fifteen minutes, Kitty in the

arms of the constable. She was barefoot, dirty and shivering with cold. Her face was bruised.

'There was nobody looking after her, and I found the poor little lass shut in the cupboard under the stairs,' the constable said. He placed the dusty letter on the magistrate's table. 'This was on the mantelpiece. It had slid behind the clock.'

'Kitty,' Callie called out softly, tears filling her eyes. Her sister gazed towards her and her glance fell on the toy cat. A smile jiggled on her face then disappeared as she gazed fearfully at Tilly.

'Ma,' Kitty whispered and began to struggle. At a nod from the magistrate the constable placed her down. She ran across to where Callie stood and hurled herself into her arms. Callie wrapped her shawl around her and the pair clung to each other, both of them weeping.

The letter was opened and the magistrate nodded. 'I'm satisfied that the truth has been revealed.' Gently, he cleared his throat. 'I think a natural conclusion has been reached, ladies and gentlemen. There is no doubt that Kitty Ingram will benefit greatly by living in a home where she is nurtured by two people acting as parents, who will love and care for her, as well as each other. I'll expect an invitation to your wedding, Miss Ingram, Mr Grace. The court is dismissed.'

'Thank you, Theron, that was a touching gesture,' she said when he came to where she stood, a smile on his face.

'A touching gesture? Good Lord, I'm not that

altruistic. I didn't propose just to save Kitty, but because I love you beyond all reasonable doubt – beyond all reason, really.'

She sucked in a breath and felt like dancing.

'Let's go and buy something warm for Kitty to wear,' he said gruffly.

Later, when Kitty was tucked up in bed and they were alone together, for Harold had disappeared into his library to pack books, and her grandmother and Trish had diplomatically offered to help him, Theron said to her, 'What sort of wedding would you prefer? One at the Friends' house, or the Anglican church?'

'What's a Quaker ceremony like?'

'First, you'll have to attend meetings for a few months, then there will be some preliminaries, mostly to satisfy the community elders that we're right for each other. There's no formal ceremony, no rituals. We'll just hold hands at a meeting and state what's in our hearts to those in attendance.'

'What's in your heart, Theron?'

He smiled and drew her into his arms. 'I'll probably say something like this: "Friends, I take this woman, my beloved friend, Calandra Ingram, to be my wife. I will love her always."'

'And I'll say: "Theron's friends, I truly adore him and will be a good wife to him. He may now kiss his beloved bride."'

To which Theron laughed, and then he did just that.